Praise for *Truly, Madly, Deadly*

"What a ride! Full of twists and turns—including an ending you won't see coming!"

—April Henry, *New York Times* bestselling author of *The Girl Who Was Supposed to Die*

"[A] tense psychological piece…Jayne delivers a healthy dose of paranoia amid the story's growing tension."

—*Publishers Weekly*

"Bored this summer? Hannah Jayne's thriller *Truly, Madly, Deadly* is sure to grab your attention the second you pick it up."

—*Girls' Life Magazine*

Praise for *See Jane Run*

"The premise is certainly an interesting one, reminiscent of Cooney's classic *The Face on the Milk Carton*…[An] entertaining read."

—*Kirkus*

"This suspenseful thriller is well paced with carefully developed characters and sharp dialogue."

—*School Library Journal*

Also by Hannah Jayne

Truly, Madly, Deadly

See Jane Run

HANNAH JAYNE

Published by Sourcebooks Fire, an imprint of Sourcebooks, Inc.
P.O. Box 4410, Naperville, Illinois 60567-4410
(630) 961-3900
Fax: (630) 961-2168
www.sourcebooks.com

Library of Congress Cataloging-in-Publication data is on file with the publisher.

Printed and bound in the United States of America.
VP 10 9 8 7 6 5 4 3 2 1

To those of us who tread water even when it seems easier to sink.

ONE

The moonlight streaked across the water as it lapped over Brynna Chase's bare shoulders. She spun, feeling the surf against her skin as she breathed in the salt-misted air. She loved the ocean at night—it was dark, like a smoky sapphire that never ended, water blurring into sky, both going on forever. The shore was out there, somewhere over her left shoulder, but she didn't care.

Erica Shaw popped up next to her, her black hair breaking the surface. She sucked in a lungful of air and grinned. "I love it out here. Hey! Stop daydreaming!" She slapped at the water, sending a spray over Brynna's head.

"I'm not daydreaming. It's the middle of the night." Brynna splashed her best friend back, and Erica reacted by making a smooth dive, her body sinewy and thin as she darted through the surf. She popped up twenty feet from Brynna, her features hidden in the darkness, her head and shoulders outlined against the pale moonlight.

"Seriously, I'd make the perfect mermaid!" Erica yelled, her voice echoing on the waves.

"Yeah, but where are you going to find two clamshells small enough for your flat chest?"

"I'm not listening to you! I'm a mermaid!" Erica dove down again, her head popping up behind Brynna, making her spin in the water.

"You're so weird!"

"Mermaid!" Erica sang again, head and shoulders going under, the dark water swallowing her whole.

Brynna kept kicking, buoyant on the water, turning, trying to predict where Erica's grinning mug would pop up next. "Erica!" she called out, spinning toward the dock at Harding Beach. "Stop playing mermaid and face me like a man!" She giggled, her voice trailing off and sounding suddenly ominous, echoing in the cove.

But the surface of the water remained unbroken, the sheer midnight blue of the surf looking darker than Brynna remembered, almost black. She kicked at the water that had suddenly taken on a bone-deep chill. Her teeth chattered. "Er?"

Brynna scanned the surface, but something inside her told her that Erica wasn't going to pop up, wasn't playing a prank.

"Erica?" Brynna dove, her strong legs driving her downward, her hands clawing as she dug through the surf. The water pushed her back, squeezing the air out of her lungs in a tight, sizzling burn. She was groping blindly, her fingers sifting through sand, raking over rocks and kelp. Finally, she pushed her eyes open, letting the upturned sand settle.

That's when she saw Erica.

Her best friend's brown eyes were wide with terror. She thrashed and flailed, her black hair a matted mess as she struggled. She was clawing at the ground, her feet driving into the sandy ocean floor.

Someone was pushing her down.

Brynna could see Erica's attacker—the long, slim legs, well-muscled as they calmly pressed through the water, the wave of sandy blond hair that now tangled with Erica's. Brynna dove for her, grabbing at the woman whose hands were around Erica's throat. The girl barely bucked, even when Brynna grabbed a fistful of her hair, yanking with all her might. Erica thrashed underneath. Every beat of Brynna's heart was a burning ache, desperate for breath, but still she grabbed at the woman, trying to look into Erica's eyes, trying to silently implore her to hold on.

That's when Erica's legs stopped kicking. Her arms fell in quiet, graceful arcs. Her fingers unclenched, lying open, a few useless grains of sand dancing in her palm. She floated weightlessly, the sand puffing around her as she landed, a perfect specimen, her eyes focused on the snatch of moonlight above her.

Erica's killer turned, and when she smiled at Brynna, Brynna realized she was looking into her own face.

• • •

Brynna woke up, coughing, clawing at her throat. She was desperate for breath.

"Bryn, Bryn, hon, are you okay?"

Her mother was there in an instant, rushing into Brynna's room, ready to shake her out of another murky nightmare.

"I'm okay," Brynna said, sinking deeper into her blankets. "It was just a bad dream."

Her mother cocked her head and bit hard on the edge of her lip, her eyes going into that pitiful, helpless sheen that Brynna had grown to hate over the last year.

"It's nothing, Mom, I'm totally fine." She pasted on her parent-approved, all-is-well smile.

"How about I make you chocolate-chip pancakes? Chocolate is good for everything from bad dreams to your first day at a new school."

Brynna flopped down on her pillow. "Ugh, there's not enough chocolate in the world for that."

Her mother paused in the doorway, silent for a beat. "Bryn, you promised. Dr. Rother said this won't work unless we all try. Your father and I are trying."

"I know, Mom," Brynna said through clenched teeth. "I was just joking."

Brynna watched as her mother's eyes studied her for a beat too long. "Five minutes then."

She waited until her mother's footsteps faded on the stairs before pulling her clenched fist from under her comforter. She dropped a palm's worth of hair into the trash.

• • •

Brynna clutched her half-damp towel against her chest and frowned into her closet. It was twice as big as the closet in her old house but it was already chock-full, even with three moving boxes—still packed, still sealed up tight—waiting on the floor. Brynna was in no hurry to empty them, whether the items inside had a home or not.

She scanned then pulled out a sweater, her fingers feeling the super-soft weave. Then remembered it was Erica's. Half of everything in her closet belonged to Erica. The other half belonged to Brynna, but one that didn't exist anymore—the "before" Brynna. When her mother's voice called a second time and a third, "honey, *come on*!" she grabbed a semi-new white hoodie and a pair of skinny jeans that had gone back and forth between her and Erica so many times that she couldn't remember if they started out as hers or Erica's.

They're mine now.

The thought pinged through her head and lodged in her chest before Brynna even knew it happened. Erica was gone; Brynna was alone, spat out to start a new life in some stupid, Podunk town full of cookie-cutter houses and kids who boozed and lounged in old abandoned farmland.

The Lincoln High kids—back when she was one of them—boozed and lounged on the beach.

Brynna salivated and shivered at the same time. She hadn't taken a drink of alcohol since her parents dragged her here, to Crescent City, and she hadn't been in the water—showers not withstanding—since she was pulled from the tide at Harding Beach. Even this morning—and every morning since—she had had to take ten deep, steadying breaths the way Dr. Rother had shown her before stepping into the hot shower. She continued the ritual while the water pounded her forehead and scalp, and she pinched her eyes shut against the wispy steam that curled around her and sucked at her breath. Every inch of rising steam was like the fingers of fog that pulled at her that night on the beach...

That night.

She wondered when—*if*—that night would ever stop being so fresh in her memory.

Brynna started down the stairs, her feet landing on the brand-new super plush carpet on the landing. It had been four weeks since the Chase family moved into the Blackwood Hills Estates—a sterile-looking pop-up neighborhood that consisted of fifty homes all stunning and yet entirely the same. The place was so new that only about a quarter of the houses were populated, and Brynna knew exactly one person in the entire development: a girl named Riley who would be a senior—one year above Brynna—at Hawthorne High that fall. Riley had invited Brynna to the movies two days after the Chase family moved in, but Brynna had declined, citing a "family thing," which was a total lie.

Brynna's mother was an artist who was constantly covered in chips of paint, and her father was a salesman who spent most of his time on planes being friendly and charming to people that Brynna didn't know. All she knew about her father's clients was that they were high-powered executives who sent expensive bottles of scotch and whiskey during the holidays, signing the cards with a mass-produced stamp.

The only "family thing" she could remember them having was when they all sat in a line on the state therapist's couch, saying nothing but silently blaming each other for Brynna's issues.

Before the dare, her parents were talking separation, but if there's anything that can bring a family together, it's a Class A Misdemeanor. The move was supposed to be a fresh start for all of them. Brynna was supposed to be better, was supposed to start new without drinking or doing drugs. Her parents would be cheerful and respectful of each other—maybe her father would even tone down his drinking in an effort to be supportive rather than hypocritical, Brynna had thought grimly.

She picked her way down the stairs, careful not to mess up the neat stack of cardboard boxes her mother had flattened, and trudged into the kitchen where her mother was staring at coffee brewing and her father was grabbing his briefcase, a piece of dry toast sticking out of his mouth.

"Have a good first day, Bryn," he muttered around hunks of bread as he made a beeline for the garage.

"Dad's going in today?" Brynna asked.

Her mother looked up, almost surprised that Brynna was there. "Oh. Yeah." She pasted a soccer-mom smile on her face and rubbed her hands together. "Excited? How about I make you those first day of junior year chocolate-chip pancakes?"

Brynna couldn't help but smile. Her mother excelled at exactly two things: oil painting and enthusiasm. While she had recently begun some sculpting work, her cooking skills were still limited to Pop Tarts and making reservations.

"Mom…"

"Okay, how about we leave now and let Grinders make you a blueberry muffin and a decent cup of coffee?"

Brynna agreed, even though the thought of a muffin or even a single drop of coffee made her stomach churn. Though the dream still hung at the back of her mind, the anxiety that was thrumming through her was focused on school now—a new school, with new people. She hoped there wouldn't be old rumors. Brynna's game plan was to blend into the background as much as possible. She would be an average girl with average grades, and when they called her name at graduation (she wouldn't be there anyway, having gotten early admissions to Anywhere But Here University), the other students would look around and wonder who she was. She didn't want to be remembered; she wanted to be anonymous.

• • •

Brynna stepped out of the car, finding her footing on the concrete. She vaguely felt her mother pat her back.

"Have a great day, hon."

Brynna heard the car door slam shut, felt the weight of her backpack pulling against her shoulders. She looked up at Hawthorne High, a sprawling, one-story expanse of too-new stuccoed buildings with flat roofs that sat before her. There was a huge cemented quad where students mingled now, bunched together in clusters on the concrete or sitting back on the perfect rectangles of Crayola-green grass that looked like they were planted for the sole purpose of introducing nature into a concrete world. Two enormous iron gates were held open and pinned back with hulking chains, and Brynna had the fleeting thought: *Are the gates meant to keep people in or to keep people out*?

She scanned the crowd in front of her—teenagers, just like her in hoodies and jeans, slashed-up T-shirts and jeans, prissy sweaters and jeans—and waited to feel their slicing stares. Their eyes would go big, but they wouldn't meet hers. She'd see them nudge each other and whisper, her mind racing to put words in their mouths: "She was so normal before the accident."

"She was the one."

"She dared Erica, but Erica never came back."

Everywhere that she went, Brynna knew the accident followed

her, branded her, and she would never be the same. She was crazy with grief, with guilt; she was messed up on drugs, on booze; she wasn't who she used to be: fun-loving, wild. All the judgment and accusation was in their eyes.

But here at her new school, no one was staring.

A few kids glanced up at her or squinted their eyes, doing their best to place her. One or two kind of smiled. Most were so focused on their friends or their notecards that they didn't even see her at all. It should have been a relief, but Brynna knew better. The dare, the accident, that night, was like a disease that would silently creep into a vein and poison her whole life. She expected it. She deserved it. Erica was dead because of her.

Brynna wasn't *popular*-popular back at Lincoln, but she and Erica were well-known. Even more so after that night. After she came back to school, people gave her sympathetic looks, and girls she barely knew linked arms with her, patted her shoulder, and told her how sorry they were. It didn't take Brynna long to realize they weren't interested in knowing her—they were interested in other people thinking that they knew her. Headlines popped up in the three-page community newspapers: *A Lincoln High Insider Tells All,* followed with someone's supposed firsthand knowledge of how "the survivor" (that's how they referred to Brynna now, as "the survivor") was coping. "We eat lunch together every day," one of the stories went, "and every day, Brynna cries on my shoulder." The source listed was a girl named Abby Hart, who Brynna was pretty sure was either a transfer student or the head of the People for Puppies Club at Lincoln. Either way, Brynna and the girl had never shared so much as a sandwich, let alone a shoulder-to-shoulder cry.

Being slightly invisible at Hawthorne High was exactly what Brynna wanted.

"Oh my god!"

The kid that Brynna crashed into was an eyebrow taller than her, with unkempt dark hair expensively cut to look that way. His eyes were a dark brown-black, but his grin was warm. He narrowed his eyes at Brynna, and she immediately felt heat at the back of her neck.

"Sorry, I didn't see you—" she started.

He shook a finger at her. "I've never seen you."

"What?"

"You're new, right?" He dashed out a hand. "Evan. Evan Stevens. Don't call me Even Stevens because it's already been done circa elementary school through three o'clock on Wednesday."

Brynna's eyebrows went up. "What happened at three o'clock on Wednesday?"

"Not important. Who are you now?"

"Uh, Brynna. Brynna Chase." She looked at Evan's outstretched hand. He immediately pulled it back.

"Not a shaker? Fine, I respect that. Supergerms and all."

Evan paused, tapping a finger against his lips as he studied her. Anxiety started to creep up the back of her neck.

"Junior. Sixteen. Doesn't drive."

It took Brynna a second to realize that Evan was talking about her. He raised his eyebrows and she stumbled. "Uh, yeah. How did you know that?"

"I'm a genius. And your student ID is sticking out." He flipped on his heel. "Come with me."

"Wait. What?"

Evan didn't answer. He kept walking with the sure step of a popular kid, and Brynna ran to catch up with him.

"Um, where are we going?" she asked once she caught up.

"You need to meet everyone. This way."

Brynna hung back for a half second, her eyes raking over Evan. He gave her a quick, impatient look, and her mind spun, processing. He didn't look at her boobs or give her the easy, cocky smile she recognized from guys who wanted to hook up with her. She shrugged and continued following.

Evan wound Brynna around the school to the cafeteria. She paused, grimacing. Evan looked over his shoulder and cocked a brow. "Oh, cafeteria for losers at your old school?" He smiled. "How cliché."

Brynna followed Evan to a round table littered with good-looking kids staring boredly into their Starbucks cups. He gave two small, tight claps.

"Everyone, this is Brynna something-or-other. Be nice; she's new."

Evan took a chair, and Brynna was left to stand in the glare of three sets of eyes regarding her with mild curiosity. She offered a slow wave then immediately felt stupid, her hand dropping to her side.

"Um, I'm Brynna Chase. I just transferred here."

"Isn't she a plum?" Evan asked the girl sitting next to him. "I discovered her." He grabbed Brynna's wrist and pulled her down into the seat next to him. "Tell us everything about yourself."

Brynna paused, her dark eyes scanning the group. She felt sweat pricking out above her lower lip, itching along her hairline.

"Where you from?" an incredibly thin girl with sharp features and a blunt-cut blond pageboy asked.

Evan pointed. "That's Darcy."

"I'm from Point Lobos."

There was a brief pause as the words came out of Brynna's mouth. She waited for them to recoil while a memory came together, to trigger that little something in their brains that remembered a news article, a tweet about the girl who survived while she watched her best friend die. *Wasn't that girl from Point Lobos?*

But no one seemed to react much. Darcy nodded, and Evan swiped a paper cup of coffee from the girl sitting next to him. His eyes cut to Brynna. "This is my sibling, Lauren."

Brynna raised her eyebrows at Evan's use of the word "sibling," and when Lauren offered her a hand to shake, Brynna tried not to stare at Lauren's sweatshirt. She wasn't successful, because Lauren looked down at herself, the emblem of a hornet in a swim cap, the words *Hawthorne Hornets Swim Team* in a circle around him.

"Do you swim?" Lauren asked.

The question shouldn't have caught Brynna off guard, but it did. "Uh, no." *Not anymore, not ever again.* "It's cool that you do though."

Evan bumped Lauren's shoulder. "Women's 500 freestyle champ. Twinsie here got the athletic ability in the fam. I got everything else."

"You're twins?" Brynna's eyes went from Lauren, with her glossy mane of Crayola-red hair and wide-set eyes, to Evan.

"Fraternal," Lauren said. "Totally fraternal."

"Aren't all boy/girl twins fraternal?" Brynna asked.

"Like I said." Evan jabbed a thumb at Lauren. "Athletic ability," and then he pointed back at himself. "Everything else."

Lauren rolled her eyes, and an enormous, stereotypical jock with the name "Meatball" stitched on his jacket sat down.

It was a flash of a second, a nearly miniscule move, but Brynna could see Evan wilt.

"What's up, fags?" Meatball asked, a wad of breakfast sandwich lodged in his cheek.

"Hey, dude, shut the hell up."

Brynna looked up to see another jock—judging by his letterman's jacket—who looked nothing like Meatball. He was slight, with close-cropped ink-black hair that looked like it'd curl if it got the chance. His eyes were an impossible sky blue and framed with lashes that Brynna would kill for.

Meatball turned his massive head up toward the new guy, shrugged, and lumbered off. The new jock slid into his vacated seat. "Sorry about that." He swung his head toward Brynna. "I'm Teddy. I don't think I know you."

"Teddy's our resident jock," Evan clarified.

Darcy shot Teddy a withering glare. "I thought he was our resident gimp."

Teddy turned to Brynna, completely unfazed, and pointed to his foot. "Os trigonum syndrome."

Brynna blinked, feeling her cheeks redden. First, she was locked in the gaze of a hot guy, and second, she couldn't understand a single word he said.

"It means he's got an extra bone," Evan said with a smirk.

"In his foot," Darcy hissed.

"Ended my football career before it even started."

Brynna smiled, and Lauren stood up, linking arms with her and pulling her up too. "Before you and Teddy go all touchy-feely on each other, how about I show you around a little bit? I'm pretty sure my sweet twinsie over there did a fab job but probably missed the important spots, like the girls' bathroom."

Brynna said some hasty good-byes and let Lauren lead her out of the cafeteria. Lauren was nearly a head taller than Brynna, with wide, muscular shoulders that Brynna knew must be from swimming. She fluffed her red hair around her shoulders and narrowed her eyes, scrutinizing Brynna.

Brynna waited for the sinking feeling to start, the trickling guilt that always shadowed her, that held her tight like a second skin. As she and Lauren walked down the deserted halls, Lauren pointing out landmarks like the administration building and the bathrooms to avoid, Brynna began to let her guard down. It only took a millisecond of easing into a comfortable space for Erica's memory to breathe down her neck and for Brynna to feel like there were a hundred eyes watching her. She zipped up her hoodie and shrugged off a chill.

• • •

It had been six weeks since Brynna's first day at Hawthorne High. People knew her now. They waved to her, asked her opinion, invited her out with "the gang." Teddy squeezed in beside her at lunch, and Evan came over almost every day. Lauren and Darcy dragged her into the girls' room for major discussions, and Meatball gave her a wide berth, whether or not Teddy was around. She was happy to be just Brynna and happy that at Hawthorne High, her secret—her guilt—could stay buried.

When her parents first moved here, Brynna had wanted to be anonymous, disregarded—a shell of a girl, trying to get through her junior year only because she had no other choice. She figured she would dutifully attend her once-weekly therapy sessions and sit through the AA for Teens (she still had to go as a condition of her parole), where all the other vacant-eyed kids tried not to look at each other. She had self-medicated her way through Erica's memorial and dealing with life after that night. She had also self-medicated herself into a DUI arrest and a habit she couldn't stop on her own.

But she had actually begun enjoying her life in Crescent City, was even on her way to having a boyfriend. For as much as Brynna tried to stay guarded, Teddy tried to break in. He waited for her after class but still gave her her space; he texted her stupid jokes and googly faces but didn't force her to talk. Her walls were breaking down, and Brynna felt something for him, a tiny spark on its way to becoming a flame.

Pep rallies, football games, school plays—it was all kind of stupid, she admitted, but still it felt good to be normal again, with a social circle, party invitations, and even a green-and-white Hawthorne High ribbon in her hair. She was staring in her bedroom mirror, trying to get the bow to sit straight on her ponytail, when her tablet pinged, signifying a new tweet.

Brynna swiped her finger across the screen, ready to tell Evan that he could never pull off a cheerleader's sweater, even if it did fit him perfectly.

But the smile dropped from her lips.

Fear, like a heavy black stone, settled in her gut.

The tweet was from **@EricaNShaw**.

Brynna touched the screen, her finger shaking, her heart thundering. She touched the little animated icon, and Erica's message popped up: **Remember me?**

TWO

Brynna snatched her hand back as if she'd been burned. The words swam in front of her eyes: **Remember me?**

Heat crawled up her spine, swallowing one vertebra after another as blood pulsed in her ears.

"What the—?"

She was reaching for the screen as she spoke, ready to delete the tweet, but the little birdie icon blinked again.

@EricaNShaw has a new tweet for you!

Every fiber of her being seemed to pull in opposite directions. Her skin felt tight, her bones like they were about to explode. Everything told her to move, to run, to flee. Her stomach turned in on itself, but Brynna had to click. It couldn't be Erica—it just couldn't.

The second tweet popped up with a gleeful little jingle that made Brynna's heart drop a little lower in her chest.

Remember me?

The bird chirped again, but there was no new tweet—just Brynna's tablet screen filling with little blue rectangles, each with the same two words: **Remember me? Remember me? Remember me?**

She mashed her fingers against the screen, her fingerprints blurring the tweets but unable to make them go away.

Remember me?

The screen kept pinging with new tweets, each note a drop of water slipping into an ocean, each word congealing into a sea of blame. Brynna was crying now, pressing her whole palm against the screen, swiping, clawing, screaming—anything to get the tweets to stop.

Erica was dead. She had been caught by the riptide and was dead. Wasn't she?

Erica's body had never been found, but there had been an official proclamation. Brynna couldn't forget—her mother picked her up from school, had taken Brynna's hand and squeezed it against her cheek.

"They're declaring Erica dead, honey."

"Did they find...?"

"No." A slight pause. "They've called off the search. It's been four days. There is no way..." Her mother's voice dropped off before she said it: there was no way that Erica could still be alive.

"Bryn?"

Brynna looked up, terrified. Her mother was standing in the doorway, one arm pressed protectively across her chest, her other hand slapped over her half-open mouth. Evan stood in front of her, his eyes impossibly wide, the little emerald H at his right eye ludicrously out of place.

"Brynna!" Her mother rushed in front of Evan and kneeled down, throwing her arms around her. "What's wrong?"

Stunned, Brynna looked down at the tablet she was still clutching. It was covered in smeared tears and fingerprints, but the screen was black.

"I got a—" She looked up at Evan, who hadn't moved from his space in the doorway. "Look." She swiped the screen back to life, and it flashed on for a tenth of a second before the CONNECT TO POWER icon started flashing.

"No," Brynna gasped, shaking her head. "It was just here. And I just took my iPad out of the charger."

Her mother let her hand fall and scooched a few inches away from Brynna. She whispered, "Are you being cyberbullied, hon?"

Brynna's eyebrows went up. "No." She dragged a palm over her cheeks and sniffed. "Sorry, it was nothing."

Brynna's heart pounded against her rib cage, but her cheeks burned with embarrassment as she looked up at Evan. His eyes were still on her, but there was no expression on his face.

"I'm sorry," Brynna said to the carpet. "It was just—"

What? Something inside Brynna screamed. *It was just what? Me going crazy? Me seeing things? Me getting a message from the dead?*

Evan didn't know about Erica. He didn't know about Brynna. And now, sitting in her new room with her new friend and on the precipice of a new life, she desperately didn't want him to know.

She focused on Evan and forced a laugh that was supposed to sound nonchalant but came out tinny and weirdly high. "Sorry."

He shrugged, his expression going back to classic Evan: unaffected. "No big. We all have our moments."

Brynna cleared her throat, her eyes cutting toward her mother. "Um, Evan and I have to get ready for the game."

Evan and Brynna watched Brynna's mother cross the room, toss a concerned look over her shoulder, and close the door only halfway. Brynna got up to nudge it shut, but her mother held firm, her hard brown eyes zeroing in.

"This door doesn't close. You've got a boy in your room and," her eyes went to Bryn's tear-stained face, "well, you know."

Brynna crossed her arms in front of her chest. "So," she hissed, "now every time I cry or get upset, I'm drinking or smoking again?"

Her mother glanced over Brynna's shoulder at Evan, who was obliviously flipping channels on the TV.

"I'm your mother, Brynna Marie. I'm supposed to worry."

A little niggling of guilt wormed its way into Brynna. She remembered the way her mother sat on the psychologist's couch, repeatedly smoothing the imaginary wrinkles in her skirt while Brynna sat icily silent, her father helpless in between, during the ten hours of state-mandated family therapy that Brynna—caught drinking and driving in her mother's car—had gotten nearly a year after Erica's accident.

"Sorry, Mom," she said on a sigh. "I'm past that."

Her mother's eyes flashed with something like hope.

"I promise," Brynna said. "Can we just get ready now?"

She watched her mother leave and turned back to Evan, pasting on the coolest, most nonchalant smile she could muster.

"So, are you excited about the game?"

Evan blinked at her. "No, but football games are a required social construct for supposedly well-adjusted teens. And speaking of well-adjusted..." His eyes cut to the discarded tablet on the floor.

Brynna swallowed hard, the weight of wanting to talk to someone—and wanting just another day of not being "that girl"—pressing against her.

"Boyfriend trouble?" Evan said before Brynna could even respond. "Jealous? Stalker? That's sick and romantic."

Brynna turned to the mirror and tugged on the end of the green-and-white Hawthorne High bow. "Yeah," she said carefully, "something like that."

Evan scooted closer to her, his dark eyes glittering. He pointed an index finger two inches from Brynna's nose and waved it. "I like you, Brynna Chase. You're dark. Mysterious. You've got secrets."

Brynna's heart started to pound even as she managed to keep her face neutral. "Secrets?"

"I can read you like a book. There's something wicked in there." He waved his entire hand now, indicating her as a whole.

Brynna's breath hitched. She stared at Evan, studying him. *There's something wicked in there...* His eyes were bright, his lips twitching up into a wry smile.

Did he know?

A cold sheen of sweat broke out all over her, and suddenly, the round collar of her T-shirt felt like it was strangling her. Brynna knew it would happen. She knew it was only a matter of time before someone at Hawthorne High figured out who she was, and the whispers would start all over again.

Everything Dr. Rother said, every breathing technique or calming technique that she had taught her, swirled in Brynna's head, rolling and tumbling in a gnarled mess. She didn't want to figure them out. She didn't want to calm down and "live through the moment" like Dr. Rother said. She wanted darkness. She wanted oblivion.

"It's not like it's going to kill you," Campbell said, his eyes half-hidden by the scruff of sand-blond hair that rolled over his forehead. "They'll just calm you down a little bit. You know, sand away the rough edges."

That's what Brynna's entire life was now: rough edges. Erica was gone. She couldn't say her best friend was dead; she wouldn't say it. It had only been eleven days and they hadn't found Erica, and somewhere inside, Brynna knew that Erica could still be alive. She had to be. Fifteen-year-olds didn't die.

"Just sands away the rough edges, huh?"

Campbell nodded and smiled. "You'll have a break for a couple hours. No big deal."

Brynna's mind still churned, that night, that dare flashing in front of her mind's eye. Every moment, she heard the splash of the water, the heavy silence as she and Erica went down, down. Every night, she dreamed of Erica, of the way she must have looked as all the air left her body.

"Do you have anything that lasts longer?"

"It's nothing," Brynna said, trying her best to shrug off Evan's questioning stare. "There's nothing...wicked...about me."

Evan digested that and narrowed his eyes. "You know you can talk to me. You know you can tell me anything."

Brynna watched Evan's eyes as they went to the tablet. Instinctively, she reached out and grabbed it, slipping the thing into her top drawer. "I know, Evan, and vice versa."

"You can even tell me what freaked you out so badly on the tablet."

She let out a shock of air and wagged her head. "It was nothing. Like you said, old boyfriend. I was just…surprised to hear from him is all."

"It's not always the worst thing in the world," Evan said, brushing a hand through his hair, "if someone from your past wants to come back to you."

Her heart did a little double thump and her stomach went to liquid. Evan must have noticed her face go pale, because he cocked his head. "Bad guy? Bad influence?"

"We should probably go." She pushed herself to her feet, but Evan didn't budge.

"Come on, B. You can talk to me. Tell me one thing—one thing that's bothering you—and I can worry about it, okay?" He offered her a small smile.

Before Brynna could stop herself, she nodded. It was as if someone took over her body and bobbled her head, and her heart wedged in her throat as she thought of just one secret to tell Evan. The problem was, there wasn't just one. Brynna's cheeks singed as she listed them off.

I killed my best friend.

I got addicted to drugs.

I drank and drove.

I got arrested.

I'm not a normal girl.

I should have been the one to die.

"You know when I said I came here because there was a crazy drug problem at my old school?"

She swallowed when Evan nodded.

"I was the crazy drug problem. I had a problem." Brynna looked at her hands in her lap. "A really big problem."

Evan blew out a long sigh, his eyes steady on Brynna's. He reached out and squeezed her hand. "And the guy—he was part of that?"

She briefly thought of Michael, her boyfriend back at Lincoln, and the reason he became just as addicted as she was: because there was no other way to reach her. He stood by her and then hung by her until they were both oblivious shadows of their former selves, drunk, high, numb.

Brynna swallowed over the lump in her throat. "Yeah."

There was a silent, pregnant pause, and then Evan smiled. "I still love you."

"Thanks."

"And seriously, you had me thinking you were some kind of ax murderer or something." He batted at the air. "Drugs? Nothing. Half the student body is addicted to something, and the other half just wants everyone to think they are." Evan's eyes shifted. "Not me, of course. I'm not stupid or a lemming."

"Are you calling me a stupid lemming?"

Evan nodded. "Yeah. Back then. But come on, you're going to

the school where a student killed another student *and* a teacher. And some other chick was like, on the run from the FBI or the German mafia or her parents kidnapped her or something. Drugs? Lame. So what was it? Oxy, Spice, Adderall, Lady X?"

Brynna sat back, a mixture of surprise and sudden comfort washing over her. She smiled. "Doesn't matter. It was lame and I'm over it. Now I'm addicted to cheap nachos, so can we please just get to this game?"

• • •

Brynna's good mood was short-lived. For every inch of comfort she took knowing that Evan was cool with her past, a needling fear poked in: *He doesn't know the real story. He doesn't know about the dare. About Erica.*

She struggled through the football game, remaining seated when everyone jumped to their feet, cheering, her head a churning mess of Erica's tweets.

No, she told herself. *Not Erica's.*

Erica was dead.

Maybe not...

The thought flashed through her mind before she could stop it, and Brynna gritted her teeth, trying to keep the memory on her periphery, out of her mind. But it crept in—the sound of the water as it broke when Erica and Brynna crashed into it. The feeling of Erica's fingers gripping hers tightly, then slowly, slowly slipping through her palm, then slipping away. Brynna thrashed, salt water floating up her nose, dripping through her teeth as she smiled. She spun, looking for Erica, feeling through the water.

But it was silent.

Dead calm.

"Hey, ow!"

Brynna blinked as Teddy pulled his hand from hers and began massaging it.

"You've got a hell of a grip," he said, his blue eyes playful.

Brynna's heart began to pound. Had she been holding Teddy's hand? Oh god, had she grabbed it?

"I'm—I'm super sorry," she said, her ponytail bobbing against her cheek as she shook her head.

"No." Teddy's hand found hers again and squeezed gently. "I like a girl who makes the first move."

The embarrassment Brynna should have been feeling was zapped, replaced by electricity that shot up her arm the second Teddy's hand settled into hers. Their bare arms touched, and the connection was there again—a hot, wonderful zing that shot through her, making every single inch of her body spark.

Evan leaned over from Brynna's other side. "Can you stop beaming for, like, fifteen seconds? I'm getting a third degree burn over here."

Teddy rolled his eyes and nudged Brynna's shoulder. "Want to get a drink?"

She felt her face redden, felt her mouth go suddenly dry. She was on probation. She didn't drink—she *couldn't* drink. She thought of the doctors and Woodbriar Rehabilitation Center where she stayed for six weeks and where they called the patients "clients." She thought of her mother, wringing her hands while her father lectured her about why "kids" shouldn't drink, his own eyes red, his breath tinged with the unmistakable scent of bourbon.

"Uh..."

"The Snack Shack only has Pepsi stuff, but there's Coke and Red Bulls in the machine in the quad."

Relief flooded over Brynna. "Oh, yeah. A Coke would be cool."

They stood up and edged through the crowd on the bleachers. As Brynna crossed in front of Evan, he yanked her down by her jeans pocket. "Don't do anything I wouldn't do," he hissed in her ear. "And if you do, I want to hear all about it."

Brynna waved him off and fell in step with Teddy. They crossed the back forty, talking about teachers and school and everything topical until they reached the main part of campus. It was darker there, the flood lights of the stadium bright in the distance.

"This place is kind of creepy at night," Brynna said, her hackles going up as they made their way through the darkness.

Teddy turned and held out a hand. "I won't let anything happen to you, I promise."

Tentatively, she slid her hand into his. There was something different about holding Teddy's hand while they were walking, while there was no one else to see them. It was tender and sweet, but secret too.

• • •

The game ended—the Hawthorne Hornets came up short in the fourth quarter—and Evan, Teddy, Darcy, and Lauren pressed in on Brynna in a tight huddle.

"Let's just go to Brewsters," Lauren said. "I'd kill for a burger."

"No." Darcy shook her head, tucking a strand of hair behind her ear. "Brewsters is crap. Isn't there somewhere else to go?"

Evan frowned. "Have you met Crescent City? It's Brewsters, the mall parking lot, or Taco Time."

"I could do a taco." Teddy was still holding Brynna's hand, and she loved the warmth but had no idea what happened next. Did she drop his hand? Keep holding it until he dropped hers?

"Oh, oh, oh! I know what we have to do. Darce, Teddy, what time do you have to be back?"

Teddy shrugged. "Midnight curfew."

Lauren nudged Evan. "Same with me and the worse half."

"I should have strangled you with the umbilical cord in utero."

Lauren stuck her tongue out at Evan, and Brynna marveled at how dissimilar they could look, even though they were born within minutes of each other.

"I would like to register a barf complaint," Darcy said, rolling her eyes. "Umbilical? Utero? Not on a Friday night. Never on a Friday night."

Evan's eyes cut to Brynna. "Curfew, Queen B?"

Brynna blinked. "Midnight."

"Then we'd better get going."

Evan grabbed Brynna's free hand and one of Lauren's. Lauren clamped on to Darcy, and with Brynna still holding on to Teddy, they were one long, wonky line being led by Evan as he stomped across campus.

"Where are we going?" Brynna wanted to know.

Lauren spun free of her brother. "Oh, that's right, you're still a virgin."

Brynna stopped, feeling all the blood rush from her face. "What?"

Teddy thumped into her and dropped her hand.

The parking lot—fifteen seconds ago littered with Hawthorne and Crescent High students screaming and talking—suddenly went impossibly quiet as if everyone, every student, every teacher, was waiting for Brynna to answer.

"Not like that!" Evan swatted at her then ducked his head close. "Although I want to hear every detail if it's a no. She means," he went on, this time theatrically and with a flourish of both arms, "you are currently on your virgin voyage of Evan's Amazing Adventures."

Teddy clapped a hand to his forehead. "Oh good god, how did I get dragged into one of these again?"

"Shut it, gimp."

Teddy rolled his eyes. "Have a little sympathy! I just watched my team get terrorized by the bottom-of-the-league Bulldogs."

"Well," Darcy said, handing Evan her car keys, "then you shouldn't have allowed yourself to get a season-ending injury before your season even started."

Brynna expected Teddy to look stung or argue, but he just narrowed his eyes and grinned. She liked that about him—he was easygoing and didn't mind being razzed. Erica would love him—would have loved him.

The group stopped in front of a sports car that looked like it belonged in the pages of a catalog or in some kind of showroom. The overhead lights bounced over the car's pristine black paint job and the inside—with fawn-colored, supple leather seats—was just as factory-new looking.

"Wow," Brynna said to Darcy, "is this your car?"

Though they had been getting closer, Darcy was the one in the group that Brynna knew the least about. She was nice enough and was in a few of Brynna's advanced classes, but the blond was quiet—or maybe it was that Evan was always so loud. Unlike the others, Darcy never invited anyone over or talked much about her parents or family. Brynna respected the girl's shy nature and never pried.

"Yup, this little beauty belongs to our Darcy—much like most of this town and half the money in this world."

"And can you believe she lets Evan drive it?" Lauren asked.

Evan rolled his eyes. "Cars are like Kleenex to the Davenports. One gets soiled, Daddy buys a new one. Come on, B. Virgin rides shotgun."

Brynna ducked into the car just in time to see Darcy, cheeks pink and eyes downcast, crawling into the backseat.

"Darcy, it's your car, you should be up front."

Darcy smiled thinly and shrugged. "Tradition is tradition, B. Better get up there."

Evan cranked down all the windows and cranked up the radio, and then Brynna was singing along with the rest of them, screaming out the wrong words to whatever song came up, kicking her feet against the dashboard during the drum solos. The night air was breezy and warm and her friends—her new life—were so magazine-cover perfect that Erica and the tweet flailed far behind, and she forgot to pay attention to the miles of road that Darcy's car ate up. She didn't notice when the breeze died down, but the temperature dropped and the air that waved over her bare arm turned moist.

When Evan made a sharp turn—and the wheels of Darcy's car spun out on a catch of sand—Brynna heard it. It was distant but distinct: the crash of waves.

She sat bolt upright just in time to see the sign, slapped over with Santa Cruz and surf decals, the name of the beach just barely visible: Harding Beach.

The memories of the night didn't have to come flooding back. She didn't have to think of the images, remember the churning surf, the way the pier looked in the darkness—because it was right in front of her.

"Why are we here?" Brynna asked, hysteria in her voice. She gripped the dashboard and the door handle, her knuckles white, her palm aching with the effort. "Why are you doing this?"

The tears were thick, choking her voice, and every synapse was shooting commands: *Run. Stay. Hide. Scream.*

Evan pushed the car into park, his face half-hidden in the darkened car. Brynna's eyes ached when the dome light sprung on, black splotches marring her vision. She was vaguely aware of Lauren, Teddy, and Darcy talking in the backseat. But when her vision cleared, it was Evan she saw, head cocked, a serene smile on his face.

"You're welcome," he said quietly.

Terror exploded through Brynna. She fought to find her voice and was finally able to utter a meek, "Why?"

"Because you looked so freaked out today, B. I thought maybe a drive by the old stomping grounds would perk you up again. You know, if you had bad memories with an old boyfriend here, you can make some new ones with your awesome new friends."

The smile on Evan's face was wide, and Brynna wanted to believe him. "You don't know—I mean, you just picked this beach?"

Evan shrugged. "It was close enough to Point Lobos that I figured you probably went here sometimes." He turned and looked toward the ocean. "It's so gorgeous. Don't you love the beach?"

"I—I—"

The day that Brynna's family had packed up the car and turned out of Point Lobos was the last time Brynna had seen the ocean. It was a speck in their rearview mirror, a churning gray reminder that Erica was dead, her body somewhere hidden, swallowed in its depths, and Brynna was alive. Crescent City was a full hour away from Point Lobos, but in California, the ocean was never that far away.

Brynna tried to inhale deeply like Dr. Rother told her, but her breath caught like a knife in her lung. She was smashed against the dashboard as Darcy, Lauren, and Teddy peeled out of the backseat. Both of the girls took off running, sand kicking up beneath their shoes.

"You coming?" Teddy asked, hand out.

"Move along, Teddy. B is mine on this one."

Brynna's head swung back and forth like she was watching a tennis match—Teddy still holding out a hand to her on one team, Evan, his hand on her knee, on the other.

Teddy shrugged. "All right, but if this guy tries to lay a hand on you, there's going to be hell to pay." His eyebrows were drawn, but there was humor in his voice.

"Noted," Evan shouted as Teddy trotted off after the girls.

When Brynna and Evan were alone in the car, he turned to her, arms crossed in front of his chest, his lips in a thin line. "What's up?"

Brynna sank back, her shoulder blades aching against the coils inside the car seat. "What are you talking about?"

Evan cocked a single brow and then rolled his eyes, clearly exasperated. "Come on, Bryn. It's the beach," he gestured absently. "Everyone loves the beach. And those who hate the beach love it at night. What's your trauma?"

She was mid-shrug when Evan clapped a hand on her shoulder. "And don't say nothing. And don't say that what happened in your room before we left was also. I'm not your mother. You can talk to me."

Brynna started to squirm, casting a short glance over her shoulder at the black, crashing waves beyond, then back to Evan's face, open, waiting.

She swallowed.

She didn't want to be *that girl* anymore.

It was her first day back at Lincoln. Everyone around her was grinning, hugging, still in flip-flops and cut-off shorts, their skin still glistening with summer tans—and they all went quiet when Brynna walked in the door. She had never done it alone before—headed through the double doors of the high school—without Erica at her side. They rode to school together, they shared clothes and everything else, but this one thing—the only thing—they didn't share was glaring, eternal, and final.

Those who would look at her offered sympathetic smiles. Most just averted their eyes. But everybody talked.

Erica and Brynna used to be a part of the whispers. People were forever leaning in, cupping their hands, whispering darkest secrets, who kissed who, where the party was, to Erica and Brynna. And they would pass it on. But that day, no one whispered to Brynna. Everyone whispered about her.

"I heard she was jealous of Erica."

"Steve says she knew about the riptide."

"I heard she's so upset, she hasn't left her room since."

"I feel like I should say something, but what do you say?"

"She really looks bad—but can you blame her?"

The whispers didn't bother Brynna so much as the fact that she faced them all alone. She pretended not to hear, pretended like she didn't care, but the only thing that rang through her head was: *I should have been the one who died.*

• • •

"Earth to Brynna!" Evan was snapping his fingers a half inch from her nose.

Her eyes focused on Teddy, Darcy, and Lauren running in lazy circles, sand exploding over their bare feet, their cheeks florid under the bright beam of the headlights. They didn't know about *that girl.* Here, she didn't have to be that girl.

Brynna slapped Evan's hand away and forced her lightest, brightest grin. "It's no big deal," she said, leaning the back of her head against the cool glass of the window. "I'm just not that big of a beach person. And it's totally freezing out there." She zipped up her hoodie and shivered against a chill she didn't actually feel.

Evan's gaze went over her shoulder. "You're absolutely right. Those three look positively hypothermic."

Evan popped out of the car and headed for them; Brynna kicked open her own car door and unsteadily put her feet on the ground, the sound of the grainy sand underneath her sneakers pricking at the back of her neck. She worked to breathe deeply, desperate to claim a second of calm as her heart hammered like a fire bell. She could hear the waves crashing outside and tried to reconcile them with the crashing waves inside her head.

She forced herself to look at the surf beyond, to look at the pier in front of her, the wooden staves drifting off into the dark water. She remembered the way the wood, pocked and cracking with age, felt underneath her bare foot. She remembered that Erica worried they'd fall through the pier rather than jump off it.

"Erica is dead," Brynna muttered, teeth clenched.

But all at once she heard the ping of the Twitter message in her head. **Remember me?**

THREE

"And then what happened?" Dr. Rother leaned back in her chair, the leather groaning as she shifted.

"Like, what actually happened, or is this like a 'See? You didn't die' kind of a question?"

Dr. Rother cocked her head, and Brynna sighed.

"It's not like anyone went into the water. I just sat on a log for a little bit." She chewed the inside of her cheek, studying the bright green fern just to the left of the doctor's ear. Dr. Rother moved her chair an inch to the left, so she was once again in Brynna's full view.

"And what did your friends say?"

Brynna shrugged and looked at her sneakers. "Nothing, really."

"Did they ask why you weren't joining in? Did they want you to hang out with them?"

Brynna looked away, trying to find something in the tiny office that she hadn't studied extensively in one of her previous sessions.

"Brynna?" Dr. Rother prodded.

"I didn't feel well, so we left after, like, an hour."

"So you spent an hour on the beach, listening to the waves. Did it bring up—"

Brynna uncrossed her legs and slumped in her chair. "I said it was like an hour. Less though."

"So forty-five minutes?"

Brynna wouldn't meet the doctor's gaze, and the doctor's eyebrows went up.

"Thirty minutes? Really, any amount of time is making progress."

That's good, Brynna thought. Because she was out of the car and back inside in less than fifteen minutes.

"And you said the breathing exercises have been helping you."

Brynna nodded, and Dr. Rother gave her a tight-lipped "yay, you!" kind of smile.

They stayed that way, Brynna plain-faced and Dr. Rother giving off her good-feeling vibes. Then she opened her mouth. "Now that you're enjoying more things at Hawthorne High, have you given any consideration to the swim team?"

Brynna felt her mouth drop open. "I practically had a panic attack at the sight of the ocean."

"A pool isn't the ocean, Brynna."

She hated it when Dr. Rother used her name and hated it more when she pinned her with that psychotherapist stare. Brynna sucked in a shallow breath. "I know. I just—I'm not ready yet. And honestly, it's not like I miss it."

But that was a lie. Lying in bed at night, Brynna couldn't get comfortable, missing the freedom that the water used to give her. It was in those long nights, in those desperate, confusing moments when Brynna thought about the drugs again, the way the memories—everything—hung on her periphery when she was high, the edges of her thoughts becoming soft, barely recognizable.

She'd lost count of how many beers she'd had. The keg was empty, tossed out on the grass like a giant soda can, and everyone around her seemed to have their own full cups or hidden flasks of booze. She needed something because the beer wasn't working. She could still see Erica's face; she could still hear her voice. She didn't have to go upstairs, back to the party, to know they were all talking about her, pointing at her. "That's her, that's Brynna Chase. She kept swimming while her best friend drowned."

She barely noticed the tears dripping over her cheeks, and she barely noticed when he sat down. She knew him from school—his name was Campbell or something—and she had steered clear of him because he was supposed to be bad. But he looked at her with a kindly smile now, with a cocked head.

"You look like you could use a pick-me-up," he said, his friendly smile widening.

Brynna couldn't remember if she replied or just nodded. But she remembered his hand, outstretched, palm up.

"Go ahead," he said, gesturing toward his hand with his chin. "This one's on me."

Brynna almost salivated, desperate for the oblivion she got from just two of those tiny little pills. They were best when mixed with beer. They obliterated everything when she took three.

But she couldn't tell Dr. Rother that. The doctor prodded, but Brynna wouldn't tell her the truth. She couldn't tell her that it was better when she smoked or drank. Not because she couldn't feel the pain, but because she couldn't feel anything. Then Brynna would think of her parents on the day she was released from rehab; they were smiling, her mother teary, but sadness overwhelmed them. Something worse than sadness—disappointment. The guilt still stung her.

Dr. Rother's eyes flicked to the clock on the back wall. She closed her file and nodded, still smiling. "I really think you're making some good progress here, Brynna. It may not seem like much, but you have gone through a significant trauma."

Being a drunken addict or daring my best friend to die? Brynna wanted to ask.

When she left Dr. Rother's office, her mother was waiting in the parking lot, engine running. Like she did every time Brynna left the office, she offered her a bright smile and a large mocha with extra whipped cream.

"Everything go okay, hon?"

Brynna nodded and took a large gulp, liking the feel of the liquid as it burned her throat. "Yeah, fine."

Her mother turned the wheel, and Brynna leaned against her seat, lazy eyes scanning the tiny town of Crescent City. There really was nothing here. A half-forgotten case of urban sprawl with a spanking-new mall that hardly anyone went to and a housing development with gorgeous homes for great prices for people who wanted to live in the middle of nowhere. She sighed and was ready to close her eyes when a clutch of bright purple fabric caught her eye. It was a hooded sweatshirt in the Lincoln High colors—a shocking, unmatchable purple with a marigold trim—and it was on a girl with a waist-length, glossy black ponytail.

Erica.

She was in a crowd, wrestling her way into the coffeehouse across the street.

"Mom, stop!"

"What? My god, Brynna, what is it? I've got coffee all over my lap."

But Brynna had already stopped listening. She kicked the door open and launched herself out of the car, barely feeling the hot pricks of liquid as her paper coffee cup exploded on the pavement.

"Erica!" Brynna called, running across the street and pushing her way through the crowd. "Erica!"

People turned with angry expressions as she bumped into them, elbowed at them, and tried to get through. But all she was aware of was the pounding of her heart and her need to find Erica.

"Brynna!" Her mother was behind her now, apologizing, grabbing at Brynna's arm.

Brynna spun. "Erica's here, Mom. She's here. I saw her!"

The coffeehouse went dead quiet, all eyes on Brynna. Suddenly, the smell of roasting beans and burnt coffee was cloying, pressing the air out of her lungs. *Where was Erica?*

"I saw her come in here." Brynna rushed to the counter where the girl behind the register took a step back. "Did you just see a girl, about my age, with a purple Lincoln High sweatshirt on?" She patted her own head. "Her hair was in a ponytail. It was black and long."

The barista held an empty coffee bag in one hand and a silver scoop in the other.

"What?"

Brynna slapped the counter. "A girl. Just now. A teenager. In a hooded purple sweatshirt." She turned. "Did anyone—did anyone see the girl who just came in here?"

"I don't know what you're talking about, sweetheart, but no one who looks like that came in here." A heavyset man with a bushy moustache that bled onto his lips answered Brynna.

"Bryn." Her mother's voice was soft, but her grip on Brynna's arm was fierce. "You probably just thought you saw her."

"No, Mom!" She shrugged off her mother's hand and addressed the crowd. "No one saw her?" The desperation in Brynna's voice was evident. *Erica was here; she was alive.* A tiny spark of hope—or was it fear?—dove through her as she looked at the startled faces around her. The blood rushed through her ears and then the quaking fear was back, the dark cloud that hung on her periphery: *It couldn't have been Erica because Erica is dead. Because I dared her, and she died.*

The line of customers had migrated toward the counter as if Brynna was a crazy person—which was how she was beginning to feel as everyone stared, but no one spoke. Finally, the boy behind the cash register—a guy who looked about Brynna's age, maybe a few years older, cleared his throat. "I've been here all morning and I didn't see a girl like that come in here," he said, his voice that sickening, soothing tone that Brynna had grown to loathe. "Maybe she went into the place next door."

Brynna felt a lump grow in her throat as the hot tears pricked at the back of her eyes. "No," she swung her head, whispering to the coffeehouse floor. "I know I saw her. She walked in here. I saw her. I know I did."

Even as she said it, Brynna began to doubt herself.

"Sorry, everyone," Brynna's mother said, addressing the crowd. Brynna watched from the corner of her eye as her mother searched through her pocketbook, then dropped a few bills into the tip jar. "I—I—" Her mother started to stammer, and each time she tried to speak was like a stab to Brynna's heart. "It's just been a long morning. Come on, honey."

The car ride to school was unbearably quiet, the miles stretching out in front of them. Finally, Brynna's mother turned to her. "Honey—"

Brynna shook her head. "I don't want to talk about it, Mom. It was just—a mistake." But even as she said it, she knew it was a lie.

• • •

"Hey."

Brynna started and dropped the books she was picking out of her locker. "Oh god, Teddy, you scared me." She pressed a hand against her chest, certain her heart would eventually press right through.

"You're really jumpy."

Brynna felt herself flush. "Um, yeah, sorry about that." She concentrated hard on gathering her books and closing her locker, spinning the combination lock. Part of her hoped Teddy would go away and let her be alone, but part of her was pulled into those warm, blue eyes, wanting to see his lopsided grin cross his face.

"You weren't at the table this morning."

Brynna waved her pink hall pass. "Appointment. Dentist. No big."

"So hey," Teddy started, falling into step with Brynna, "I wanted to ask you—"

"Brynna!" Evan was shooting toward them like a hurricane, kids bending back in his wake. "I've been looking for you, like, everywhere. Please tell me you have last night's trig homework."

Brynna looked apologetically at Teddy but was glad for the interruption. With Evan, everything was a screaming drama, and his loud theatrics amused Brynna, but more so, his involved stories and perceived personal tragedies stamped out any thought other than Evan.

"Yeah, no problem." She turned to Teddy. "See you later?"

There was something in his eyes that Brynna hadn't seen before, but he nodded and silently turned away.

The rest of the school day—only lunch and three more classes—passed uneventfully, and Brynna was happy. Or she would have been if the image of Erica disappearing into the coffeehouse—and then disappearing altogether—wasn't still etched in her mind. Even as she was being jostled through the crowd of rushing students talking over her, slamming lockers, and the chorus of get-to-class bells, her mind rolled over and over the scene in the coffeehouse and the girl with the long, black ponytail. The second the bell rang, she snatched up her bag and made a beeline for her locker, then dug through a stash of old test papers and Chapstick tubes until she found her cell phone.

Her fingers shook as the phone downloaded her messages and email—a whole slew of messages about nothing in particular, and not a single one from Erica. Brynna's shoulders ached as if an enormous weight had been taken off them.

"All right, Bryn, it's homecoming season," Evan said as he glided up behind her. "What are we going to do about it?"

Brynna blinked and blinked again, forcing her mind into the hallway, forcing herself to look at Evan. "Homecoming?"

Evan rolled his eyes. "That's what I said."

She started to smile. "You care about homecoming season?"

"Maybe. Got a problem with that?" Evan crossed his arms in front of his chest.

"Uh, no..."

Lauren stomped down the hall, eyes narrowed. "Brynna Chase, I hate you so much right now."

Brynna's stomach folded in on itself and she felt her eyes go wide. She knew that, eventually, someone at Hawthorne High would figure out what she did, who she was, but she wasn't ready for it. Not now.

"What—what did I do?"

Lauren glared. Though Evan swore that they both had the same color hair once, Lauren's was bright red now, with dipped black ends. They both had pale, fine-boned features, but even side-by-side, one might mistake them for distant cousins—not siblings and definitely not twins.

But with Lauren's teeth-clenching glare, she looked more like her twin than ever. Evan had the lighter, more fun personality but eyes that could slice you with a look. Lauren tried to be as bubbly, but she had a streak of her father in her: intimidating and argumentative. He was a top-notch lawyer, and Brynna had no doubt that when Lauren grew up, she would be too. She had a way of telling jokes that were a little too serious and poking fun about things no one joked about. Basic questions sounded accusatory coming out of her mouth. Evan blamed it on the fact she never got over being the younger—by six minutes—twin.

"It's what you didn't do." Lauren pushed an index finger in front of Brynna's nose. "You never told me you were, like, a massive swimmer."

Evan gaped. "What?"

"Oh, yeah, your Queen B here has been holding out on us."

Brynna took a miniscule step back, heat washing over her as she crashed into the bank of lockers. "Where did you hear that?"

"Darcy works in the office third period, and your old school sent something over to you. I heard it was your varsity letter for the Lincoln swim team."

Brynna clamped her jaws shut certain, if she didn't, her thundering heart would burst out of her mouth.

"Okay, that has to be a mistake. Bryn hates the water. Don't you, Bryn?"

Lauren mashed her palm against her brother's chest. "They don't give *varsity* letters to freshmen who hate the water." She turned her eyes on Brynna. "So?"

"I, uh, I did swim—for a little bit, over at Lincoln."

Lauren's eyebrows went up. "Varsity?"

Brynna's blood thundered in her ears, and a snapshot of Erica, darting through the water in her Lincoln-purple swimsuit, shot across her mind. "It was a really bad team. Everyone made varsity."

"You must have spent an awful lot of time on the bottom of the pool ignoring, like, everything. Because (a) Lincoln High is beachside and word is that your coach actually makes his team practice in the ocean, and (b) Lincoln was division champions, like, forever."

"Unlike our own Hawthorne Hornets," Evan said, slinging an arm around Lauren. She glared at him. He wrinkled his nose and tossed a glance toward Brynna. "Hornets aren't exactly water insects."

"That's why we totally need you! You have to try out. Hell, you probably don't even have to try out. You own a bathing suit, you're on the team."

"No, no," Brynna started, feeling a bead of sweat itch its way down her stomach. "I—I don't swim anymore."

Evan shrugged. "You're going to have to swim either way."

Brynna felt like she *was* underwater—drowning—the air being forced out of her lungs. "What are you talking about?"

"Swim test."

Brynna looked from Evan to Lauren. "What swim test?"

"The one you need to graduate. Everyone has to take one. It's so lame. Jump in, float, go to the bottom, swim across the pool, and no bikinis."

Heat snaked up the back of Brynna's neck. Just the thought of getting into the pool made her seize up, made her heartbeat start to race.

The pool that was once so freeing to her was like a cellblock now. And water, that moving, churning being with icy, clawing fingers, had taken Erica away, and Brynna knew that it wanted her too.

Brynna forced herself to breathe and prayed that her knees wouldn't buckle. "Why do we need a swim test to graduate?"

This time Evan and Lauren both shrugged. "I don't know. Probably some holdover from the olden days. Or like, 'Send your kids to school! They might die here, but they'll know how to swim.'"

Lauren raised her eyebrows. "Well, they've got something there. Bullets are crap in the water." She swung her attention back to Brynna. "So? You'll do it, right? If you're on the swim team, you automatically pass the swim test. Unless you drown." Lauren laughed at her own joke, a loud kind of guffaw that made Brynna want to hate her.

"Sorry, Lauren. Like I said, I don't swim anymore."

Lauren abruptly stopped laughing and put her fists on her hips. "Why the hell not?"

Brynna wished that Evan would say something, would drag her out of this horrible inquiry, but he did nothing, looking at her with an open face.

She snapped her locker shut and spun the dial. "I just don't." She slipped away from Lauren and Evan without looking back over her shoulder. She didn't need to look to know they were staring at her.

Brynna was out past the double doors and had cleared campus in less than fifteen minutes. Hawthorne High was situated on a huge expanse of rolling green hill bisected with paved paths the students were supposed to walk on but never did. There were bald patches of grass, mostly under the craggy cypress trees from years of kids hanging out, and the usual detritus that came from high school: crushed soda cans that never quite made it into recycling, wadded up McDonald's wrappers under a poster of a fat owl saying

"Give a hoot, don't pollute" that was tacked to a metal trash can. Everything whirled by Brynna. She was walking fast but aimlessly, just needing to move her body—to feel her legs, to propel herself *somehow*. If she could walk, maybe she could leave everything behind. She crossed campus then turned and started again, walking until her legs ached. Sweat was rimming her hairline and breaking out on her upper lip when her phone rang. She glanced at the number on the screen and caught her breath. Butterflies turned into bat wings and stabbed at her stomach. It wasn't the phone number that unnerved her—she didn't recognize that—it was the area code. Six-two-one. Point Lobos.

With a shaking hand, Brynna slid a finger across the screen and pressed the phone to her ear. "Hello?"

There was nothing but static at first, then the high-pitched screech of a girl and a round of far-off laughter.

"Brynna?"

The breathy voice that answered her made Brynna's stomach drop into her shoes.

"Erica?" Brynna's voice was pleading. "Erica?"

"Drink this!"

There was a garbled response, and Brynna realized that the people on the phone weren't talking to her. She heard their indistinct voices and the jostling of the phone as if it was in someone's pocket. She was about to hang up, to chalk the thing up to a random butt dial, when she heard a voice—distinct, sharp.

"No, no, no, my turn!"

She knew the voice from somewhere—didn't she?

Laughter. Something popping. Another voice.

"Okay then, go!"

It wasn't Lauren or Darcy, but she knew that voice too. The first girl laughed then started up again.

"Okay." A muffled, drunken snicker. "I dare you to take off all your clothes and jump, right now."

Ice water shot through Brynna's veins. She wanted to drop the phone, to run. But she was paralyzed, phone pressed to her ear.

"Where? What the hell are you talking about?"

"You. Take off your clothes. Walk your fine little butt to the edge and jump. Come on, Erica…"

The voice belonged to Brynna.

She strained to hear over the thundering sound of her blood as it pulsed in her ears. Every cell in her body was electric, moving so fast that Brynna felt like her skin would explode. Sweat broke out over her upper lip, dampening her palms, and her chest ached, begging her to breathe.

She remembered every second.

In her mind's eye, she could see pictures of that night, of all of them—Erica, Brynna, Ella, Michael, and Jay, bare feet pressed in the sand as the fire crackled in front of them. Behind them, screams, laughter, and the soft music as the end-of-summer party went on. Erica was winding a stray piece of Lincoln-purple crepe paper around and around her hand. Michael kept hiccupping. Brynna leaned against him, breathing out the saturated sweetness of breath soaked with some kind of punch that made her eyes cross.

"So you want me to get buck naked and jump off the pier? First of all, the water is, like, eight degrees."

Ella started to crow like a chicken.

"It's August. The ocean is, like, sixty-eight degrees."

There was a muffled, masculine voice, and Brynna remembered Michael nuzzling into her neck, saying something disgusting about sixty-nine. Holding the phone against her ear, she shivered and pulled back, thinking of his beer-soaked lips kissing the spot behind her ear. Then, the feeling was warm and sensual; now, just the thought sent ice water down her spine.

"Okay." Brynna listened to her own voice sounding foreign on the phone. "No nakedness. In your clothes."

Erica said something muffled, and Brynna's heart started to speed up as memory filled in the gap.

"Just because you dare people to do stuff doesn't mean they have to, Bryn. You don't rule the world."

She remembered the way she felt then, her body made lithe by the liquor, her skin hot from the fire, from Michael's body heat.

"Prove it!" Brynna sang back to her friend.

Brynna took a few steps back on the lawn as if the scene was still in front of her. The chill that ran through her was gone, replaced by a searing heat that oozed into every pore of her body. She felt the fist knotting in her chest. She knew what came next.

"Come on." Brynna could hear sand shifting, bodies moving. She knew that was when she rolled onto her knees and eyed Erica hard. "You said dare, you have to do it, you big baby. It's not my rule. It's the world's rule."

The soft cackle of her friends' agreement.

Erica's silence.

"Okay, okay, fine. I'll totally do it with you since you're such a massive wimp."

"Bryn, for a best friend, you're a super huge ass. But if I have to do it, your big assiness is coming in with me."

"'Kay, but you both should really take your clothes off. They could be a water hazard." Jay's warning was equal parts drunken and lascivious.

"Okay, so, there's no way I could, like, do something else?" Erica again.

"Come on, wimp. You're doing it."

She knew she didn't want to hear anymore, but she couldn't get her arm to move. She was paralyzed in the makeshift park, the phone pressed against her ear.

Erica's groan. "Fine. But I'm shaving off your eyebrows when you fall asleep."

There was a silent pause, and Brynna remembered her and Erica running down the beach. Her toes itched as if the sand were still there. Her palm twitched, remembering the way she pulled Erica along.

We were laughing, Brynna reminded herself. *We were both laughing.*

There was more static on the phone as if someone was fumbling or moving with it. The sound of the ocean was more clear now, the rhythmic whoosh of waves pounding shore.

"Time to step out of your comfort zone, E!"

"May you get eaten by a great white, Brynnie."

Brynna was there again, standing on the dock, the sliver of yellow moonlight washing over her and Erica as though it were dawn. She felt Erica grab her hand this time.

"If I go down, you're going down with me."

Brynna dropped the phone and slammed a hand over her mouth as the crash of the water flooded the earpiece.

They jumped.

Tears filled her eyes and the line went dead.

"Ms. Chase?"

Brynna whirled and threw her arms up instinctively. She was shaking so hard her teeth were chattering, and although her mind was registering someone standing in front of her, that was where recognition stopped.

"Brynna?"

She felt a soft touch on her forearm and stepped back.

"Just breathe."

"Mr. Fallbrook."

Brynna's English teacher was standing in front of her, his head cocked, his normally shining blue eyes clouded. "I'm sorry if I scared you—are you okay?"

Mr. Fallbrook looked barely old enough to be a teacher and had the high school girls following him around Hawthorne High in a panting, giggling line. His hand was still on Brynna's arm, soft, barely touching her, but her heart was still thudding so hard it hurt, and she wanted to tell him everything. He was an adult; he could make everything all right.

"Um…" Immediately she heard the echo of Erica's voice on the phone, the definitive tone of her own as she ordered her friend to jump. "It was just—I just…" She stared down at the phone dumbly then used the back of her hand to swipe at her tears. "Nothing. Thanks."

His hand dropped from her arm, but his concerned expression didn't break. "Shouldn't you be in class?"

"Shouldn't you?"

A small smile touched Mr. Fallbrook's lips. "I'm a teacher and I have a free period. You're a student and you have…?" He raised his eyebrows.

"P.E."

"Look, if there's something wrong, you can talk to me, but you're going to have to go back to class eventually. If you're not feeling well, I can write you a pass to the nurse's office."

Brynna grabbed her phone from the grass. She shoved it into her back pocket and sniffed, trying her best to settle herself into some semblance of a non-hysterical mess. "That's okay. I'm fine, really." She shouldered her bag and started to walk, making a straight line for the school building. "Thanks," she called over her shoulder. Mr. Fallbrook stood, watching her go.

She was met at the double glass doors by Evan. He was framed perfectly on the other side of the glass, arms crossed in front of his chest, a sharp, scrutinizing look marring his features.

"What was that all about?" he asked as he stepped through the door. His brown eyes grazed over Brynna and immediately brightened. "Oh my god. You've been having an affair. You're pregnant with his love child."

Brynna was taken aback and found herself laughing. "No."

Evan frowned, running a hand through his rumpled brown hair. "Nothing good ever happens around here."

"What are you doing out of class?"

He shrugged. "Same thing you are. Ditching."

"I wasn't—"

"Come on."

Brynna wanted to stop him. She wanted to find a dark corner, dig the phone out of her pocket, and listen to the call message again and again, as if every second, every staccato note of the conversation, wasn't already etched in her head. But Evan linked her arm and dragged her toward the student lot.

"Wait," Brynna said as they approached the edge of the grass. "Fallbrook is out here. He knows I have P.E."

Evan put a hand over his eyes, shielding the sun. He did a quick scan. "I don't see him. Besides, Fallbrook remembers what it's like to be young. He's not going to report us. He's not been at Hawthorne long enough to get bitter and start hating his students." He waggled his eyebrows. "He's still fresh. So come on!"

Once Brynna was strapped into the passenger seat and Evan had cleared the Hawthorne campus, she tried to focus on him, on the road in front of them, but Erica and Michael and Ella and Jay kept whispering in the back of her mind.

"You said dare, you have to do it!"

"It's not my rule. It's the world's rule."

"Earth to Queen B!" Evan said, snapping a finger a half inch from her nose. "Want to get something to drink?"

She snapped to attention, eyes wide as she stared at Evan's profile. Immediately, she could feel the hard burn of something smoky and dark as it slipped down her throat, singing away the memories, her reality. Her mouth started to water, and she could feel an icy cup in her hands, could feel the way her stomach churned with the first few swallows of vodka or whiskey or rum.

She was supposed to be over that. She was supposed to be better now.

But it wasn't the alcohol she craved; it was the oblivion that came with it. She knew she was breaking every rule they had forced her to learn at rehab. She knew that she was breaking her probation. She didn't care.

"Yeah, I do."

Evan flashed a wide grin at her and flipped on his blinker. "Great. I know the best place."

FOUR

The silence in the car was palpable, at least to Brynna. The waves kept crashing in her head, and all she could focus on was a drink, something to drown out the voices.

She leaned over and nudged the radio up. Evan shot her a glance and turned the volume back down. "If I didn't know better, I'd think you didn't want to talk to me."

Brynna gave a halfhearted shrug. "So Lauren didn't want to come out today?"

"She's already out. Mom picked her up to get her head shrunk."

"Lauren sees a therapist?"

"Yeah. Sometimes I'll drive her, but it's over off Sand Dollar and there is nothing out there."

"Sand Dollar?"

Brynna thought of the turns her mother took when she dropped her off at Dr. Rother's office. She closed her eyes and visualized the street signs: left on Harper, left on Cole, right on Sand Dollar.

"Do you know who she sees?"

"I don't know, some lady. It's not like I engage the crazy."

Does Lauren see Dr. Rother too?

Brynna started feeling like she was hearing information she wasn't privy to. She knew she shouldn't, but she couldn't help herself. "Why does she go?"

Evan shrugged. "I don't know, chick stuff, I guess. Or probably like how she's depressed because she can never measure up to her beloved twin brother. Who knows? Maybe she's a serial killer."

A tremble went down Brynna's spine, and she forced a laugh. "You're joking."

"Of course I am. She's my sister." He turned the wheel easily. "I think I'd know if I was sharing my bathroom with a socio."

Brynna laughed with Evan, but there was still something nagging at the back of her mind.

Evan slowed the car, the wheels crunching over the gravel. He pushed it into park, and she looked up, surprised.

"Where are we?"

"This is officially downtown Crescent City. Try not to become a coked-up heroin addict."

"Coke and heroin are two different things."

"What's that?" Evan asked as he fed quarters into a meter.

"Uh, nothing. So, why are we here?"

"Because." He pulled open the glass door in front of them and she followed. "You are going to tell me everything you've been hiding from me."

Brynna glanced up at the hand-painted sign above the front door. There were swirls and big hippie flowers, the name *By Joe!* painted in swirly white script.

He yanked her down onto a leather couch in the coffee shop that looked like it was born on a movie set. Two overhead fans turned lazily, slightly moving the warm, coffee-soaked air. Tiny round tables dotted the room—which could have been only ten feet wide, tops—and against one of the latte-covered walls was a heavy wood bar with curlicues of brass design going the whole length down. Ivy and leafy vines trailed from a hodgepodge collection of coffee pots set on the table next to the couch, giving the whole place a sort of coffee-jungle-type vibe.

"Where did you find this place?" Brynna asked.

"Sometimes I need to get away." Evan stood. "I'm getting you their special. It's called Cocoa Bananas. Coffee, chocolate, banana, malt, pixie dust, eye of newt, whipped cream."

"Sounds delicious," Brynna deadpanned.

She tucked her legs underneath her and sunk into the butter-soft leather of the old couch, immediately liking the private vibe, enjoying the enveloping warmth of the place. She was comfortable enough to forget that Evan had dragged her there in an effort to force her secrets out of her and that she was about to down a horrible-sounding coffee drink rather than a mind-numbing shot.

When he came back with their drinks—two behemoth mugs oozing whipped cream and chocolate sprinkles—Brynna was in a relaxed state. Even more so when she took her first sip.

"This sounded disgusting when you described it, but it is incredible."

"There really isn't any eye of newt in it. That was a joke."

She nudged him gently. "Dork."

"So." Evan got comfortable, situating himself so he was facing Brynna full on. "Spill it."

The nervous twitter that the comfort of the room had stamped out was back, full force. The sweet, chocolate liquid turned to acid, burning in her stomach. "I don't know what you're talking about."

"Are you bipolar?"

Brynna pulled back, stunned. "No."

"Then there is something going on with you. Are you doing drugs? Do I have to go all public service announcement on your ass?"

She wrinkled her nose. "No, of course not. On both counts. I'm fine, Ev, seriously."

"Nope. You were all fun, bubbly Bryn and then, *kapow!* You're terrified of your own shadow, and you've worn the same hoodie and jeans to school three days in a row."

She looked down at the jeans in question. "You noticed that?"

"Everyone noticed. Darcy was going to host an intervention."

"There is—"

Evan put a hand on her shoulder. "Spare me. If you're going to say that there isn't anything wrong, then it's been nice knowing you."

Brynna gaped. "Seriously? If I don't spill some stupid secrets to you, you're going to stop being my friend?"

But Brynna's indignant act dropped the second she saw the look on Evan's face. It was sad. Kind.

"I want to help you, B. I care about you. If something is bothering you, it's bothering me too."

A hint of a lump started to form in her throat. "Does everyone else feel this way too?"

"Lauren and Darcy? No, they couldn't give a crap. Teddy, I don't know about. So come on, B, what's going on with you?"

Brynna put down her mug and studied a blue ink stain on the leg of her jeans. Part of her wanted to tell Evan everything, to let someone shoulder a tiny bit of her burden, even if it was only for the duration of a car ride and a cup of cocoa-malt-banana-coffee. But the other part—the louder part—rallied for her to drop her coffee and run, or to make up something, some lie that would appease Evan so she could keep his friendship—and her secret.

Internally, Erica, the dare, that night would follow Brynna forever. She would never be able to dismiss what had happened, would never be able to overcome her grief and her guilt. If she hadn't dared—then prodded, then pulled Erica into the water, Erica would still be alive. If she had gone back in the water again, maybe she could have saved her best friend.

Erica was the pretty one, the fun one, the smart one. Brynna was just the girl who survived.

"Okay, look. I'll tell you a secret first, and then you'll know that we're bound together forever and you can tell me yours."

Brynna nodded, glad just to have a few more minutes while Evan looked away, worrying his bottom lip. Finally, he sucked in a dramatic breath and focused his eyes on her.

"No one else knows this, B, okay?"

"Okay, just between us."

He closed his eyes for a long beat and then blurted, "I hate corduroy."

Brynna gaped. "Seriously? That's your enormous, earth-shattering secret? That you hate fabrics?"

He held up a finger. "One. I hate *one* fabric."

Brynna rolled her eyes but found herself smiling.

"It's serious!" Evan smirked behind his coffee mug and took a long sip. "Okay, also—"

"If you're going to tell me you hate seersucker too, I'm going to beat you with this coffee mug."

"I don't know what seersucker even means. My secret is that I hate corduroy. I hate the shoosh-shoosh sound it makes when people walk. Also, I'm gay."

He kept his focus on her, and Brynna could nearly see the cogs working in his head behind his bright, wide eyes. He was sitting up ramrod straight and holding his breath.

"Okay," Brynna said.

He let out a chocolaty, banana-scented whoosh of air. "Okay? That's your response?"

Brynna blinked innocently. "Who am I to judge what kind of fabric a guy likes?" She grinned. "Honestly, I kind of had an idea."

Evan shrugged, his cheeks going pink.

"So no one else knows? Not even Lauren?"

He stared into his cup. "Honestly? Lauren and I aren't that close. We shared a womb, but other than that, we don't have much in common." He paused, sipping the last bit of coffee. "Everyone thinks they know that I'm gay, I guess. But no. You're the first person I've actually come out to." He let out another long breath and laughed at the end. "Felt kind of good." His face went slightly serious. "Do you want to lecture me on going to hell or whatever? Do you hate that I lied to you?"

"Well, I am crushed that we'll never get married and have lots of tiny, corduroy-hating babies, but I guess I can just continue to casually date Teddy…"

"Thanks," he said softly. "You're a really good friend, B. My best friend. And don't worry; I am going to be just as understanding and supportive when you come out as heterosexual. Is that your secret?"

A slight chuckle. "No."

"Tell me."

Brynna tried to think of a funny and light response for Evan, but all she could think about was the dare. The humor slid right out of her, and she chanced a glance over the rim of her coffee cup. Evan's eyes were still fixed and warm. With the soft leather couches and the cozy, coffee-scented air, she felt a comfort she hadn't felt since before that night at Harding Beach ever happened.

Brynna sucked in a determined breath. "Back at my old school… back at Lincoln, um, there was this party at the end of the summer. We were partying at this beach house—the whole school was. A few of us broke away and went out onto the beach. It was late, way past midnight."

Evan's eyes flashed and he scooched closer, setting his mug down and pressing his hand, palm warm from the coffee, against Brynna's.

"Go on," he whispered.

"We were just screwing around. Drinking and whatever."

Like the flames of the bonfire, the memory flared up, images flicking up in her mind's eye. She felt Erica's bare skin pressed against her as they sat shoulder to shoulder on the beach, giggling.

She saw the red party cup propped up by the sand, smelled the swirling fruit punch and alcohol smell.

"Someone"—she couldn't bring herself to say Erica's name—"someone went into the water. A girl. She drowned."

Brynna peeked up at Evan who was sitting, rapt. His eyes were wide and he was pressing a hand over his open mouth. "Oh my god, B. And you were there? You were on the beach when this happened?"

She bobbed her head without thinking about it. "Yeah."

"That must have been awful for you! To watch one of your classmates drown." He shuddered. "Did you see the body?"

Brynna stared straight forward, not really seeing anything. "No. They said she got caught in a riptide. They said it probably swept her under and..." She cleared her throat but couldn't force herself to go on.

"And it probably sucked the body out to sea. Did they ever find it? Probably not, right, because of currents and sharks and stuff? Ohmigod, Bryn, no wonder you're all jumpy lately. Is this, like, the anniversary of it? Or, no, it's not summer. Her birthday or something?"

Brynna wanted to say something about the call, about the tweet, but the static in her head drowned every thought out. All she could do was shake her head from side to side.

"That's not everything, is it?"

Brynna snapped her gaze back to Evan then dipped her head again, feeling the weight of her secret closing in on her.

"She was my best friend."

"Who was?"

"Erica. The girl who died. She was my best friend, and she jumped into the water because I dared her to jump with me."

Brynna held her breath, waiting for Evan's face to harden. She was ready for him to spring to his feet and walk out the door or to point an accusing finger at her and call her something horrible.

Finally, after a beat that lasted a lifetime for Brynna, Evan said, "B, you don't think you're somehow responsible for Erica's death, do you?"

Brynna couldn't have answered if she wanted to; her heart was lodged firmly in her throat.

"Because that's completely ridiculous."

"But I was the one who dared her."

"And who are you, the Queen of Sheba? Erica didn't have to go through with it."

The pounding was beginning in her head. "I made her. I told her she had to."

"So you roofied her, carried her limp body down the beach, and dumped her in the surf? Then you're right. You did it."

"No, but—"

"But nothing. She jumped because she wanted to. And you obviously thought it was fine because you did it too. No one could blame you."

Brynna paused, her teeth pressed against her lower lip. "I think someone does though."

"What are you talking about?"

She clasped her hands hard, suddenly hyperaware of every noise in the coffeehouse: the hiss of the steam escaping the espresso machine, the weird, new-agey music that was barely audible, the tink and clatter of coffee mugs being stacked on the counter.

"B?"

"Someone—someone tweeted me from Erica's account. It said, 'Remember me?' over and over again."

"That could be anyone, you know, it could mean anything."

"And then someone called me and it—" Just the echo of the voices on the phone stung her. "It was a recording of us that night. Right…right before everything happened."

"Someone's playing a joke on you. That's all it is. Someone is playing a really awful joke on you. It's probably some horrible ass from your old school. Some idiot who thinks he's being funny."

Brynna wasn't sure if Evan was trying to convince her or himself.

"Did Erica have any siblings or anything? They could have easily had access to her accounts and stuff."

She shook her head. "No. Well, her father was married before, but his stepson was, like, ten years older than us. He never lived with Erica or anything."

Evan tapped his foot on the hardwood. "B—what is it?"

Brynna swallowed hard. "What if—what if it's not someone from my old school? What if it's Erica? What if she's back?"

FIVE

Brynna nearly dropped her mug when her cell phone started blaring. She glanced down, certain it was Erica, and blew out a semi-relieved sigh when she recognized the number.

"Hello?"

"Oh, Brynna, thank god. Where have you been? Why weren't you answering?"

"Dad?" Brynna inched back as though her father were standing in front of her. "Uh, I was in school. I can't use the phone until school is over."

Her father sounded exhausted—and irate. "You got out of school over an hour ago."

Brynna's eyes went wide. "I did?"

"Your mother and I have been worried sick. She came to pick you up and you weren't there. She's been driving around looking for you, and I was just about to leave the office and—Brynna, what's wrong with you?"

"Nothing, Dad. I just lost track of time."

He let out a long, exasperated sigh. "You know we had a deal."

A lick of anger sparked in the pit of Brynna's stomach. "I know, Dad," she said slowly, trying to keep her voice even. "I wasn't doing anything. I just—" She thought of telling her father about the tweet but just as quickly dismissed the idea. Her parents would probably move Dr. Rother in with them and give Brynna a drug test with her Cheerios every morning and a breathalyzer check at lunch. "I was just," she thought fast, "watching the swim team practice."

There was a long pause, and Brynna imagined her father, pushed back in his enormous leather office chair, pulling out his legal pad and writing himself a message: *Brynna—late—on drugs?*

"I'm really sorry. I guess I just got caught up. The team is doing heats." She pinched the bridge of her nose, trying to stave off the headache that was already starting. "I'm helping the coach keep time."

"The swim team, huh?" Her father's voice took on a note of interest, and Brynna envisioned him scrawling a second note: *swim team—better?*

"It's over in twenty minutes. And Evan's here. He could drive me home."

Another pause. "You're still in trouble, young lady. Your mother will be waiting outside the gym when the swim team is through."

• • •

After a "we're all trying to learn together" lecture from her parents and a grounding, Brynna retired to her bedroom and braved a hot shower that was more panic-inducing than relaxing. Wrapped in her robe, she crossed her room, her fingers brushing over her iPad. Should she check?

She swiped the thing on, and when she got to her mailbox, she let out the breath she didn't know she had been holding. The only tweets were from Lauren with a few responses from Teddy and Darcy. Nothing serious.

Nothing from Erica.

She glanced down at the phone and scrolled to the call log, finding the number with the Point Lobos area code. She hit the send button without waiting for her heart rate to climb or that little inner voice to tell her to stop. There was an odd crackle as if her call was going through actual wires and being connected, and then she heard the first ring. It shot a chill straight through her.

What would I say to Erica?

I'm sorry.

I should have let the dare go.

I miss you.

Is it really you?

Images of Erica pinballed through Brynna's head while a second ring sounded. She remembered Erica with pigtails when they step-touched on their first day of dance class. Erica licking her greasy, salt-covered fingers after she ate all Brynna's fries when Brynna never even offered. The way Erica's eyes looked when Brynna said, "I dare you." Wide. Round. Scared.

There was a click on the other end, and someone sucked all the air out of the room.

"Erica, is that you?" she stuttered into the phone.

There was more static and then, "Phillips Mortuary, may I help you?"

Brynna felt the phone as it left her fingers. The gentle sound of it thudding on carpet seemed to reverberate through her skull as if it was the loudest sound on earth. She wanted to scream—but she was paralyzed, the cloying scent of thousands of white lilies stinging her nostrils.

"Hello? Phillips Mortuary?"

There were flowers everywhere. White lilies, which Erica hated, and piped-in classical music, which Erica hated even more. Would have hated, Brynna corrected herself. Erica was dead—that's what they kept telling her. Erica—caught in a black-and-white toothy grin from the cover of the Phillips Mortuary Memorial program—glared up at Brynna, her dark eyes smoldering, accusing.

"It should have been you..."

It was Erica's voice, barely a whisper, but Brynna would almost swear she felt her best friend's breath tickling her ear.

People started to file in then, uncomfortably silent, holding their breaths as they took their seats in front of an empty casket that was supposed to represent Erica. Brynna couldn't stand it any longer, sure that if she stayed one more second, the overwhelming smell of dying flowers would strangle her.

Brynna was terrified. She was confused.

How could the call have come from the mortuary?

She was crazy, she was guilty, she wanted *not* to feel. She spun around the room, her eyes darting toward all of her old stash points: in the box spring, in her jewelry box, a bottle stuffed in her boot. It may have been illegal and unhealthy, but she didn't care—having her heart beat through the roof and her skin pricking with fear couldn't be healthy either. Her lips felt dry and sticky, and she was tearing through her things now in case something had been forgotten, been carelessly tossed into a box: a lone pill, a fat green tablet of leftover Oxy to obliterate the facts, make her float away from memory. Maybe she had left one of the mini vodka bottles she used to stash in her purse. They were barely a taste, but it was something, something to quell the aching in her chest, the way her every cell seemed to fold in on itself with want.

"Brynna?"

Her mother's voice floated up the stairs, and all at once, Brynna remembered that she was in her new house, in her new room, in her new life, and she was supposed to be better. She was supposed to deal with problems with deep breathing and talking to "peers she could trust." Brynna looked around at the detritus of an almost-binge. Her head started to pound, and there was a lump in her throat.

"Pizza will be here in fifteen minutes."

Brynna swallowed hard and pushed herself off the floor, pressing the mess back into her closet.

"Okay, Mom."

Fifteen minutes was all she needed.

Brynna fished her phone from the mess and redialed the number, breathing deeply as she paced. This was a mistake. A misunderstanding. She couldn't have heard—

"Phillips Mortuary."

It was the same female voice that answered the time before, but this time, it was fraught with annoyance.

"Hello, is anyone there?"

"Hi." Brynna forced the word out. "Hi, I'm sorry. I—I just received a call from this number."

"That's impossible, miss. There are no outgoing calls on this number."

Brynna blinked, straightened. "No, but I just did. I just redialed it and now I'm talking to you."

The woman let out a sharp sigh. "You can call me, but I can't call you. This number doesn't make calls. That's from the office line—"

"No," Brynna said, sweat heating up the back of her neck. "No, someone just called me."

"I'm sorry, ma'am, but—"

"Erica. Do you know Erica?" She knew she sounded desperate—crazy, even. And as tears pricked at the back of her eyes, that's how she felt.

"I'm sorry, ma'am. I can't help you."

The dial tone droned in Brynna's ear as everything came crashing down around her.

"No." She dropped the phone and pressed her palms against her ears, terrified that she would hear something, that the phone would ring again, and this time, it would be Erica. *Still alive, or back from the dead?*

A tiny voice in her head tried to reason with her: it was a weird ping from the cell phone tower. It was a snag in the service. But all of that was stomped out by the sickening terror that wracked her. She wasn't sure when she started crying, was even more surprised when her parents rushed through her bedroom door and gaped down at the mess on the floor. Brynna was pressed so hard against her bed that the iron bar of the frame was digging into her flesh. It hurt, but it was real and tangible and it was better than the pain of memory, of disembodied voices and mysterious phone calls.

"Brynna, Brynna, honey, what happened? Are you okay?"

She was trembling completely now, biting so hard into her lower lip that her mouth filled with the hot, metallic taste of blood. Brynna blindly shook her head from side to side.

Her mother came to her side immediately, but her dad stood in the doorway looking both parts helpless and angry. He used one hand to pick up her laptop and the other to unplug it.

"You're supposed to be grounded."

"Adam, can you forget about the rules for two seconds? Something happened to Bryn."

"I understand that, but forgetting about the rules isn't going to help her." His eyes flicked over Brynna's, but she was too scared to care. She wanted to curl into her mother and cry, to let everything out, every last detail of the last fourteen months. But she couldn't. She was supposed to be better. She was supposed to be starting a new life.

But something from the old wouldn't let her go...

"There was—I got a call from—" Brynna looked at both of her parents, each one wearing an expectant expression. She couldn't tell them.

They'll know you killed her, a little voice at the back of her head whispered. *They'll know you're crazy,* another one confirmed. *They'll have you locked up...again.*

Brynna dropped her head into her hands, using her fingertips to grip at the skin on her forehead as she pinched her eyes shut.

"I just got scared is all."

She didn't have to look up to know that the loud whoosh of air she heard was her father trying to regroup. She wasn't surprised when she felt her mother's palm on the back of her neck, gentle and warm.

"That's okay, Brynna. We know that this is difficult for you."

But Brynna didn't want to hear another Dr. Rother-ism. She was tired of hearing her mother utter phrases from the Alateen handbook—the one handed out to the parents of every teen in Alcoholics Anonymous, empty words that were meant to be helpful or inspiring but only made Brynna want to escape all over again. She was tired of her father working hard to act concerned when Brynna knew the only thing he was doing was biding his time until his next trip, until his next flight where he could be a thousand miles away from his drunken, screwed-up daughter.

"I'm sorry," she said, pushing away from her mother. "I'm sorry I worried you guys. I think I should probably just get some sleep. It's been a long day."

Her mother eyed her suspiciously but eventually kissed Brynna's forehead and got up to leave. Her father blew her a kiss and offered a "sleep well, honey," and they both shut the door, leaving Brynna in silence. She crawled to the wall and clicked off the lights, then made her way into her bed, not bothering to change her clothes or take off her makeup. At least in sleep, she wouldn't have to think.

• • •

"Bryn! Bryn, is this going to be an every morning thing now?"

Brynna's mother was standing a half inch from her bedside. Brynna tried to open eyes that felt glued shut.

"What?" she finally mumbled.

She heard her mother smack the top of the alarm clock, quieting the fuzzy quips of two morning DJs as they screamed about something. Then there was a hand on her arm, shaking her violently.

"Okay, okay, I'm up!" She propped herself up on one elbow, her body screaming in protest as every muscle tightened and ached.

"You look awful. Did you sleep at all last night?"

The details of the previous night flooded back, and Brynna's eyes were wide now, blinking at her mother. She cleared her throat. "Uh, no, I slept fine. Just tired, I guess. Sorry about the alarm clock."

Brynna threw her blankets off and went straight for the bathroom, her mother's eyes hot on the back of her neck. She didn't want to face her, was afraid that every detail of last night's call was written on her face—or at least the guilt of it.

"I'll be downstairs in a minute," she called over her shoulder as she turned on the faucet, hoping her mother would get the message and go away.

Brynna stepped under the hot stream of water, letting it break over her head and cascade down her shoulders. The hot water felt like pinpricks on every inch of skin. Brynna was still cold, still trembling as though she had jumped off the pier into that frigid water just last night.

• • •

"Well, look what the cat dragged in," Lauren started.

"Or barfed up," Evan finished with a good-natured chuckle. "What happened to you?"

Brynna slumped in her seat, the mingling scents of cafeteria food and student bodies making her stomach churn. She snapped to attention every time she heard a sound—the ringing of a cell phone, some girl's shrill laughter—and as a result, she was exhausted, her own body weighted and pulling her down. She propped her chin in her hands, too tired to even offer Evan and Lauren a good quip back.

"Bryn, seriously, are you sick or something?" Darcy's voice was soothing at her ear, and Brynna shook her head, then glanced at the concerned faces of her friends.

"No," she finally muttered. "I just didn't sleep well."

"For, like, the last thirty days?" Darcy said, poking her fork into something that vaguely resembled mashed potatoes.

"Leave her alone, Darce. So, who's ready for homecoming shopping?"

That snapped Brynna to attention. "What? Homecoming shopping?"

Now it was Lauren staring at Brynna. "Don't tell me you forgot. We talked about it yesterday. I left a message on your phone."

Brynna's mouth went dry. "On my phone?"

Lauren screwed up her face. "Uh, yeah. How else do you send a message? Carrier pigeon?"

Evan reached over the table and fished Brynna's phone out of her purse. "Duh. See? Three missed messages."

The hairs on Brynna's neck pricked as blazing heat raced down her spine. She watched, every action in molasses-slow motion, as Evan hit the "call voice mail" button and pressed her phone to his ear. Before she could consider what she was doing, Brynna launched herself across the table, slamming her phone from Evan's hand. It landed with a shattering thud on the ground, and Brynna, balancing on her belly on the tabletop, was half-covered in Evan's mashed potatoes and the dregs of Lauren's mocha.

"Holy overreaction, Batman!"

"Bryn, what the hell?" Evan kicked his chair back and stood, picking bits of mashed potato from his T-shirt.

Darcy and Lauren had hands pressed to their mouths, but Brynna could hear their stifled giggles, because the rest of the lunchroom had gone astoundingly quiet.

"I'm…sorry?" It was more question than apology, and Brynna wriggled herself off the table, ignoring the mashed potato scales that arced off her sweatshirt. She crumpled to her knees and started gathering the remains of her phone. Evan jumped down to join her, putting a hand on her forearm. His eyes were wide and smoldering brown when she looked up at him.

"What was that about? Did something else happen?"

Brynna eyed him for a short beat before shaking her head curtly. She knew he would tell her again to brush the call off. She wished she could.

The students in the lunchroom picked that perfect moment to get over Brynna's James Bond maneuver and went back to talking, screaming, laughing—making enough merciful noise so Brynna couldn't explain even if she wanted to.

Darcy laced her arm through Brynna's the instant Brynna stood up. "I'm pretty sure wearing mashed potatoes is against the Hawthorne dress code. Come on, I'll get you a pass and you can get into the locker room."

Brynna let Darcy lead her from the lunchroom. She didn't bother to look back.

"Um, so I guess you're a pretty private person, then?" Darcy asked once they stepped into the deserted hall.

Brynna's lips were still Sahara dry. Her throat felt constricted, but she forced herself to talk, offering a giggle that was supposed to sound carefree but came out tinny and staid.

"I think it was just some weird, Pavlovian reaction," she lied. "My brother used to steal my cell phone and broadcast all my messages."

Darcy was silent for a beat, her arm still wrapped around Brynna's. She didn't look at Brynna when she said, "You don't need to lie to me."

Brynna stopped, certain the thud-thud-thud of her heart would give her away. "I'm not lying. Why would you think that?"

Darcy dropped Brynna's arm and kept walking, the hall long and empty in front of them. "Because you don't have a brother."

Brynna had to jog to catch up to her. "He's my stepbrother."

"Sure. Fine. Whatever."

"Darcy!" Brynna put her hand on Darcy's shoulder and forced the girl to face her.

Darcy blinked. "I work in the office, Bryn. I've seen your records. I know you're an only child."

Brynna's thudding heart jumped into her throat, and her lungs felt like they were going to collapse. The lockers all around her seemed to close in, and the smell of industrial cleaner from the shiny hallway floor was sharp in her nose, almost suffocating. *Darcy had seen all her records?*

Thoughts spun in Brynna's brain. Did Darcy know why Brynna came to Hawthorne? Did she know about Erica? Could she have been the one—?

Darcy's eyes were a clear, pale blue. With her white-blond hair and little ski-jump nose, she looked like a pixie. With her wire-framed glasses and her cardigan sweater, she looked like a little, perfect-student pixie. Brynna swallowed. "What else do you know about me?"

"I know that you transferred from Lincoln High where you were on the swim team, that you're horrible in math and earth science, and that you have to see a psychologist."

"Do they always give that kind of information to student aides?"

Darcy flushed barely pink for a brief second before slipping right back into her normal confident vibe. She shrugged. "It's no big deal."

Darcy said the last while ushering Brynna through the glass double doors of the administration office. Brynna looked around, suddenly anxious, suddenly extremely aware of her surroundings. She took in the burnt-orange, industrial-style carpet that seemed to only exist in high school offices and breathed in the slight smell of pencil shavings and office supplies. Muted music came from one of the desks, something with a cheery, Spanish beat that seemed remarkably out of place among the cubicle walls and office furniture that was all done up in shades of gray. There was a series of trophies and fading pictures of Hawthorne Hornets, going all the way back to the class of 1980. Brynna briefly wondered what happened last year, where those kids were, but immediately forgot about them as she looked away. There were the usual antismoking and antidrug posters that featured sad-looking kids from 1979 posted on either wall, plus a newer-looking antibullying one with cartoon kids ganging up on a single loner.

Brynna snapped back to reality as the double doors snapped shut and Darcy made her way behind the big desk where she pulled out a pink pad of hall passes.

"Hey," Brynna whispered, so low she wasn't sure if Darcy could hear her.

Darcy looked up, blond eyebrows rising and disappearing into her bangs. "Hm?"

Brynna looked around again, taking in the two boys sitting outside the principal's office, one ripping at the bottom of his shorts, one eyeing her with a look she didn't like. Brynna stepped closer to Darcy.

"Can I talk to you for a second?"

Darcy shrugged, giving her the universal sign for "spill it."

Brynna paused, and Darcy took a step closer.

"Could you, like, not say anything about my record?" She felt dumb saying it, feeling the heat singe her cheeks. Really, she didn't care if the group knew about her bad grades, but if they knew she was in therapy—that she *had* to see a therapist according to the Crescent County District Attorney's office—she knew the questions would start.

"Why were you doing drugs?"

"What did you talk about in rehab?"

"Why did the police send you there?"

Though she could answer all their questions without mentioning Erica out loud, Erica always came up, always seemed to whisper in her ear. "Tell them, Bryn. Tell them what you did to me. If you weren't guilty, you wouldn't have needed to numb yourself…you wouldn't have needed to get rid of me…again."

Brynna could almost see the flash of anger in Erica's eyes then, and it always shot a jolt of ice water through her veins.

She shrank back from mentioning anything about her past at all.

Darcy was silent for a beat, her blue eyes seeming to consider Brynna's wish, seeming to weigh whether she wanted to side with her.

Finally, "Why? It's not that big of a deal."

Brynna felt a momentary flash of relief. "I just…" She fumbled with her hands. "Just want to start fresh and all."

"Whatever. As an office aide, I'm sworn to secrecy anyway."

"You are?"

Darcy's smile was easy. "No. Anyone can be an office aide. I'm pretty sure the only requirements are that you have to be a student here and you have to know all the letters from A to Z. In order. Don't worry though"—she patted Brynna's shoulder—"your secret is safe with me."

Brynna offered her a small smile.

Darcy wrote out the pass, and Mrs. Nunez, the head secretary, initialed it and handed it back. Darcy held it out to Brynna.

"You know where the locker room is, right?"

Brynna took the pass and tucked it in her back pocket. She nodded, her eyes never leaving Darcy's. Darcy smiled as Brynna left the office, but Brynna wasn't so sure the smile was kind.

There was no one in the locker room when Brynna stepped in. Its cinder-block walls were long and colorless, lending an air of inescapability to the place. There were windows every few feet, long, narrow rectangles placed high enough up the wall that any light they brought in dissipated far above the girls' heads. The fluorescent overhead lights constantly buzzed, and the yellow light they offered seemed only to accentuate the overall gray.

When the girls were lined up at their lockers, their chatter and laughter bounced off the walls and the flashes of color—someone's brand-new fluorescent pink bra, the green of a Hawthorne High cheerleading uniform—cut through the overall grimness and made the room bearable. The scent of their perfumes, scented body soaps, and flowery deodorants almost masked the smell of mildew and wet cement. Now, the odor was almost overwhelming, and every step she took seemed to amplify into a grating smack of rubber flip-flop.

Brynna wrinkled her nose and picked her way around the long wooden bench that bisected the rows between lockers. It was the middle of the school day, and though it was an unintelligible din, she could hear students bustling about outside. She had snatched her cell phone before Evan had a chance to scroll through it, and Darcy had mostly agreed to keep her secret. There was no reason for Brynna to feel uneasy, but walking through the shadowed rows of the lockers, her heart fluttered and her hackles went up.

Brynna steeled herself and went directly to locker 127 where her gym clothes—a pair of yoga capris and the required Hawthorne Hornets green T-shirt—were wadded on top of a pair of last year's sneakers. She yanked the T-shirt out of her locker, sputtering and coughing when something flew out with it.

Brynna looked down at her sweatshirt. It was covered in fine grains of sand. They were all over her jeans too and blanketing her toes, crunching underneath the soles of her shoes as she moved.

She looked back into her locker and took an involuntary step back. The blood started rushing through her veins as streams of sand flowed from her locker.

Brynna pulled everything out—yoga pants, sneakers, socks—and the rivulets came faster, pooling at her feet.

There was a mound of sand on the bottom of her locker; it was easily three feet tall.

Brynna could feel the prick of tears, the tight lump forming in her throat. What was happening? Who was doing this to her?

"Someone from Lincoln," she whispered, trying to moisten her sandpaper lips. "It has to be." She shook her head, dusting the sand from her sweatshirt and jeans. "Someone's stupid idea of a stupid prank."

But even as she thought it, her brain was working fast: someone from Lincoln would have to drive at least forty-five minutes to fill her Hawthorne locker with sand. That was a long way to go for a prank.

But it's possible, Brynna pushed back. It's possible.

The revelation did nothing to stop the tears that rushed down her cheeks; it did nothing to calm the thunderous pound of her heart.

Remember me?

The image of Erica's words burned their way into Brynna's eyes.

Remember me?

Was it a plea or a warning?

Suddenly, the sand, the locker room—everything—fish-eyed then blurred in Brynna's vision. Her skin seemed to tighten, her bones threatening to break. She sat down hard on the metal bench, eye level with the base of her locker. Half the sand was gone now, exposing a tiny strand of purple. Brynna leaned forward, gingerly pinching the ribbon between thumb and forefinger. She gave it a subtle tug, rubbing the fabric between her fingers. But it wasn't fabric.

It was a short length of deep purple crepe paper.

SIX

"Erica?" she whispered.

Feeling a shiver that cut all the way to her bones, Brynna tried to grip her locker door to smack it shut, but her fingers shook and her palms were slick with sweat. She tried to drop the crepe paper but it stuck to her palm. When she was finally able to move her hands, she yanked the paper from her skin and gaped, losing her breath. The bright, brilliant, Lincoln High purple of the streamer bled into her palm. A smear about the size of a quarter looked like it was burned into her flesh, like a spot of blood that could never be washed off.

"No!"

The word came back to her, echoing off the cinder-block walls and sounding more and more desperate each time it came back.

She thought she heard someone giggling.

"Hello?" What was meant to be a yell came out a tortured, choked sound. "Is someone in here?"

No response except the pitiful echo. Brynna stood statue still for what seemed like a millennium but must have been less than a minute. She pinched her eyes shut, trying to breathe deeply, trying to remember whatever the hell it was that Dr. Rother told her she was supposed to do. Her chest ached and her lungs popped with fire. She couldn't pull in a breath, couldn't force air between her lips. She felt like she was running a marathon while breathing through a straw. Sweat beaded at her hairline, shot like pinpricks all over her skin.

"Hello?" This time it was a barely a whisper, and Brynna immediately prayed that no one would answer her, that the bell would ring, that students would come flooding in. Anything to get her out of this moment, to get her out of this locker room where her feet felt cemented to the ground.

Footsteps sounded behind her—a shuffling, unsure sound—and Brynna whirled, the crunch of her sneakers grating against the spilled sand sounding a thousand times louder than it should have.

She pressed her hands to her chest, trying to force in a breath, when no one was behind her. But still her lungs failed her. Her eyes started to water and pain started at her temples, shooting fire bolts behind her eyes. She knew she had to sit down. She knew she should press her head between her knees. She knew that she couldn't force her body to do either of those things.

Brynna let out a choked sob as an unassailable fear washed over her. There was someone with her in that locker room, someone watching her struggle to breathe, someone watching her shiver and cry. Someone who had no intention of helping her.

Brynna saw her knuckles go white as she gripped the open door of her locker, her wet palm sliding down as her knees gave out. She landed with a hard thud on her butt and pulled her knees into her chest.

Breathe, breathe, breathe.

Blood, like ocean waves, crashed through her ears.

Breathe, breathe, breathe.

Her thundering heart pounded against her thigh.

There's no one else in here. There's no one else in here. Breathe.

Brynna had almost convinced herself, was almost breathing normally, was feeling the slowing, normalizing pace of her beating heart.

"There's no one else in here," she whispered to herself.

Finally, using the lockers behind her for leverage, she stood, walking on shaky legs toward the bank of sinks at the front of the locker room. She rounded the corner when she heard one of the automatic sinks start flowing, the water rushing so hard into the basin that it splashed a fine mist onto the concrete floor. There was no one in front of the sink.

It snapped off as Brynna approached it.

Swallowing hard, she peeked into the basin where a single tube of lipstick lay, cap off, the bright red color leaving streaks on the white porcelain. Brynna didn't need to check the label to know what color it was or what brand. It was Erica's color, Erica's brand.

Across the mirror, written in the candy-apple red that Erica adored so much, were the words, *I haven't forgotten you, Brynna.*

A starburst of heat exploded in front of her eyes. Her whole body went rigid. She doubled over and dry-heaved, the image of her sneakers below her swirling and blurring with her tears.

"I have to get out of here. I have to get out of here!"

Brynna crossed the locker room like a shot, at some point having enough presence of thought to snatch up her bag and continue to breathe. She burst through the double doors and peeled through the now-crowded halls. All around her, kids were talking and laughing and yelling, but it all faded to a cacophonous din in her ears. She walked with purpose but aimlessly, as the halls of Hawthorne High bowed in different directions. Everywhere she looked were faces she couldn't recognize, faces that clearly didn't recognize her. The crowd, the walls, all started to close in on her until she burst through the double doors that led to the back quad, doubling over and desperately sucking in huge gasps of air. Pinpricks broke out along her fingertips and palms, and Brynna closed her eyes, feeling a single bead of sweat drip down the center of her back. Her chest was tight. Her heart slammed against her rib cage so hard that she was sure it would crack.

"Panic attack," she whispered to herself. "I'm having a panic attack."

She heard Dr. Rother's voice echoing in her head: "Concentrate on your breathing, Brynna. Focus."

Focus, Brynna commanded herself. *Focus on your breathing and your shoes and the cement in front of you and not the sand, not the churn of the surf that seemed to always crash. Concentrate on the here and now. You're here, at Hawthorne High, and Erica is dead.*

That last word—*dead*—echoed in Brynna's mind, and she couldn't concentrate. She fisted her hands and stepped forward, trying to focus on something, some stupid rote action that would free her mind from the panic cycle. She took another forward step then started a slow jog toward the football field and the back forty, concentrating only on her footsteps, only on covering ground.

She climbed up the bleacher stairs and pinned herself into a corner, the high walls of the structure guarding her against the wind. She crumbled, letting the tears fall rapidly now, not caring when her soft cry went to spastic hiccupping.

Why would Erica do this to me?

The sound of muffled laughter and someone coughing snapped her back to reality. Heat washed over her cheeks, and she used the heel of her hand to wipe away the tears that were already drying. Muffled voices went around again, and bile climbed the back of Brynna's throat—was she really going crazy?

When a snake of cigarette smoke wafted up from the open slots between the bleachers, she glanced down, her heart speeding up as she noticed a group of kids sprawled out on the hard-packed earth, smoking. One was holding a water bottle that Brynna knew wasn't water. The girl took a large swig and passed it to the guy next to her who mumbled something and took a swig of his own.

Brynna glanced down at the broken face on her phone while her mind shattered into millions of images—all of them Erica, all of them her and then *not* her—one minute laughing, splashing, the next minute, gone.

Numb the pain…

Brynna's mouth watered. Her head pounded. She could dull the pain again, just this one time. She swung her legs down, but everything froze when she heard the laughter. It was high-pitched and funny, the kind of laugh that made you giggle too. It was too loud, too distinct.

It can't be Erica.

She was on her feet then, vaulting over the metal guardrail of the bleachers. Her feet hit the hard-packed ground with a thud, and all the kids huddled under the bleachers—there were three of them—stopped what they were doing and glared at her.

There were two scrawny boys that Brynna vaguely recognized from school and a tall girl with fake platinum blond hair. She was holding a cigarette a half-inch from her pale, chapped lips, and Brynna watched, mesmerized, as smoke curled up in a lazy trail.

The taller boy shoved the blond behind him and gestured to Brynna. "Want something?" His voice was sharp but not unkind as his dark brown eyes went up and down Brynna's body.

Her muscles tightened, and the back of her neck pricked with sweat.

The blond peered around the boy. "Travis, who's she?"

Brynna could smell the sharp tang of vodka mixing with ash on the girl's breath. She immediately recognized the glossy sheen in her eyes, the unfocused stare of someone who just got high.

Hours seemed to pass as Brynna stood there, thinking, until Travis hitched his chin. "Hey." His eyes went over Brynna's shoulder and she turned, seeing Evan cutting through the grass, coming right for her. When she turned back to Travis and the two others, they had shrunk back into the shadows of the bleachers, their backs turned on Brynna as they walked away.

"What are you doing out here? Seriously, we sent out a search party." Evan stayed just outside the shadowed border of the bleachers, arms crossed over his chest. "You know the only people who hang out here are the freaks and stoners."

Brynna's stomach shifted. "Yeah, well..."

He held out a hand. "Come on."

It was like the first day of school all over again, and Brynna wondered whether Evan thought that too. She took his hand and let him pull her onto the grass. He immediately squeezed her palm and they began to walk.

The almost-tardy bell rang and students buzzed around, rushing toward classes, and Brynna, strangely, felt herself looking forward to walking into a room crowded with students. She was ready for some normalcy in her day, and the din of student chatter calmed the constant questions that pinballed through her mind.

"Hey! I was hoping to run into you," Teddy said, his face lighting up when he saw her.

Brynna could feel herself blush and hoped she no longer looked as ghoulish as she did in the locker room.

"We were taking a breather," Evan answered.

Teddy tossed him a noncommittal glance then went back to Brynna. "Walk to Fallbrook's with you?"

"Yeah." She turned to Evan. "See you after?"

"Yep."

"So, Bryn—"

"I've been looking all over for you!" Darcy cut right between them, her slick pageboy nearly slapping Teddy in the face. "Sorry, T." She turned back to Brynna. "I went looking for you in the locker room and you, like, poof, were gone. What happened to you?"

"Oh, I—"

"Look, Darcy, I need to talk to Brynna," Teddy cut in.

The final bell cut them all off.

"Into class," Principal Chappie yelled as he zigged through the hall. "That means you three," he said, pinning Teddy, Darcy, and Brynna with an authoritarian glare.

Brynna tugged on the back of Darcy's sleeve as they pushed into Mr. Fallbrook's class.

"Hey, when you were in the locker room," Brynna started.

"You're in my classroom, guys, zip it." Mr. Fallbrook looked slightly annoyed, but Brynna knew it was more for effect than anything else. Darcy was already ignoring her, sliding primly into her seat and batting her eyelashes at Mr. Fallbrook.

Brynna slid into her desk and tried to catch Darcy's eye. Her pulse throbbed with curiosity: did Darcy see the lipstick on the mirror in the locker room too?

Teddy leaned toward Brynna. "Hey, I just wanted to ask you—"

Mr. Fallbrook tapped on the blackboard. "Ms. Chase, apparently Mr. Higgins has something so important to tell you that it trumps whatever I was planning on teaching." He crossed his arms in front of his chest and leaned against the edge of his desk, hitching his chin toward Teddy. "So, go ahead, Mr. Higgins. We'll all wait."

Brynna's skin burned white-hot as every eye turned toward her and Teddy, eyebrows raised expectantly. Teddy glanced at Brynna, his cheek pushed up in that half smile, then leaned toward her.

"Oh no." Fallbrook stood. "If it's that important, we should probably all know."

Brynna closed her eyes, the embarrassment total. Teddy stood up. "Thanks, Mr. Fallbrook, it is important. I need to know if Brynna will go to the homecoming dance with me."

A ripple of laughter and "awws" went through the room, and Brynna glanced around, nervous. She caught Darcy's eye, and Darcy immediately looked away, her mouth held in a hard, thin line.

"Well?" Fallbrook asked.

"Uh, yeah. Yeah, Teddy, I'll go with you." Giddiness washed over Brynna, and she could feel little pops of warmth thrumming underneath her skin.

"All right, fantastic. Now everybody get to work."

• • •

The rest of the school day passed uneventfully, and Brynna was glad. By sixth period biology, her stomach had de-knotted itself and her heartbeat was back to its normal, non-rib-slamming pace. When the final bell rang, she made a beeline for her locker and grinned when she saw that Teddy was already there.

"Hey, what are you doing here?"

He held up a sad-looking daisy. "Flower delivery guy." He offered Brynna the flower, which flopped when she took it.

She smiled anyway. "Uh, don't take this the wrong way, but you're not very good at your job. Aren't you supposed to keep these in water or something?"

Teddy clutched at his chest. "You're breaking my heart, lady!" He straightened. "Would you like a ride home?"

"In your refrigerated flower truck?" Brynna mimed thinking hard. "It would be a treat. But no thanks. My mom is picking me up."

"Ah, the mother. Much like the fake phone number."

"No, really, my mom is picking me up. You can even come out and meet her."

Teddy waited with Brynna at the front of the school until her mother pulled into the roundabout. When the car came to a stop, Brynna linked arms with Teddy and pulled him toward the car.

"Hey, Mom, this is my friend, Teddy."

Teddy waved. "Hey, Mrs. Chase."

Brynna's mother offered a thin smile and a curt nod. "Nice to meet you, Teddy. Bryn, we're kind of in a hurry."

Brynna turned to Teddy and waved. "See you tomorrow." She tucked the daisy behind her ear. "And don't put me on your list of references for your new job."

Teddy laughed then jogged across the grass while Brynna plopped into the passenger seat. "He gave me a flower." She tossed her backpack over the seat and belted herself in while her mother stared at her, eyes wide.

"Uh, something the matter, Mom?"

Her mother took a short, quick breath and then pushed the window button, the driver and passenger windows sliding down two inches each. Brynna pulled her hoodie tighter across her chest and went to roll her window back up.

"Mom, what are you doing?"

"You've been smoking."

Brynna gaped as her mother calmly pushed the car into drive and pulled away from the curb. "No, I haven't."

Her mother kept a careful eye on the road in front of them, refusing to look at Brynna.

"Mom." Brynna tugged on her mother's sweater. "Hello?"

The light in front of them turned red. "Don't lie to me."

"I'm not lying!"

Her mother turned in her seat. "Brynna, I can smell it all over you. Does that boy smoke too? Is that why?"

"Teddy? No, Mom."

"Brynna Marie, I'm really getting tired of—"

"So am I, Mom." A small flicker of anger in her belly turned into an overwhelming flame. "I was sitting on the bleachers and there were kids smoking underneath me. *I* wasn't smoking. *They* were."

Her mother slowly stepped on the gas as the light changed but said nothing.

"Mom, I swear."

"I want to believe you, Bryn."

"Then you should." She pressed her fingers into the dashboard. "It's not like I'm Dad."

Brynna's mother's head snapped toward Brynna, her eyes shooting venom. "Your father is of legal drinking age, young lady. You will leave him out of this."

"So forty-five, that's the legal age to be a functioning alcoholic?" She knew it was low, but the hypocrisy of her parents—her father, with the faint smell of bourbon on his minty-fresh breath, and her mother, pretending it wasn't there—infuriated Brynna.

Her mother took a deep breath, presumably to calm herself, and Brynna felt a stab of jealousy. When her father was drunk, out entertaining, Brynna wasn't the only one left behind—her mother was too.

"I'm not going to smoke. I'm not going to drink. You stuck me in that stupid rehab for six weeks. Do you think I would just go back to—" Brynna crossed her arms in front of her chest, the frustration hot in her cheeks.

"You father and I did not 'stick' you in rehab, young lady. You did that yourself. And smoking, drinking, any of that violates your probation and our deal."

"You think I don't know that? God!" Brynna slammed herself back in her seat, edging as far away from her mother as she could get.

"When we go home, you're heading straight for the shower. Leave your backpack downstairs on the table."

"You're searching me again? Mom—"

"We had a deal."

"But it wasn't me. I didn't do anything."

Her mother kept quiet, dark eyes focused hard on the bare road in front of them.

"So if I happen to sit next to someone who smokes, then I go back into lockdown? This blows."

"You know what? I don't want to have to search your stuff any more than you want it searched, but that's where we are, right? And if you were just 'sitting' in the smoking section, you won't have any cigarettes or lighters in your bag, and you won't have anything to worry about, will you?"

Brynna was taken aback. Her mother's cheeks were flushed and she was gripping the steering wheel so hard her knuckles were white.

"I thought we were past this, Brynna."

A memory tugged at the back of her mind.

Everything was white at Woodbriar, white and sterile so that the few things that were supposed to be "cheery" or "inspirational" and were brightly colored stood out like circus elephants.

She sat out on the verandah on one of the white wooden rocking chairs and looked over the perfectly manicured lawn and the snakelike driveway that cut through the boxwood and carefully trained roses. The garden was supposed to give the place a hotel, resortlike feel, but after six weeks of meetings and therapy and rehab and "activities," Brynna knew that every branch and leaf at Woodbriar was cut according to a precise master plan to give the illusion of natural freedom while guiding "clients" along a specific path.

When her parents drove up and got out of the car, they looked too happy, too eager, and it made Brynna cringe against the hardwood back of the rocker and grip the armrests until her fingers ached. She didn't know if she was better yet. All she knew was that the "old Brynna," the one they were so happy to see, didn't exist at Woodbriar.

When her father picked up her luggage, he looked down at it awkwardly, and Brynna knew what the staff at Woodbriar had told him about aftercare: "guardians" needed to check their children's bags and quarters daily because even though they've gone to Woodbriar, it didn't mean they were cured.

Brynna and her mother drove the rest of the way in silence, Brynna scrupulously studying the passing scenery as if the banks of trees and dried grass were something new and spectacular. As they entered the wrought-iron gates of the housing development, she stared at each house gliding by her window, even as she watched her mother's reflection watching her. When they pulled up to their house, a hulking, homey place that looked just like every other house on the block, Brynna was out of the car, skulking up the driveway and through the front door before her mother even turned off the car.

She went directly to the kitchen where the oven and stove still boasted the slip of protective blue plastic—her mother didn't cook—and slammed her backpack onto the granite countertop.

She stomped up the stairs, vaguely hearing her mother as she fumbled with the phone, no doubt calling to report to Brynna's father. The thought of her parents having a hushed conversation about her, about Brynna's "relapse," sent a new wave of anger through her, and she slammed her bedroom door with a satisfying clap.

If she were a normal girl, she would have gone directly to the shower to scrub the smoke out of her hair, but the idea of standing under a spout of hot water shot her anxiety through the roof. Instead she slumped down on the carpet, with her knees tucked to her chest, and cried.

Dr. Rother would have said something about using this opportunity as a "learning moment," but Brynna felt tortured and crazy and a dozen other flying emotions—none of them good. But somewhere, way in the back of her mind, she didn't blame her mother. Every other millimeter was equal parts seething and terrified.

Even if she wanted to go to her parents about the tweet and the phone call and now the stunt in her locker, she couldn't. They thought she was lying again, doing drugs and drinking. If she were to tell them that she thought Erica was still alive, they'd pat her knee gently and send her right back to Woodbriar.

Brynna crawled across her floor and pulled a cardboard box out from the depths of her closet. She upended it and watched as a shower of ribbons, most red, very few blue, fell out, along with swim meet stats, a few old pictures, and some forgotten trinkets. She picked up one of the photos. It was so old the corners were soft and bent, and Brynna and Erica grinned out at her, the massive blue expanse of swimming pool behind them. They were each holding their ribbons, Erica her bright blue first place and Brynna her blood-red second place, and they both looked so happy, arms entwined, sunlight glittering in their eyes.

Erica was always better than me. The thought niggled into Brynna's brain, and just as quickly, she chased it out. *Erica was my best friend. We were always happy for each other, no matter who won.*

But it was always her that did.

Maybe I wanted to kill her. Maybe I needed her to die.

Brynna pressed her fingers to her forehead as if she could pull out the errant thoughts. They ached behind her eyes.

"I didn't mean to," she mumbled out loud. "Erica, I swear, I didn't mean to." For fourteen months, Brynna prayed that Erica knew that. But here, in her new house and new life in Crescent City, she found herself wondering if someone else had heard.

Someone had left the sand—and the purple crepe paper—for her to find. Someone didn't just want Brynna to know that they were there that night. They didn't just want Brynna to know that they blamed her. This person wanted her to pay.

Brynna's mind spun as her blood pulsed.

Erica's name flashed in her mind and just as quickly was washed out by the pounding of the black night surf. Erica's hand was in hers, and Brynna was tugging.

"You are the biggest wimp!"

"Because I won't jump off a pier? Lame."

"You're scared."

"You're stupid."

"I'll do it. I'll even do the real dare." Brynna yanked off her bikini top and waved the hot pink scrap of fabric over her head triumphantly. The kids on the beach—figures half-illuminated by the dying firelight—hooted and hollered. Someone laughed; someone jumped up and danced in the sand. Far away, the music swirled, mellow from this distance.

"Really?" Erica cocked an eyebrow and waved a thick lock of ink-black hair over her shoulder. "You're brave because you're standing on a public dock with your knockers out?"

Brynna threw her head back and laughed. Everything was funny and warm and coconut scented. It was Erica's shampoo, caught on a wispy ocean breeze.

"You and your knockers are coming with me." Brynna clamped a hand over Erica's wrist, and Erica pulled back but laughed, collapsing onto the dock.

"Don't put those things near me!"

"Jump," Brynna chanted. "With me. It'll be, like, our yearly ritual. The two of us against the world."

Erica was sitting back on her haunches. She cocked her head, considering. "The two of us?"

"Together. For life." Brynna spun.

"Until death do us part?"

Brynna laughed. "We're not getting married, dork."

Erica tossed her head back so that her long hair pooled on the dock. "You and me, forever and ever, right?"

"Sirens of the surf." She held out her hand.

Erica stood and slid her hand into Brynna's. "Promise me."

The stars blurred before Brynna's eyes. The punch she had drunk—something fruity laced with something fierce that burned its way down her throat—was making her whole body warm. "Promise what?"

"That you'll never leave me alone."

Brynna was breathing hard, her eyes itchy and dry. She couldn't remember if she ever answered Erica's question.

SEVEN

Brynna padded down the stairs when her mother called her for dinner. Both her parents were already seated, and Brynna could see her bag, moved to one of the barstools. Her parents had clearly gone through it.

They said nothing to her when she sat; her mother just scooped a spoonful of whatever takeout she had gotten and plopped it onto Brynna's plate. Brynna was going to say something. She was going to wait for an apology, an admission that the only things they found in Brynna's bag were her books, her binder, and a couple of errant highlighters. But no one said anything.

Each day after the wardens at Woodbriar did their methodical check of Brynna's bags, her pockets, and her room and came up empty—or "clean" as they called it—they left without saying a word too.

Brynna stiffened and poked at the food on her plate.

After dinner, she was back in her room attempting to study. The new house was just a little bit bigger than the house in Point Lobos, but everything about the Blackwood house was brand new—new carpet, new appliances, even new landscaping that was perfectly watered and well maintained. The house should have been cheerful with its soaring high ceilings and model-home furniture, but it still gave Brynna the creeps. There were only a few families living in the neighborhood, and the "For Sale" and "See Me!" flags on the houses across the street snapped in the fall wind. During the day, the houses were occupied with families carrying brochures and hopeful-looking children. At night, the houses were unmistakably vacant, the windows gaping and black. Brynna squinted as a pair of headlights washed yellow light over her room and then watched out the window as the red taillights of the car traveled up her street, only to disappear around a corner. There was no one outside, but she couldn't shake the feeling that someone was out there, lurking in the dark, watching her. She yanked the blinds closed, but the feeling didn't go away.

She went back to her history book, but her mind kept wandering until she smacked it shut and peeked out the window once more.

No one there.

But something in her mind kept nagging her…

Finally, in a rare moment of bravado, she slid on her phone and dialed, vaguely surprised that her fingers still remembered Erica's number. She counted the rings until the familiar tones started chiming: "This number has been disconnected. If you feel you have reached this message in error…"

It should have been comforting. It should have been another bit of tangible proof that Erica wasn't alive, that she wasn't hanging around in the dark, calling and haunting Brynna.

She paused for a beat, then dialed a second time, listening to the shrill ring without holding the phone to her cheek. When someone answered, she snatched it up.

"'Lo?"

Brynna paused for a beat too long.

"Hello? Is anyone there?"

She cleared her throat and worked to keep her voice as bright and even as possible. "Hey—hi—Ella, it's me, Brynna. From Lincoln?"

There was a long pause. "Seriously?"

Butterflies flapped knife-edged wings in Brynna's stomach. "Yeah, sorry I haven't really been in touch. With the move and all…"

"You haven't been in touch with me, you mean." Ella didn't try to hide the bitterness in her voice, and Brynna felt trapped, wounded. She felt the need to explain—and defend.

"I'm really sorry—"

"Whatever. Why are you calling me?"

Brynna knew she should ask after Ella, inquire about her life and about school, but all she wanted were answers. "So, I got this weird tweet the other day."

"Wait. I don't hear from you for almost six months, and you want to talk about some weird tweet?"

"It's just that—"

"Brynna, you walked out on us. You just up and left. Of course, that was after pretty much dumping us at school."

Brynna bit down hard on her lower lip. "I know. I'm sorry, it's just that—"

"Do you know what happened when you left? I mean, you just disappeared."

"I was in rehab," Brynna blurted, the humiliation burning all the way to her scalp. Her mind immediately reeled back to her crumpled car, the flashing red and blue lights, the police officer who helped her stumble along until he snapped the cold metal cuffs on her. She remembered the throbbing in her head, the way the whole scene swirled in front of her eyes. "I had to. I couldn't talk to anyone after. I couldn't see anyone." She hoped that Ella wouldn't ask questions, would assume that Brynna "couldn't" see her old friends because her doctor or the parole officer told her so—not that she couldn't face them.

Ella was silent for a beat on the other end of the phone, and Brynna counted the seconds. When Ella spoke again, her voice had a slightly softer edge to it—but just barely.

"You just abandoned us. All of a sudden, you disappeared. And after Erica"—Ella sucked in her breath—"people started to talk."

Brynna's hackles went up. "What do you mean, they started to talk?"

"People said you were dead, Bryn. They said that you offed yourself because you killed Erica."

Pain sliced through Brynna's chest. "I didn't—"

"And then, know what? They started blaming Michael and Jay. People started to tell me that I was next. Or that I was in on it. My parents made me see a shrink, and the cops came to school asking questions."

There was real angst in Ella's voice, but she tried to drown it out with spitting anger.

Brynna's lips felt numb. "But everybody knew that she—everybody knew that Erica—"

"Erica what? Drowned? Maybe. There was no body. You were the one who said she was dead. You said it. Maybe it was because you were the only one who actually knew that she was."

Brynna's head started to throb. She pinched her eyes shut, trying to block out the images that came seeping in, but they were there, clear as day.

"Erica is dead, Brynna, you have to know that."

Brynna shook her head. "No one knows that. They never found a body."

She hated the way Dr. Rother needled her with her gaze. It was like she wanted to cure her, to make her happy, by destroying her first.

"The police have declared Erica Shaw dead. Say it, Brynna. Say that Erica is dead."

Brynna shrunk into her sweatshirt, angling her head so that her just-dyed, so-blue-it-was-black hair hung over her eyes. "I don't think she is," she said to the scuffed toes of her black leather boots.

Dr. Rother let out a long sigh, making it obvious that Brynna wasn't grieving right. "Once you admit it, once you admit what happened—that Erica jumped into the water and was drowned by a riptide—then you can start letting go."

Brynna looked up at that, the idea of being free of Erica's deathly pull holding some appeal to her. She had spent months trying to block out Erica's accusing eyes, the way her fingertips felt those last few seconds before she drifted away.

"Is that true?"

*"Once you admit that Erica can no longer be alive—*is *no longer alive—then you can begin grieving her properly. This"—she gestured*

toward Brynna, almost shuddering with her distaste of her rumpled hair, oversized sweatshirt, and filthy jeans—"this isn't healthy. This isn't what Erica would want for you."

Part of her wanted to jump to her feet and scream at Dr. Rother, to scream that she had no idea what Erica would want. But part of her started to break. Part of her was desperate and exhausted and wanted peace.

"Go ahead and say it, Brynna. Say that Erica is dead. You need to begin to accept that."

Erica is dead. *The words felt sour on Brynna's tongue. "Erica..." she started.*

Dr. Rother's pale blue eyes were on her, an unwavering, expectant stare.

"Erica..." Brynna tried again. "Erica...is...dead."

"Are you even listening to me?"

"Wha—" Brynna sputtered, crashing back to the present.

"You said she was dead and then you started to hang with those—those *losers*—and we had to deal with everyone talking like we were criminals. Do you know what that's like, Bryn? Do you?" Ella's venom poured through the phone, and Brynna's heartbeat sped up. "I hope you're super happy throwing us under the bus so you could start a new life as a goodie-goodie in, where was it? Crescent City?"

"I'm sorry, Ella. I—I—was going through my own thing. I should have—"

Brynna was cut off by Ella's slicing breath. "What do you want anyway, Bryn?"

She paused for a beat, everything inside of her telling her to hang up, to stop feeling. She steadied herself. "I got this tweet. It came from Erica's Twitter account. Do you know anything about that?"

"No. I mean, probably someone just took over the account or the handle or something. Her account was probably deactivated last year."

Ella's lack of concern didn't lessen Brynna's. "You don't think maybe—maybe that Jay or Michael were playing a joke or something?"

There was a long pause on Ella's end of the phone. Every millisecond it went on ratcheted up Brynna's tension.

"Jay doesn't go to Lincoln anymore. And, well, you know all about Michael."

Brynna sat on the edge of her bed. "What do I know about Michael?"

"Did you call just to lie to me and play the super innocent chick? You have a lot of fucking nerve, Brynna."

"Please—tell me. What happened to Michael?"

There was a long pause, and Brynna dug her teeth into her lower lip, willing Ella to respond and praying that Michael was safe.

"Michael. The *anonymous* phone call to his parents? I bet you thought that was pretty damn funny. They sent him to North, you know. That wilderness camp? It's supposed to be for super messed-up kids—real druggies and, like, psychopaths. But now, thanks to you and your middle-of-the-night tips to his parents, he's stuck there. For *six months*. I really didn't think you had it in you, Brynna."

"I don't! I didn't!"

"Who else then?" Ella snapped. "Someone else with your caller ID?"

Brynna gaped. "My caller ID? It wasn't me. It didn't come from me. I didn't even have my phone the whole time I was at Woodbriar."

"Sure. Another girl must have taken your phone to make the call. That makes sense."

Terror and confusion pricked at Brynna's skin. "I don't know—I don't understand. But I know I didn't make any anonymous call. Why—who—what happened? What did they say?"

Ella sucked in a razor-sharp breath. "Are you one of those—what do they call them? sadists?—who like to re-witness their crimes? Okay, sure, I'll play. The Peytons get an anonymous call in the middle of the night saying that Michael has been doing drugs—like, hardcore drugs."

Brynna closed her eyes, a lump growing in her throat.

She got high. *She* did the hardcore drugs. Michael just wanted to be with her—and he wanted to stop her.

"You—I mean, Ms. *Anonymous*—even told them where Michael supposedly hid his stash. Of course, they looked and voila, Oxy. Speed. Even some coke, I think, not that we would really know what that even looked like because none of us really did hardcore drugs. None of us except you, I mean. Nice work on getting the police involved too; that was really awesome of you. Was that all part of your twelve-step program, Bryn? Making amends?"

Brynna wanted to fire back that Michael had done drugs—hard stuff, like she did. Oxy, speed, ecstasy, coke—she knew because she did it with him. The weeks after Erica died. She made him do it.

She was drunk and high, and the sick was crawling up the back of her throat, but the rest of her felt fine. Not fine—nothing. Her body was there—probably—but she was a tired, slightly smiley mess, curled up on her bed.

And then Michael crouched down in front of her.

It was hard to get her eyes to focus completely—or maybe the edges of Michael had grown soft and fuzzy anyway—but Brynna tried, noticing the downturned curve of his mouth.

"I'm not doing this with you, Bryn. Not anymore. I basically threw the whole match. I wasn't even messed up, but that shit stays with you, I know it does." His voice got soft as his lips pressed together, hard. "Look at you, baby, you're a mess. You've got to stop this."

There was a soft weight on Brynna's leg, and when she looked down, she saw that it was Michael's hand, pressing warmly. The sensation was nice at first, but then it sent the bugs crawling—tiny feet hammering through her veins, skittering across her skin. She brushed him off and yanked her knees to her chest, wrapping her arms around them. There was blood on the heel of her hand. She couldn't feel any pain, didn't remember any, but there was a thick, red scratch there, a thousand tiny lines cross-hatching through her skin, each crossing oozing with its own bubble of velvet, red blood.

"Do you hear me, Bryn?"

The fat, red droplets were racing each other, this one going faster, this one getting bigger, this one finally breaking into a blue-red rivulet that trickled over the delicate skin on her wrist.

Michael was still talking. Brynna knew that, but the blood—the way it danced and tickled—was intoxicating, and she was drawn. It made her happy to see the red freeing itself from her veins, from the tight restraint of her body. She wished she could do that. She wished she could be free.

"I love you, Bryn, but not like this."

The blood moved slower now, the lush color turning to a dirty rust as it congealed and settled. Brynna's own heart seemed to slow with the motion, and when she looked up, Michael was gone.

Brynna's voice was barely a whisper. "Michael got addicted to drugs?"

"No," Ella spat. "*Someone* just said he did. And planted a huge stash on him. Gee, wonder who that could've been?"

"I never called Michael. I never called his parents."

"Of course you didn't! It's just damn convenient that he gets picked up right as you move to another city. What an alibi! 'I was living somewhere else; it couldn't possibly have been me!'"

Brynna's mind was reeling as Ella began hurling insults. Who could have called in Michael? Why would they have done that?

"Ella—" Brynna tried to break in, but Ella wouldn't let her, going on in a breathless chatter.

"Why'd you do it, Bryn? Jay and I have been trying to figure it out. What did you get out of it? Or were you just feeling awfully lonely as the only drugged-up loser in the loony bin?"

"I wasn't in—it was a rehab program. The court made me go."

Her head was throbbing, each pulse telling her it was futile to answer, even to defend herself. "I would never do that to Michael. He knows I wouldn't do that to him."

"So is that why you're calling? Because I'm next on your little hit list? Off Erica, get rid of Michael, and now me? A little pissed because when you went off the deep end, Michael came to me for comfort?"

Brynna swallowed hard. The thought of Ella and Michael together really didn't bother her. But the thought of an anonymous call, Michael being sent away, and everyone from her past thinking that she "offed" her best friend did.

"Don't ever call here again, Brynna."

Stunned, Brynna held the phone to her ear until the little electric beeps sounded.

Brynna lay back in her bed, her emotions roiling inside her. Was the same person that was targeting her targeting her old friends back at Lincoln? She couldn't take a second reviling phone call, but she could do the next best thing. She slid out her laptop and tapped in her password. A cool breeze washed over Brynna as her computer sprang to life with the usual cache of cheerful wallpaper and no new messages.

"At least there's that," she whispered to herself.

The night outside was an eerie, moonlit silver the next time Brynna looked up. She stretched, hearing her bones pop and crack as she put her laptop aside and peeled her legs from their pretzeled position. She had trailed Jay, the other kid who was at the campfire that night, on the Internet, holding her breath and silently praying that he wouldn't have been disfigured in some horrible accident or suddenly have gone missing. Thankfully, he was a senior at another high school now, an all-star forward on the football team, and had been awarded a scholarship to an impressive university. He was fine, and other than her cancerous anger, Ella was unharmed as well. Michael could very well have made his own way into the wilderness program—the anonymous call could have been a lie or someone who knew Michael well. But knowing that her old friends were safe didn't make Brynna feel any better.

• • •

The next two days passed uneventfully for Brynna and she was glad. There were no messages from Erica, no "gifts" appearing in her locker. The calm was nice but unnerving. Brynna prayed that Erica—or whoever was pretending to be Erica—was done with her, but that sounded too good to be true.

When Brynna came down for breakfast the third day, her mother was already awake, already covered in her almost-to-her-knees painting smock, and on the phone. Her auburn hair was pulled into a sloppy topknot, and a half-dozen pencils were angled inward, keeping the mess in place. Brynna could see that her mother's hands were already covered in paint, which meant she had started working even before Brynna woke up. She was grinning into the phone, and Brynna wasn't sure if her mother's happiness came from the fact that her father had left this morning on yet another business trip or something else. She clicked the phone off when Brynna walked in.

"Guess who has great news?" her mother said with a flourish.

Brynna poured herself a bowl of cereal. "Who?"

"You!"

She cocked a slightly interested eyebrow and flooded her Cheerios with milk. "How do I have great news? I've been asleep."

Her mother dropped a napkin on Brynna's lap. "Don't talk with your mouth full. You have great news because"—she pressed her lips together in an approximation of serious expression—"I talked to your guidance counselor and your P.E. teacher about your swim test requirement."

Brynna set down her spoon. "And? Are they going to let me skip it?"

"No. They can only waive it if you join the swim team at Hawthorne."

"That's my great news?"

"No. I told them about your phobia."

She gritted her teeth, hating that word.

"And they agreed to give you extra practice time in the pool."

The single bite of cereal seemed to expand in Brynna's gut, pushing her insides out. She didn't want more time in the pool. She didn't want to "practice" not being crazy while a class full of other girls looked on, wondering why Brynna was such a freak.

"Mom, that sucks. That's the worst thing—"

Her mother held up a hand. "The P.E. teacher agreed that you could practice after school in the indoor pool. There won't be any other students there with you. Dr. Rother said that you just need to get comfortable in your own time. This way, you'll have the whole school year to practice."

Brynna blinked, still in disbelief. It seemed like a good idea in theory, but even here, sitting at the breakfast table in her house, Brynna could smell the overwhelming stench of chlorine, could feel the burn of her lungs as water rushed down her throat.

"You have to pass it to graduate, Bryn. I told you I could talk to the guidance counselor and Dr. Rother can write a note..."

"No." It was out of her mouth before Brynna could stop it. "No. I need to...I want to get over this." She looked up at her mother who had a look of pity and pride on her face.

"You don't have to, Bryn."

Brynna wanted to agree with her mother, wanted to give up the whole idea of getting in the water again, but something deep inside—maybe it was her stubbornness, maybe it was a small piece of her old self—pulled at her to try. She didn't want to be pinned down by her fear her entire life.

"Are you sure?" her mother asked.

Brynna took a deep breath and nodded, half grateful that her mother had made the effort.

"Mrs. Markie said you can get in the pool today." She bit her lower lip. "I know how hard this is going to be for you. I can come down and—"

"No. No. The only thing more humiliating than running away from water is running to my mommy."

"I do want to make this easier for you, hon. I thought this might help." She plucked a shopping bag off one of the chairs and handed it to Brynna.

Brynna looked inside and tried to swallow. "You got me a bathing suit?"

"You got rid of all your other ones, and I thought this one was kind of...nice."

Brynna pulled the suit out. It was a navy blue one-piece with red-and-white polka-dotted piping and red stitching. The neck was cut lower and the legs cut higher than she was used to with her usual utilitarian swim team suits. All of those were Lincoln High purple or club swim team blue, and Erica had the same ones, matching Brynna suit for suit.

Brynna looked at the hopeful smile on her mother's face and felt a twinge of guilt. She wanted to be better for herself, but she wanted to be better so her mother would stop worrying about her.

"It's cute, Mom. Thanks."

Brynna finished her breakfast and gathered her shoulder bag and the new swimsuit. She tried to shove the suit and a towel in with her books, but the result was a huge, awkward bulge. At Lincoln she had a swim bag—between two years of high school swimming and five years of club, she had a half dozen. But again, just the thought of her old bag was too much to handle, so she shoved the towel and the suit back into the bag it came from and carried it with her to school.

All around her, students were bustling with homecoming excitement, and the Hawthorne halls were covered with construction paper leaves in fall colors. Lauren and Darcy descended upon Brynna the moment she stepped on campus.

"So, so, tell us, B, we're dying to know. What's your homecoming dress like?" Lauren asked.

"How do you know I'm going to homecoming? I don't think I even said anything."

Lauren rolled her eyes and Darcy looked away. "Duh, the whole school heard about Teddy's mid-class invitation. Cutest. Thing. Ever. Right, Darce?"

Darcy shrugged, and Brynna got the distinct impression that Darcy wasn't happy.

"Who are you going with, Darcy?" Brynna said, trying to make the girl the center of attention.

Darcy sighed and looked incredibly put out. "Oh, I don't know yet. I'll figure it out." Her eyes cut to Teddy, and Brynna watched Teddy look at his shoes. A little flick of jealousy went up in the back of her head but she pushed it away. Teddy and Brynna hadn't made any official proclamation, but it was pretty well known that wherever Brynna was, Teddy wasn't far. They were as close to being boyfriend and girlfriend as they could get—and they would have been together, Brynna suspected, if she could put all this guilt behind her, if she could just turn the page and be one hundred percent normal again.

Despite Darcy's reaction, Brynna really was excited to be going with Teddy. The signs for the homecoming dance were everywhere, and though they weren't officially dating, it was becoming common knowledge that Teddy and Brynna were together.

"Bryn, your dress?" Lauren said, snapping her fingers anxiously.

"I actually haven't even thought about it yet."

Lauren gaped, her crayon-red hair shaking. "That's unnatural."

"Don't worry." Evan showed up out of nowhere and slung one arm around Brynna's shoulders and the other around Teddy's. "It's not like we're going to let Hawthorne High's premier couple show up in trash bags. We'll get the whole thing sorted. Shopping trip this weekend." He grinned.

"We're the premier couple?" Brynna asked skeptically.

"In!" Lauren said.

"I guess," Darcy nodded.

"Dress shopping?" Teddy held up his hands. "I'm out. I know you're all fashion-forward and everything, E, but I plan on wearing whatever the rental place hands me."

Evan swung his head toward Brynna and lowered his voice. "Don't worry; I'll make sure to get him in something black and from this century."

"I don't know," Brynna said with a sly smile. "I think Teddy could totally rock one of those powder blue, frilly collar tuxes."

"I'm going to pretend you never said that so we can continue being friends." Evan narrowed his eyes and did the universal "I'm watching you" sign before he, Lauren, and Darcy melded into the swarm in the hall.

"So," Teddy said, his fingers lacing with Brynna's, "hang out after school?" His smile was hot chocolate warm, and it shot a zing throughout her as she slid the combination on her locker. Her good mood was immediately cut short when she saw the swimsuit bag sitting there.

"I forgot," she said, shoving the bag back into her locker depths. "I have to make up a test after school."

He shrugged. "No big. I'll wait."

"No." She rested her hand on his bicep. "No, that's okay. I'll probably take forever. Maybe later, okay?"

A trace of annoyance flittered across Teddy's face, just long enough for it to register with Brynna. "Whatever," he said nonchalantly, pulling his hand from hers. "See you later then." He gave her a quick peck on the forehead and turned on his heel, her hand immediately missing the warmth of his as he walked away.

Brynna had forgotten the exchange with Teddy in the hallway—and so had Teddy, it seemed—by the time the lunch bell rang.

The lunchroom was a maelstrom of voices, blaring cell phones, and silverware clattering. The constant noise and the warm, familiar scent of a high school cafeteria were oddly comforting to Brynna—as if in the flurry, she could shake off her guilt, as though it wouldn't be able to find her among the moving bodies.

Teddy was pressed up next to her, and with every breath, she could smell his fresh, soapy scent. Evan was on her other side, fork full of tater tot raised as he argued with Lauren about a movie.

Darcy sauntered up and set down her bag then flopped down next to it with a groan.

"Well, hello to you too," Evan said.

Darcy yawned. "Don't start with me. I bombed my geometry test, which means adios to my car for a week."

"And Daddy won't let you take the jet?"

"Anyway, Teddy," Darcy returned, cutting through Evan with her gaze. "Room for one more in the car today? I don't have a ride home." She pouted, and Brynna could feel the heat rise in her cheeks.

"Actually Darce, I'm on two wheels today. But I suppose if you want to ride on my handlebars."

Brynna straightened up. "My mom's picking me up. I'm sure we can give you a ride home. I've…got a few things to do after school lets out, but it beats sitting on someone's handlebars." She forced a smile, willing to suffer whatever consequences—even letting Darcy know she was "practicing" in the pool—to keep Darcy away from Teddy.

Darcy's eyes cut to Brynna's, a glint of hardness in them. "Really, Brynna? You're sure your mama won't mind?"

"Lay off, Darcy," Evan said, leveling her with a stare. "Not everyone's father's a Pulitzer Prize-winning photographer."

"Nominee," Teddy coughed into his hand.

Brynna could see the fire redden Darcy's cheeks, going all the way up to her scalp, making her pale blond hair look like wispy flames. She snatched up her bag and turned on her heel, stomping out of the cafeteria in a puff of couture perfume and haughtiness.

"You guys are a couple of asses, you know that?" Lauren said, giving the boys a halfhearted glare. She gathered her things too, threw out her trash, and went out after Darcy, but with far less angst and storm.

"Well that was fun. What's next?" Evan asked, grinning.

Teddy planted a chaste kiss on Brynna's cheek and grabbed his tray. "I've got an English test to make up, so I'll see you two later." He wound through the room, going the opposite way the girls went.

Evan gave Brynna a soft elbow to the ribs as she stared into the remnants of her lunch. "Don't worry about Darcy. She can be a real bitch. It's no big deal not to have a car."

"A car would be useless for me," she mumbled.

"Wait. Do you not even have your license?"

Brynna spun back to that night, almost a year after Erica's death.

Her father was gone—as usual—off to close a deal or open up some airport bottles, and Brynna was stuck at the Gallery on Main, a pompous shop full of blond wood and thick glass where her mother's paintings hung under gooseneck lamps. There was soft music playing, something just slightly jazzier than you'd hear in an elevator, and people milled about in dark suits and cocktail dresses, eating petit fours, drinking wine, and talking in muffled voices about the paintings. Brynna was in her own formal wear, a black shift that her mother set out for her that used to hug her curves but now hung shapelessly, her arms and legs sticking out like thin, pasty twigs. She had given up trying to be pretty a long time ago, and so her dirty blond hair was pulled back in a ponytail and her lips were only red because of the wine she kept swilling. Her mother was busy being The Artist, so she didn't notice when Brynna swiped the first glass, and from her perch halfway behind the registration desk, no one watched her swipe the second and third. When the bottle was gone, Brynna's stomach was grumbling, so she took the keys from her mother's purse, went to the parking lot, and slid behind the wheel. She was six hours into Driver's Training, so she knew what to do, guiding the big car out of the lot and into the street. It was dark but lights were flashing everywhere—headlights, traffic lights, streetlights—and they all blended together in one bright, blinding mess. She meant to park the car right along the sidewalk—she could walk the rest of the way to Burger Town, but the car lurched and someone screamed, and then even when she hit the gas, it wouldn't move. She could hear the engine run, she remembered hearing it rev until blood dripped into her eyes, turning everything outside the windshield a thick, deep red. She remembered the sound the scissors made as the paramedic sliced through her seat belt—weird and sawing—and she thought it would be faster. She was being jostled and moved, and her head hurt and the red wine had made her lips dry. She just wanted something to eat. She wanted the flashes of light to stop.

"She's going to be okay, Ms. Chase. She's going to be just fine."

The masculine voice floated down to Brynna, and she opened an eye. Her blood-tinged gaze found her mother standing at the side of the car, one arm across her chest, one hand pressed against her open mouth. There were tears in her eyes.

Then Brynna heard the clink of the handcuffs, the metal tightening around her wrists.

"No, I don't have my license."

"Why not? Were you prairie people where you were from? No, wait. You lived by the beach. Boat people?"

He grinned, and Brynna sucked in a breath. "Because I got arrested for drunk driving when I was fifteen."

She waited for Evan to gape, but he didn't. He just threaded his arms in front of his chest and nodded appraisingly. "Well, aren't we the bad girl?"

"It was stupid and I can't believe I did it, and now I can't get my license until I'm twenty-one." She felt the sting of humiliation on her cheeks. "Promise me you won't tell anyone?"

Evan leaned into her. "Your criminal past is safe with me,

Queen B. Any more secrets you want to lay on me while I've still got half a Coke?" He shook his half-empty can.

"Not that I can think of. But maybe you can tell me why Darcy seems to hate me on cue?"

"Teddy. They kind of used to date."

Brynna blinked. "What? He never told me that."

"Well, honestly, he wasn't so much dating her as she was dating him."

"That makes absolutely no sense."

Evan nodded. "It made sense to Darcy. She was constantly glued to him, and so they were sort of dating by proxy. Or by proximity."

"Group dating? Like, Teddy and Darcy and you and Lauren?"

"I just threw up a little in my mouth. That's my sister, B. But don't even worry about Darcy. She's totally harmless, and you've got the guy." He gave her a slick smile, tilted his head back, and finished his soda in one swig.

EIGHT

When the final bell rang, Brynna tried to be ready for it, but every second afterward seemed to race too quickly as she retrieved the swimsuit bag from her locker. She avoided all of her friends, unwilling to face any additional questions, and slipped into the nearest girls' room she could find. She had no intention of going back into the locker room, even knowing that this close to school's end, the place would be packed. She tried not to remember what was scrawled on the mirror in there, but lately her head was so filled with the things she didn't want to think about, the few things she did—homecoming with Teddy, shopping with Evan—had no room.

Everything she did made a horrible racket, metal and concrete reverberating a thousand times over while her heart pounded out a drumbeat that trumped everything else. Her swimsuit pinched at her skin; the slick material once like a second skin was now foreign and cold and deeply uncomfortable. She grabbed her swim cap and goggles and had a brief flashback of the hundreds of other times she had done the exact same motion: swiping both from her swim bag, dangling the goggles between her two fingers as she waited for Erica to finishing sucking in her stomach and glaring at herself in the four-by-four-inch mirror stuck to her locker door.

"If I could lose three more pounds, I would be unstoppable," Erica said, brushing a palm over her already flat stomach.

"If you lost three pounds, you'd go straight down the drain in the showers."

Erica clamped her hands together and batted her eyelashes. "But you would rescue me, wouldn't you, my shining prince?"

"Sure," Brynna said, her front teeth clamping over a snag on her thumbnail and biting down hard. "I'll get right on that—becoming a prince, growing a penis and all."

"Ew!" Erica beaned Brynna with a wadded-up towel. "Who says 'penis'?"

Brynna could still hear her and Erica's fading laughter, and for a brief second, she almost felt soothed by the memory, comforted by the fact that right after that exchange, they both snapped on swim caps and goggles and took to their lanes, slicing through the water, their bodies taking over. But she didn't feel that way anymore.

She slid her jeans and sweatshirt back on over her suit, concentrating especially hard on the techniques that Dr. Rother had taught her. She couldn't help thinking how proud her shrink and her parole officer would be, knowing that she was not only learning but "applying" techniques for "relaxation and reengaging." The thought made her stumble. It wasn't that long ago that she would go running into any body of water within a twenty-mile radius. It wasn't that long ago that she only wondered whether her parents were proud of her—not a shrink or a parole officer.

"Things change," Brynna muttered under her breath.

The halls were still peppered with slow-moving students and teachers straightening their rooms, so Brynna was surprised that when she pushed through the heavy double doors to the poolroom, it was empty.

The overhead lights were on full force, the bright yellow light reflecting off the water. She waited for the panic to overcome her, for the choking grief to storm in, but to her absolute shock, Brynna remained calm. She slid out of her jeans and sweatshirt and turned back to the pool. Her blood pressure ratcheted up a notch with each step she took toward the glassy water, but it didn't cripple her.

Brynna stared at the pool and worked hard—using every technique Dr. Rother had ever taught her—to see exactly what was there: a pool. A pool with a flat, glasslike surface and a clear, white bottom, illuminated by a blue-tinged light. No darkness. No waves. No riptides. Just a swimming pool.

Brynna took the first step, the water making a sucking sound as she dipped her foot in. She glanced down, relieved to see her foot underneath the water's surface, her red toenail polish as bright and cheery as it had been above water.

"Nothing hiding under the surface," she said aloud.

She was waist deep, and her anxiety level was staid. The pool water was only disturbed by her movements, and even then, it was only tiny, two-inch ripples that cascaded over the water. She could see her limbs, she could see the bottom, she could see out in front of her.

"I can do this."

Brynna snapped on her swim cap and goggles and dipped lower, the water swirling around her elbows, then her chest. She stood there, waiting to feel the enveloping comfort that the pool had always given her. She hoped it would flood back but knew it would be a long shot, since her heart was still keeping an ultra-quick, steady beat as she stood there.

She remembered wading in side-by-side with Erica, just before they took their lanes. They would make faces at each other and snap the other's goggles, jumping and slicing through the water. There was nothing left of that lightness.

She forced herself to walk in deeper until the lukewarm water batted over her collarbone and then her chin. She let her foot leave the bottom and started to gently tread water. Her limbs were blooming with warmth, and her natural ability took over as she drifted a few inches farther toward the middle of the pool. The sound of the water, of her body moving through it, reverberated through the tiled poolroom and bounced back at her. So did the heavy sound of the double doors clicking shut. Brynna snapped her head toward the sound, and then everything went dark.

The overhead lights snapped off, and she was blinded by the sudden darkness, by the little explosion of hot, white light that bloomed in front of her from the sudden change of glaring bright to pitch blackness.

"Hello?" she called out, her meek voice floating back to her.

"Hello? Someone's in here. Can you please turn the lights on again? Please?"

She started to kick harder as the panic rose in her chest. She could feel the adrenaline oozing into her blood stream. The same adrenaline that used to shoot her across the pool weighed her down now, and the side of the pool—the steps—seemed to get farther and farther away as Brynna kicked.

And then there were the fingers.

Hundreds of them, clawing at her skin. Dead, clenched hands, marble cold, ripping at her throat. Tearing at her hair. Slicing across her swimsuit.

There's nothing here in the pool with you, Brynna. You're imagining this. You're panicking.

She worked to breathe, to let herself see that she was alone in the water, while her mind spun on, conjuring up corpses in the water pulling her under. Her panic threw her off balance.

She felt the slick step disappear, and she was tumbling, the water pressing against her chest pushing her down, pulling her under. The water dripped in between her clenched teeth. It snaked into her nostrils, and she struggled to breathe. She sucked up the water, and it doused the burn in her lungs and then made it worse. Her hair swirled and snarled in front of her eyes as the sound of water, the pound, the rush, whooshed through her ears. She was screaming and coughing and clawing, trying to keep her head above water, trying to figure out which end was up.

Find your footing, find your footing, find your footing. Her inner voice was screaming, desperately trying to be heard over the whoosh of water. She tried to work over the panic. And then her hand hit something solid.

She felt the sting of the concrete slapping her palm first, then gripped at the cement, feeling her fingernails catch. She winced as they broke but still she struggled to pull herself toward the cement ledge of the pool. She kicked and clawed, and then there was a hand on hers.

A savior.

Brynna's head broke the surface—or she thought it did. When she opened her eyes, everything was black. She launched herself toward the ledge, toward the hand holding hers, but it was like there was a wall. She pressed, and the wall pressed back. Her eyes began to adjust and she knew where she was—inside the pool, inside the school.

But why was it so dark?

There was a figure at the edge. Crouching, examining Brynna with a cocked head and one hand out, gripping hers.

Erica?

Brynna blinked, the water, like tears, running over her cheeks.

"Erica?"

The water seemed to still, and Brynna's voice echoed back to her. "Erica" raised her head, but her face was still shadowed, her dark hair tumbling over her cheeks and chin. She leaned down closer to Brynna rather than pulling Brynna toward her and pulled her hand from Brynna's.

Then Brynna felt the palm on her head.

"Erica?" she asked again.

She felt the pressure first. Erica's fingers were splayed over Brynna's skewed swim cap as her palm pressed down on her head, pushing Brynna lower, lower. Brynna thrashed at the water as it once again invaded her nostrils, her mouth. She felt it rushing down her throat, and she wrenched her eyes open, staring up through the water to see Erica, both arms outstretched now as she held Brynna under the water. Brynna writhed. Her lungs stung. She tried to kick out of Erica's reach, but Erica's grip only tightened, strands of Brynna's hair breaking in her fist.

Suddenly, breathing didn't seem so hard anymore. The water that pushed and pulled against her was a smooth, cool cradle, and Brynna was getting tired, so, so tired.

No.

Her eyes flew open, and she made one more pitch away from Erica. She heard each individual strand of hair breaking, felt the cool water rush over the fresh bald spots on her scalp.

She was free.

Brynna didn't think. Her body took over, and she was slicing through the water with a speed and ease she had never known. She gripped at the side of the pool and launched herself out, gasping, crying, coughing—*desperate.*

Even in the pitch darkness, Brynna knew that Erica was just a hairsbreadth away. She turned, ready to dart for the door, but the arms clamped around her first, pinning her own at her sides.

"Brynna!"

Brynna opened her mouth to scream, but just like the dream, nothing came out but a tortured gasp and a vile dribble of ingested pool water. She willed her arms to move, her hands to claw, her legs to kick, but someone was shaking her, moving her.

"Don't do this, Erica!"

Brynna's voice echoed, a crisp, clear sound bouncing off the tiles.

And all at once, the viselike grip released and the whole room came alive in too-bright, blazing lights. Brynna was on her butt on the tile floor, huddled in a wet mess, and someone was rushing toward her. Fear welled up once again but was immediately doused when Brynna heard Teddy's voice.

"Bryn, Bryn, calm down, it's just me." Teddy dropped to his knees and Brynna watched, dumbfounded, as the knees of his jeans darkened from the puddles of water he leaned in. He snatched her towel from the bleachers and wrapped it around her trembling shoulders, pulling her close. Instinctively, her arms were out, palms pressing against his chest.

"No, don't." Brynna launched to her feet and whirled around. "Where is she? Where is she? Did you see her when you came in?"

Teddy stood up, wringing the towel that slid off Brynna's shoulders. "See who? What are you talking about, Bryn?"

"Erica." The name was out before Brynna could think about it, could weigh whether or not she was ready to call out Erica or call out her ghost.

Teddy's blue eyes clouded. "There was no one else here."

"No. She was here. She was here!" Brynna's hand went to her head as her eyes filled with tears. Her hand closed on the tender strands, and she tugged one lightly, feeling a tuft of wet hair coming off in her palm.

Teddy's mouth dropped open. "Brynna, don't." His voice was soft and his fingertips brushing over her raw scalp were softer.

"She was here."

Teddy spun, looking. "Stay right here." He jogged toward the bleachers and bent, scanning underneath. "Did you see where she went?" He came at her, grabbing her by the arm. "We have to get you to the police or the principal. Did you see her? What did she look like?"

"It wasn't—I didn't..." Brynna looked at the hair in her palm, and her stomach churned, bile itching the back of her throat. "She was here. She tried to—she tried to kill me. Erica did."

"We have to call the police."

"No." Brynna stopped Teddy, her hand on his arm. "We can't—we..." She paused, for a moment wishing that Teddy would understand her without her having to explain. "We can't call the police."

Teddy swallowed slowly, his Adam's apple bobbing as he did. "You said her name was Erica. Who is she?" He put his arm across Brynna's shoulders and guided her to the bleachers, pulling her down beside him. "Is she from a different grade or something?" His eyes caught Brynna's and flashed; he stared down at his palms. "Is there something you're not telling me?"

Brynna's lips felt numb. "No, no. She was here." It was barely more than a whisper, but the statement seemed to hang in the air between them as Teddy's eyes scanned the concrete around the pool. There was nothing there. No wet footprints, no water droplets. There was nothing except for the square of wet concrete where Brynna pulled herself out of the water.

She blinked up at Teddy. "You didn't see—"

He shook his head, something like sadness or apology in his eyes. "I didn't see anyone else in here, Bryn."

Tension stiffened Brynna's spine. "Then why did you come in here? Were you—"

The apology in Teddy's eyes immediately vanished. His cheeks pinkened in the dim light. "I wasn't stalking you or anything. I was just coming back from football"—he pointed to the discarded sporting goods at the door as if for proof—"and I heard screaming."

Instinctively, Brynna's fingertips washed over her throat. "Screaming?"

"I looked in and saw that it was dark. But I heard you—I didn't know it was you then—scream again, so I came in and you were just coming out of the water. What happened? Why were the lights off? You weren't swimming out here alone, were you?" He looked strangely skeptical. "In the dark?"

A tremble coursed through Brynna, and she felt the sting of tears behind her eyes, that heavy tension of holding back tears pressing on her temples. "I don't know what happened," she whispered.

Teddy stared at her for a silent beat before pulling Brynna into him. His cut-grass smell and warm sweatshirt comforted her, and something inside her broke. She was suddenly crying silently, body-wracking tears that strained every fiber of her being. Teddy brushed his lips over Brynna's forehead then rested his cheek on her head, his arms engulfing her completely until she couldn't cry anymore.

• • •

"Come on, I'll drive you home," Teddy said.

"Actually, my mom was going—" She glanced down at her cell phone and slid the text message icon. "Well, she's going to pick me up in forty-five minutes."

"I'll take you."

Brynna fell into step with Teddy then paused. "Didn't you tell Darcy you biked today?"

Teddy looked sheepish. "I may have kind of lied."

Brynna raised her brows.

"Darcy can be kind of…rough. Besides, I saw she got a ride home from one of the guys on the baseball team anyway. She's never really hurting for help."

She smiled, feeling a modicum better. Teddy didn't want to be with Darcy. Not at all. The thought made her warm, even as her skin stayed ice cold.

Teddy drove Brynna, still wrapped in her towel, home. She wore her flip-flops and clutched her goggles and swim cap in one hand, her backpack hugged in her other arm. She worked the stitches on her backpack strap, the movement rote and comforting even as the nubby fabric rubbed the skin on her fingertips raw. Teddy tried to speak every so often, and Brynna wanted to respond but her eyes—her mind—were so consumed with finding Erica that every movement outside the dark car windows made her jump, made her already queasy stomach roil.

It was Erica, the voice in her mind repeated.

It couldn't have been Erica, another voice countered.

They never found her body…

"It's this one, right?"

Brynna jumped, her heart hammering against her rib cage. "W-what?"

"This one." Teddy's eyes cut across Brynna's face as he glanced toward her house, hulking in the darkness.

"Oh, yeah, right." Brynna hadn't realized how long they had driven, how far they had gone. She gathered up her things then looked at Teddy. "Hey, how did you know which house it was?"

Teddy shrugged nonchalantly. "You told me you guys were one of the only lived-in houses out here, so I kind of assumed."

Brynna nodded, feeling slightly ashamed for questioning him. "Oh. Well, thanks for…the ride…and everything." The interior of the car was dark, but a sliver of silver moonlight illuminated the hard planes of Teddy's face. It made his light eyes look dark, like deep, jeweled pools, and Brynna instantly feared she would go under.

She wanted to lean forward and kiss Teddy, to get lost in that prickly feeling that came when his lips founds hers, when his arms wrapped around her. She could feel his heartbeat then, thundering with her own, and she felt safe, connected. But this was a different Teddy and she was a different Brynna: naked, exposed. Teddy didn't lean in to kiss her, and his gaze only grazed her as he turned to stare out the windshield directly in front of him.

He thinks I'm crazy. He—knows—I'm crazy.

The reality hit Brynna like a solid pop to the chest, and she nearly lost her breath, finding the door handle and pressing herself out into the cool night air before she could. She gasped, but the sound was snatched away by the roar of Teddy's engine as he revved it, the red taillights of his car like sharp, accusing eyes fading into the blackness.

The house was dark when Brynna sunk her key into the lock, and inside, the only light was the pale gray glimmer of a television on in the family room.

"Mom?"

Brynna stopped in the doorway, one leg twisting around the other. Her mother was sunk into the fluffy brown sectional, an afghan pulled up around her shoulders.

"Hey, Bryn." She leaned forward and clicked on a lamp, the room filling with a soft, yellow light. Her eyes immediately darkened. "Oh, honey, why are you still in your swimsuit? You're going to catch your death."

Her mother rushed to her and replaced Brynna's sopping towel with the afghan, tucking it around her shoulders and piling her wet hair on the top of her head. Brynna's teeth chattered.

"You're freezing. Go upstairs and take a hot shower and I'll make you something to eat. Soup?"

But Brynna stayed rooted to her spot.

"Brynna? Did you hear me?"

Brynna swallowed, her thoughts crashing. Everything inside her pulled, but she couldn't keep quiet anymore. She knew she was going to break. "She was there, Mom," she said simply.

"She? She who?" Her eyebrows went up.

In her mind, Brynna said it. *Erica.* But in reality, she couldn't press the word, her best friend's *name,* over her teeth. As much as she wanted to, as much as she wanted to put it out there, she couldn't say it.

Her mother stepped closer. "Who was there, Brynna?"

Brynna's eyes looked over her mother's head while her mother tried to catch her gaze.

"Erica," Brynna finally whispered.

Her mother looked away, and immediately, Brynna recoiled, her whole body thrumming with the knowledge that she had done something wrong, said something wrong. Her mother wouldn't understand. She would think Brynna was crazy.

Maybe I am crazy.

"There was no one here, Bryn." Teddy's words came back to her and she shuddered, pulling the afghan tighter.

"Honey." Brynna's mom reached out for her hand, gently pulling her toward her. "Erica is gone. She's dead, sweetie. I know it's hard—I know. But you have to accept that. The sooner you accept—"

The chatter of Brynna's teeth spread through her whole body, and she was trembling now. "How do you know?"

"How do I know what?"

"That Erica is really dead."

Her mother looked taken aback. "Honey—"

"They never found her body. They never found anything."

There was something in Brynna's mother's voice—exasperation? Desperation? "Brynna, there is a riptide on Harding Beach. Everyone knows it. The fact that Erica didn't, that her body didn't—the fact that we didn't find her only proves that she can't be alive. She drowned, honey."

"We never looked for her. No one did."

"That's not true, Brynna. The police did. They sent out divers and—"

"And still no one found her."

"They could only go out so far. The riptide is that dangerous."

Brynna shook her head. She could understand the words, and intellectually, she knew the idea that Erica could still be alive was farfetched at best. But the tweets and the sand, and now the dark figure. Her scalp started to sting where Erica had ripped out her hair.

"But what if she didn't, Mom? Just, what if? What if she came back—and she's mad at me?" Brynna's lower lip started to tremble and the tears started to fall, making hot tracks down her ice-cold cheeks. "What if she wants to hurt me?"

Brynna could see her mother working out her response. Finally, "Even if that were at all possible, Bryn, Erica wouldn't be mad at you. She wouldn't want to hurt you. It was an accident. Erica knows that—she knew that, honey."

An accident I caused, Brynna wanted to shout. Erica wouldn't have jumped if it hadn't been for Brynna's dare. She wouldn't have jumped and Brynna wouldn't be standing, dripping in this strange new kitchen, certain that her best friend wanted her dead. If it hadn't been for her, everything would have been fine.

"Are you okay, hon? Should I make another appointment with Dr.—"

"I don't want another appointment, Mom."

Both Brynna and her mother were silent for a long beat while something unspoken hung in the air.

"Erica's dead, Brynna. You need to accept that. You just…do."

Brynna thought about telling her mother about the pool, about Erica, but even with the scratches on her arms and the unrelenting fear that Erica was there, was after her, Brynna couldn't overcome the aching fear that she was going crazy and her parents would give her a one-way ticket back to Woodbriar.

Brynna turned without speaking and started up the stairs. Her head was pounding and her eyes were dry and itchy from the chlorine, and she wanted nothing more than to peel her still-damp swimsuit off, but the second she walked into her bedroom, she paused. The feeling was overwhelming and immediate: someone was there. It was nothing obvious—she didn't see or hear anything, but still the certainty slammed into her with all the subtlety of a brick wall.

"Hello?" Brynna asked, clicking on the light. "Anyone here?"

There was a fresh pile of folded laundry on her bed, but everything else was the same, everything else in its place—except her tablet. It was propped up against her pillows, longwise, as though it would spring to life with an ad for new sheets at any moment. Brynna licked her lips and checked over her shoulder as fists of dread crashed into her chest. Staying as far as she could from the device, she leaned over and swished the screen on then blew out the breath she was holding.

The page displayed was AskAnything.com, a website where Brynna and some of her friends posted random homework and general questions that were answered by a sea of geniuses or wisecrackers somewhere in the cyber-universe. She used the site regularly and let out a wild little giggle, knowing she must have left the site open—until she snatched the tablet up. Someone had asked a question:

QUESTION FROM: BRYNBE51: How long can someone survive adrift at sea?

The question had been asked from her account.

She scanned, finding a litany of answers.

DJQUIMBY: Depends on the H2O temp

FXRCR: 3 days w/o fresh water. 1 month w/. Unless theres sharx! : O

D24MJ: Do u have a raft/life jacket? If yes, much longer.

SPARKLESUZY: Sharks! Ahhh! :]

YES2ME: Hope you kno how 2 swim!

ERICANSHAW: You tell me.

NINE

Brynna blinked at the screen, feeling her stomach churn. She swallowed, this moment, this life of hers dropping into slow motion as the world went on at a whirring pace around her. Someone was watching her. Someone was haunting her.

Before Erica's death—just every once in a while—there had been a niggling jealousy that stabbed at the back of her mind. When Erica swished by Brynna in the pool, overtaking her at the last second to win. When Erica mastered a stroke the first time out while Brynna struggled to perfect it. How everyone happily revered and assumed Erica's first place status and Brynna's second.

She would always cheers to Erica, sipping her drink while Erica beamed and people complimented her. At first, it was just the fun of the celebration, the party—a little slug of beer to raise or something fruity and red to mask the alcohol taste. Brynna would have a few sips and set the cup aside when the sting of jealousy subsided. But week after week, the sting started to last, and the booze helped to soothe it. But still, she would stop drinking, determined to beat Erica the next time. She knew she could. She knew she deserved it.

Not jealous, Brynna thought. *Competitive. Competitive, not murderous.*

The last thought rang hollow in her mind. She had a vague memory of something she learned in sophomore biology about how the brain could trigger things—thoughts, desires—and the body could act on them. Afterward, the actions would be expunged from the person's memory. *Lacunar amnesia*, Brynna recalled. Selective memory loss.

Suddenly, her mind's eye was flooded with memories: the sick slap of flesh hitting water. The underwater sound of thrashing. The way Erica's hair felt—slippery and fine—as it slid through Brynna's fisted hand. The pale, waxy look of Erica's skin as her body floated downward into the depths of the Pacific Ocean, so calm, so peaceful, her slightly parted lips, and eyes, wide open, staring at Brynna with the moonlight reflected in them.

How would I know what Erica's hair felt like? How would I know what she looked like? I have this image of her—Brynna closed her eyes, trying to stamp the ghastly image out—*where did it come from?*

Heat surged up the back of Brynna's neck, and she was racing through the room, clawing her way to the bathroom. She doubled over and vomited, tears and sweat commingling and dripping from her chin as she heaved.

The images in her head came from her dreams, because once Erica hit the water, Brynna couldn't see her anymore. Could she? She fell against the wall, her back sliding until she landed on her butt with a hard thump. She could feel the cold tile shoot a chill up her spine as she thought about the dreams where Erica was floating down below her. Was it a dream or a deeply hidden memory suddenly shaking loose? Brynna pushed up to her knees and vomited again.

At some point, Brynna's mother rushed through the bedroom door and fawned over her, coaxing her into her pajamas and tucking her into bed. Her mother was still in her paint-covered smock, and when she leaned down to rest her palm on Brynna's forehead, Brynna breathed in the heady, earthy scent of the paints and the bitter bite of turpentine, the smells that always comforted her as a child.

"I told you sitting around in that wet bathing suit was going to get you sick." Her mother leaned over her, pressing a cool, damp washcloth to Brynna's forehead. "I thought you've been looking a little pale lately, a little off."

Brynna nodded and looked away.

"Soup?"

She looked up into her mother's eyes, her forehead creased with worry. Brynna never realized how much older her mother looked than she had just fourteen months ago, how now when her hair was wound in the messy topknot, there were streaks of gray between the auburn. Her eyes were lined and tired-looking, and although part of Brynna wanted to curl up in her mother's arms and tell her everything—everything—she couldn't. Her mother looked so fragile.

"You don't have to wait on me, Mom. I'm really okay. I just… ate the cafeteria food today." She offered a small smile. "Not going to make that mistake again. I think I just want to go to sleep."

Her mother's eyebrows went up. "It's barely nine o'clock. You must be sick."

She blew her a kiss, clicked off the overhead light, and shut the door with a soft click. Brynna stared at the ceiling for exactly five minutes before sleep hit her like a solid wall. She slept fitfully, dreaming of Ella screaming at her, her teeth jagged and blood-stained as she snapped her jaws at Brynna. Shards of black water crashed into her subconscious, and Ella's screams were snatched away by the pounding sound of waves crashing on sand. Erica was there and then she wasn't, and Brynna reached out to her, their fingertips brushing then separated by miles of water. Erica would come back again and the whole thing would repeat. Each time it was comforting and then terrifying, and dream Brynna screamed until her throat was raw, and then she began to sink. She felt the water lapping over her, and this time, she welcomed it. She closed her eyes and gave in to the soft lull of the ocean, to the caress of the waves. The undulating surf was like soft hands pressing her down, and as the water invaded her nose, dripped down her throat, and poured into her lungs, Brynna felt herself letting go. She didn't struggle to breathe, and the twilight behind her eyelids grew darker and darker as the water took her over. She couldn't hear the waves anymore. She couldn't hear Ella's screams. She could only feel the blissful tug of the water…

Then all at once, a hand wrapped around her arm and yanked her up until the sunlight blinded her and her wet body shivered in the chilled air. Brynna yawned then blinked.

"What?"

Her alarm clock was blaring and her sheets were rolled in a matted mess at the end of her bed.

"Holy crap."

She raked a hand through her hair, the unsettling remnants of the dream still hanging on her periphery. She sighed and glanced around the room, her room, with all of her things lined up and set just as she had left them—but something felt off. Kicking her bare feet over the bed, Brynna stepped onto the plush carpet and immediately sat back down.

Her feet were wet.

Fire zinged through her body, but Brynna worked to shake it off. She glanced over her shoulder at herself in the mirror and started, her heart seizing in her chest.

Her biology book lay open on her desk. Perched on top of the splayed-open pages was a pair of glasses. From where she sat, Brynna could see them glitter, could see the sunlight bounce off the tiny pool of water they sat in. She made a beeline for them, snatching them up.

They were Erica's.

Though nondescript to the casual observer, Brynna would know them anywhere. Erica had painted the inside of the plain black frames with the hottest, pinkest nail polish she could find. She used to say they represented the "diva inside."

Brynna started to tremble. The eyeglasses were wet, the saltwater smell unmistakable. A fleck of kelp wrapped around one edge of the frame. She turned, glasses in hand, but stopped cold when she saw the footprints on the carpet: Dainty. Barefoot. Wet.

Her heart slammed against her rib cage, and she started to cry, her eyes watering acidic tears over her cheeks.

"Erica?"

She remembered the dream and stared incredulously at her arm, waiting to see a burn or bruise from where Erica's hand had grabbed when she yanked Brynna from the water—but there was nothing there.

"Erica is dead," Brynna started. "Erica is dead." She rocked and chanted the sentence to herself like a mantra—or a prayer.

• • •

Trepidation shot through Brynna when she set foot on campus the next morning. She wasn't sure if Teddy told anyone about what happened—if he said that he had found Brynna nearly drowned or that he found the "new girl" wrestling with an imaginary ghost from her past. Everything about her felt vulnerable, like walking through a crowded room with a tender sunburn, and Brynna didn't want to see anyone so she skirted the main halls and walked the perimeter of the building. That was where she was when she saw the janitor outside of the poolroom's double door. He had a pair of long-handled pipe cutters in his hands and was working at something shoved through the door handles. Brynna paused, watching.

The janitor stopped mid-cut and took her in with disapproving eyes. "Help you?"

Brynna scratched her cheek. "What—what are you doing?"

The janitor made the cut, and Brynna watched a chain slide out from the door handles and land in a snakelike coil in the dirt. "Isn't it obvious? Some idiot chained the poolroom doors together."

Bat's wings punctured Brynna's stomach. "When?"

"Last night. Did almost all the doors. I don't know what's wrong with you guys."

Brynna was too shocked to be indignant, to point out that the entire school didn't chain the doors together. She licked her bottom lip and tried to steel herself, gripping the edges of her books so tightly her knuckles went white.

"Which doors, exactly?"

The janitor stopped then and looked Brynna full in the face, his eyebrows turned down in two black slashes. "Every one but the one interior door in the senior hall. Locker room doors, outside door." He leaned over and snatched the broken chain off the ground, giving off a huge cloud of dust. "Do me a favor, huh? Tell your friends these little pranks are really a pain in my ass." He stalked off, and Brynna stepped back, stunned.

If only she could believe that last night was just a "little prank."

She started down the hallway, glancing down at her vibrating phone. It was another text from Teddy, and a wave of guilt shot over Brynna as she slid the phone to the off position. Brynna had been avoiding Teddy's texts and calls since last night. It wasn't that she didn't want to talk to him; it was that she had no idea what to say. She had mumbled on and on about a dead girl trying to drown her when there was no one else in the pool. Teddy was sweet and had tried to be understanding, but how long would he go on understanding Brynna if she kept acting so crazy?

"There you are."

Brynna turned and sucked in a breath, face to face and nearly a hairsbreadth away from Teddy. His eyes were an intense blue and his hands were on her shoulders—firm but careful. Brynna's heart started to thud.

"Uh, hey, Teddy." She managed a small smile.

His hands dropped to his sides, and her shoulders were cold where his hands had been.

"So you have been avoiding me."

"No, no." She pressed her palm flat against his chest, feeling the beat of his heart in her hand. She wanted to throw her arms around him and live by that steady, constant rhythm. "I mean…yes. I kind of thought it would be best."

"For who?"

Brynna was taken aback by the slight edge in his voice. "Well, for you. I mean, I—clearly—am nuts or something—"

"Or something." A smile kicked up the edges of his lips.

"I'm sorry, I just didn't think you'd want to be labeled as the guy with the crazy girlfriend."

The second she said the word "girlfriend," heat flashed over Brynna's cheeks and all the way up to her hair.

"So you're my girlfriend now?"

Her heart was lodged securely in her throat, and Brynna thought that if she was going to die anyway, now would be the perfect time.

"I—I didn't mean—I just meant girl, who's a friend…"

Teddy held up a hand stop-sign style. "Nope. Stop there. I like girlfriend."

Now Brynna's heart sped up for a different reason, and she felt the grin spread across her face, pushing up her earlobes.

"I like you," Teddy said.

"I like you too."

He slung an arm around her. "So we're in agreement."

"Yeah, but about last night—"

Teddy pressed his index finger to his pursed lips. "Shh. Your less-than-stellar swimming abilities can be our little secret."

Brynna fell into step with Teddy. Their hands hung by their sides but close enough so that their fingers brushed. The feeling of Teddy so close trumped all the negative feelings Brynna was having, and she reveled in the few minutes of between-class happiness.

Teddy yanked open the door for her. "After you."

She smiled, warmth climbing up the back of her neck. When Brynna stepped into the room, her eyes cut across the chalkboard. She found her seat, pulling her Mr. Fallbrook-mandated "journal" out of her bag.

Fallbrook's AP English class was required to "loosen up" with a daily writing prompt. He would write a statement or a topic on the board, and before anything happened—before papers got turned in or excuses were given for papers not being turned in—students had to write at least a full two pages in their black-speckled comp books on the topic. He checked them once a week and actually read what they wrote, so giant handwriting or a series of "I feel very, very, very, very strongly about this topic" wouldn't fly.

Brynna actually liked the routine, and the prompts gave her a way to throw all her thoughts and energy into something other than what was going on in her head. Today, however, was an exception.

In Fallbrook's blocky writing was the daily writing prompt: *Write about a time you were really scared.*

Brynna opened her notebook, her pen sliding through palms that were already clammy.

How about now? She wanted to write.

I was really afraid that night when I came out of the water.

She felt the water breaking over her face, the choppy waves at her shoulders, sinking into the loose-weave fabric of her summer T-shirt. She could taste the salt water on her lips.

Her lungs were burning, pulling. It didn't seem that far out when they walked the pier, but swimming back to shore was another thing entirely. Brynna stopped kicking and started to tread, her legs working as she spun in a circle, searching the slick top of the black water for Erica.

"Erica…" she sang.

But there was no Erica.

"Come on." Brynna slapped at the water, cold droplets landing on her eyelashes and lips. "Fine, be that way." She turned and started to swim toward shore again, certain that Erica, the stronger swimmer of the two, was already padding through the wet sand at the water's edge, cursing Brynna's name.

Brynna pounded through the water, feeling the slight tug of the surf pulling her backward. But she cupped her hands and stroked until her shoulders ached and her knees banked against wet sand close to shore then stood up, letting the weight of the water drip off her as she reached the pillowy dry sand. Her heart was thundering, and she was breathing hard but smiling, tasting the salt on her lips.

"Whew!" She threw her hands up in a victory V and danced around the beach, wriggling her butt and shaking her head. "That was awesome!"

Michael, Ella, and Jay were jogging toward her, hooting and whistling. "Nice job!" Ella crowed.

"Weren't you supposed to be naked?" Michael said, that sly grin not skipping a beat. He hiccupped softly, a burst of sugar-sweet, alcohol-scented breath commingling with the salty beach breeze.

"I took my top off. You must have blinked and missed it. Your loss." Brynna stopped dancing and wrung the water out of her hair. "Okay, where's the big cry baby? Is she hiding because she doesn't want to admit that that was totally unreal?"

Michael tossed Brynna a towel and jutted his chin toward the water. "She's still out there."

Brynna pulled the towel around her and turned to look. "Really? I thought for sure she'd beat me in."

"Well...there you go. She's faster in the lanes and you're faster in open water. 'Cuz you're like a shark!" Michael snapped his jaws before planting a smacking kiss on her cheek.

Ella scratched her head, squinting. "I don't even see her."

"Erica's like a snake in the water. You don't even see her coming and then bam! There she is."

"Okay," Jay said, "then where is she?"

Brynna walked down the beach, letting the water crash over her ankles. "Erica?" She cupped her hands around her mouth. "Erica!"

The only answer was the sound of the waves smacking the wet sand.

Brynna turned and glared at her friends. "You guys are so stupid.

Where is she? She came in way before me, didn't she? Is she trying to make me think she's dead? Trying to prove some kind of Erica-point?"

Ella's face was wan. "No, really, Bryn. She didn't come in."

"You're lying."

Now Michael shook his head, and the action shook something loose in Brynna. "Really?"

"Seriously. Didn't you see her when you guys came up the first time?"

Brynna's chest started to tighten. Sweat beaded along her hairline and upper lip, even as she shivered in the night air. "I—I think so."

"How could you think so? That was five minutes ago," Jay said.

Brynna looked at her trio of friends and the hard, worried looks on their faces. "I know but I—I mean, I'm sure I did." She spun back to the surf. "Erica!"

Jay was stripping off his shirt and Michael kicked off his flip-flops. The sound of their bare feet slapping the sand reverberated through Brynna's head. She took one look at Ella, chewing on her bottom lip, and dropped her towel, cutting ahead of the boys and diving into the foam-covered waves.

Brynna plunged under the water, feeling the sting of the salt water as she opened her eyes. The water at Harding Beach was murky even in sunlight, and at night, she was met with a wall of blackness. Her feet hit the sandy bottom, and Brynna launched herself, head and shoulders breaking water. "Erica?"

Her voice joined the chorus of Michael and Jay's. Brynna spun in time to see Ella running up the beach, her figure becoming smaller as she broke the wall of swaying kids on Jay's back patio.

Brynna dipped back under the water, groping blindly, her fingers sifting through sand, her arms being slapped by kelp as she swam. Underwater, she started to cry.

Erica is playing a trick, *she told herself.* Erica is trying to teach me a lesson.

It seemed like hours passed, and every muscle in Brynna's body was screaming in exhaustion, rallying against the pain of pushing against another crashing wave, another swell of surf.

Then she felt the hand on her shoulder.

"Erica!"

Brynna opened her mouth and grinned, feeling the cold water slide through her teeth. The hand tightened on Brynna's shoulder, pulling her back toward shore. Brynna pushed off and broke the surface, gulping in a deep breath of salt-tinged air in time to see Michael in front of her, dragging her behind him.

Brynna looked around for Erica and felt her heart swell with relief when she stepped onto shore and spotted Jay swimming in.

A thousand feet seemed to pound the beach, and Brynna spun back to the beach house, seeing half the party vaulting toward her, led by Ella. Her cheeks were red and her lips drawn.

"Come in!" someone called. "Get out of the water and come in!"

"What's going on?" Brynna asked. "Where's Erica?"

"You can't swim there at night," the same voice said. "There's a goddamn riptide. Get out of the water!"

Brynna blinked. "A riptide?"

Jay trudged out of the water, eyes darting across the sand and slicing through the group of kids. "Where's Erica?" he said.

"I couldn't find her, man," Michael answered.

Heat raced up the back of Brynna's neck, and her stomach started to churn.

"Brynna?" Ella asked.

Bile itched at the back of Brynna's throat, and the world dropped into slow motion. The waves took their time swelling and curling; their crash was gentle and calm as fingers of frothy water crawled toward her feet before being sucked out again by the tide.

Somehow, Brynna knew someone was talking to her. She could vaguely hear the sound of her name, could vaguely feel people touching her, but she felt like everything was encased in cotton. Cotton stuffing her ears and muffling sound, cotton keeping her a thousand miles from the arms that reached for her.

"No." She was finally able to push the word over her teeth. "No!" The towel that someone had slipped over her shoulders flopped into the sand, and Brynna was pushing forward, pushing through the crowd. "I have to get Erica. Erica!"

She barely felt the water as her feet plunged into it, as it slapped against her calves. "Erica!" she was calling, straining to be heard over the surf. "Erica!"

She was waist-deep before Michael grabbed her, bear-hugging her around the waist and yanking her backward. But Brynna fought back, clawing for the water, trying to dive out of his arms.

"My best friend is out there! Let me go! You have to let me go!"

She dug her toes into the wet sand, praying for some traction, but Michael just hauled her backward as if she weighed nothing.

"Erica!"

Terror like an icy hand gripped at Brynna's heart, and she struggled to breathe, her eyes darting across the undulating water. Every swell was Erica breaking through; every crash was Erica kicking her legs.

"She's out there," Brynna whispered, the tears burning over her chapped cheeks. "I have to find her."

Somehow, the paramedics made it down the beach with flashing lights and wailing sirens that Brynna didn't hear. A medic asked her some questions; she jostled out of the blood pressure cuff he tried to slap on her.

"No," she mumbled.

This isn't happening.

Fear like a lead weight settled in her gut. Her skin felt too tight. Erica was here. She was here.

Brynna turned out toward the water again, breaking away and darting for the crashing black waves, but someone was gripping her, the pain of their hands at the crook of her elbow surging up to her shoulder.

"Brynna—don't." It was Michael, his eyes a flat black.

Brynna looked over him and saw two police officers stepping out of a squad car parked on the sand. They looked so out of place with their drawn faces and pristine black uniforms, pant cuffs clouded with sand, but Brynna beelined for them anyway.

"Have you found Erica?"

The younger of the two officers, with a buzz cut and thick, black slashes for eyebrows, scratched his head. "Ma'am?"

The other officer pushed in front of the first and looked down at his phone. "Are you Brynna Chase?"

Hot tears clouded Brynna's vision. "Yes, but it's Erica. Erica is the one who's missing. She's—" Brynna turned toward the water, something breaking inside of her.

Erica was gone.

Past the breakers, the ocean was glass-topped and flat. The red and blue flashing police lights reflected off the water, a terrifying stained glass window, the image searing itself into Brynna's mind forever.

TEN

"All right, guys." Mr. Fallbrook began erasing the prompt on the board, looking over one shoulder to address the students. "Close your journals and pass them to the right. You know the drill."

Brynna felt her breath catch as the corner of the first journal was nudged against her arm. She looked down at the blank page in her own journal and back up again, feeling her cheeks redden. A blank journal entry resulted in an automatic zero for the day, regardless of how dazzling a student was in the hour that followed. With Brynna's mind splintering in so many different directions lately, her grade was already suffering.

She printed the prompt on the top of the page and then hastily wrote the words, "I don't remember ever really being afraid."

It was a flaming lie, of course, but Brynna wasn't ready for the kind of attention "I don't remember the last time I felt safe" would draw. She glanced up at Mr. Fallbrook who raised his eyebrows at her. He was one of the younger teachers on the faculty and certainly one of the most handsome, with an easygoing personality and a quick wit. He was the kind of teacher a student could talk to.

But not Brynna.

She gathered her classmates' journals from her right and shoved hers under the stack. Although the daily writing prompts required far more than she had given, she hoped at the very least Fallbrook would give her partial credit for writing something.

The class passed uneventfully while Brynna held her pen poised, ballpoint tip pressed against her paper. When the bell rang, she looked around with a start as kids around her started gathering up their things. She did the same thing, but the motion was rote, done out of memory rather than necessity.

"Uh, Brynna, wait."

Mr. Fallbrook shimmied his way through the students to reach Brynna's desk.

She sank back into her seat. "Yeah?"

"Is everything okay with you?"

Cold broke in her chest. "Wha—what do you mean?"

Fallbrook shrugged. "I don't know. You just seem kind of off lately."

Brynna looked at her hands in her lap. "Oh. That. Just studying a lot. There's so much, you know, homework."

"And you've been working really hard."

Brynna pumped her head, sensing a quick getaway. "Transcripts. College and all."

Mr. Fallbrook pressed a finger against the notebook Brynna was about to leave behind. "These today's notes?"

She felt the heat rise again as she glanced at the notebook, the page completely blank except for the date written in the top left-hand corner. Brynna smacked thc notebook shut and stood quickly. "I'm sorry, Mr. Fallbrook. It's just been a rough day. I promise I'll do better tomorrow." She edged backward down the aisle, bumping her hips and bag as she went.

"If anything's wrong, you can talk—"

But Brynna was out the door and into the hall before he had a chance to finish.

• • •

Brynna squinted through the passenger-side window as her father pulled the car up into the school driveway. She opened the door when he stopped, engine idling, and scooched into the front seat.

"What are you doing here?"

Her father's eyebrows went up. "You're not happy to see me?"

"It's not that. It's just that Mom usually picks me up. Did you get back early or something?"

"Yeah." He pushed the car into drive, and they made the right onto Blackwood Highway. "I finished up earlier than expected and hopped the first flight out."

Brynna's hackles went up. Her father was too casual in his explanation, too buttoned-up to jump an earlier flight. He wasn't the "surprise" kind of father who showed up at swim meets or soccer games, and even if he was changing, was ready to pay attention to his family, he wasn't the car-pooler type.

"Your mother actually had an errand to run, so I volunteered to pick you up. Besides, don't you think it's about time your old dad saw his kid's new school?"

Brynna glanced back over her shoulder, feeling her lip snarling. "And how did you find the Hawthorne High parking lot, Dad?"

He shot her an icy look. "I'm trying, Bryn."

They drove the rest of the way in awkward silence, her father cutting glances at her every few miles or so, Brynna with her arms crossed in front of her chest, consumed by fury. When they crossed through the heavy wrought-iron gates of Blackwood Hills, she turned to him.

"Why now, Dad? Why are you 'trying' now?"

He was silent until they pulled into the driveway of their house, and Brynna was sure he wasn't going to answer her. Then he let out a low sigh as if he were the one being haunted. "Can we talk about this inside, Bryn? Your mother is in there. We should talk as a family."

He got out of the car, and Brynna followed. Her stomach twisted, and the few bites of lunch she had managed expanded in her belly, shooting a heavy wave of nausea through her. "We really don't need a family meeting for you to tell me you're getting a divorce."

Brynna's father snapped around so quickly she ran into him. His eyes were glittering pinpoints, and from their close proximity, she could smell the faint odor of scotch on his breath. It made her stomach tighten even more. He glared at her for a beat but then closed his eyes, pinching the bridge of his nose. When he opened his eyes, there was true sadness in them, and something inside Brynna's chest broke. This was her family; these were her parents. Her life was already fragmented and upended, and her parents' divorce would only guarantee more of the same. She felt a lump grow in her throat, sudden dread growing in her belly.

Her eyes went around her father to the closed interior door where Brynna knew her mother was sitting beyond. She didn't want to go inside. She wanted to get back in the car and reverse all the way back to Point Lobos, to before the dare, even before she'd ever met Erica. This was all her fault. A simmering anger swallowed up the cancerous guilt, and she felt vaguely relieved, having someone to be mad at. If it weren't for Erica, Brynna's parents might have learned to be happy. Brynna might still be happy.

She followed her father through the door and into the kitchen where her mother was seated at the kitchen table, her hands wrapped around a steaming mug of tea. She wasn't wearing her painting smock, but Brynna could see chips of paint around her fingernails, a fading white streak down the length of her jaw. She looked as though she had been interrupted while working, and now she sat, stone still, her watery eyes red-lined and unfocused.

Brynna dropped her bag and rushed toward her. "Mom? Are you okay? Is everything okay?"

Her mother made no response, and for a brief moment fear and anger clawed at Brynna's chest. "Mom?"

"Oh, Bryn, you're home. Can I make you some tea?" She smiled thinly, but Brynna could see her blink away tears.

"Have a seat, Bryn."

Her father pulled out a chair while her mother fiddled around the kitchen, preparing a cup of tea that Brynna hadn't asked for. When she set it in front of Brynna, she looked from her mother to her father and growled, "If you're getting a divorce, just tell me."

A fat tear rolled down her mother's cheek, and her father wouldn't look at her. "This isn't about your mother and me, hon."

Brynna felt her mother's hand on her own, squeezing with almost no strength. "It's about Erica, honey."

Everything in front of Brynna went black. Her tongue went heavy in her mouth, and her jaw went slack, every muscle, every vein, every cell turning into lead weight. "You know?" Her own voice was unrecognizable. "You know what she's been doing to me?"

All at once, every image shot in front of Brynna's eyes, like heinous snapshots, horror after horror: *Remember me?*, the eyeglasses, the dark form in the water, the nightmares, that night on the pier. She felt her bare feet itch as they left the splintered, salt-water-licked wood; she felt the lightness as her body vaulted through the air; she felt the tug of Erica's arm as their fingers laced together. Then the black chill of the water as it swallowed them both up, feet-knees-hips-shoulders-head, the darkness settling over them like a death mask until there was only calm.

Brynna was crying, hiccupping, her breath locked in her chest. "Ever since we got here, Erica has been watching me and following me and leaving me things. She blames me; she hates me! The day in the coffee shop, that was her, wasn't it?"

Her parents exchanged startled glances, and her mother started to cry harder. "No, honey, no." She shook her head, her auburn hair swirling.

Her father took her hand, his grip firm and comforting. "Erica is dead, Brynna—"

"No!" Brynna was on her feet so fast that the chair she was

sitting in went clattering to the hardwood floor bchind her. "I told you, she's here! I've seen her!"

"No, honey. They found her." Brynna's mother's soft voice hitched. "They were able to identify her remains. Erica is really gone, honey."

Color and sound exploded all around Brynna. It would have been loud, overwhelming, if her head hadn't been filled with cotton or the rushing sound of her own blood, or whatever it was that was stifling every sound, vaulting her further and further away from her parents, from her warm kitchen and her lukewarm cup of tea.

"What?"

"A coroner the next county over from Point Lobos recovered"—Brynna's father bit his lip, carefully considering his words—"some remains, a few months after Erica drowned. They were classified as a Jane Doe since there was no identification found."

"Remains?"

Remains weren't people, Brynna thought, *and they certainly weren't fifteen-year-old girls.*

"You don't want to know the details, honey. They're not important."

Brynna pressed the pads of her fingers against the cool wood grain of the kitchen table. Connecting with something—anything—made her feel real, even as everything inside of her wanted this moment to be fake.

"I want to know, Dad." Her heart was a steady drumbeat. "I need to know."

He cleared his throat and shifted his weight in his chair then tossed a glance at Brynna's mother who nodded almost imperceptibly.

"Erica had been in the—"

"Erica's body," Brynna's mother corrected, her eyes fierce and fixed.

"Right, sorry. Erica's body had been in the water a long time, Brynna. The water, the animals… Honey, they had done a lot of damage to Er—the body. She wasn't found all at once. It took them some time to identify and confirm the remains that they did have."

Brynna's stomach heaved and she was at the sink, gripping the tiles as she vomited. Her stomach doubled in on itself and then revolted, and tears were sliding down her cheeks as her body convulsed. Vaguely, she could feel her mother stroking her hair and telling her things would be okay. She could hear her father's heavy footfalls as he paced behind her, clearing his throat the way he always did in a weird attempt to convey concern.

When her stomach calmed or there was nothing left inside her, an icy chill shot through Brynna, even as her body broke out in a sweat. Her teeth were chattering, and all her muscles were spent as though she had just run a marathon. She fell back against her mother and let her hold her; she didn't react when her father wrapped his arms around them both. Her mother cried, stifling little mewling sounds while her father cried silently. Brynna just stared at the grain of the hardwood floor, eyes itchy and dry.

• • •

Brynna lay in her bed, staring up at the ceiling, watching the shadows swirl in the dark. Knowing that Erica was found wasn't the relief she thought it was going to be. As long as Erica was *out there*, she could have been out there, alive. As terrifying as the recent taunts and messages had been, there was a sliver of hope, somewhere deep down, that Erica was responsible. Erica could be mad at Brynna—hell, she could want Brynna dead—but Erica would be alive. And, Brynna believed, if Erica was taking out her anger on Brynna, it was fine because she deserved it.

But now...

Erica was dead. It was that simple and that horrifying. Brynna's best friend was dead, and in a matter of days, they were going to dump her in a box and bury her under six feet of earth. Her fingertips burned, knowing that the last time she touched Erica, as their fingers pulled apart in the cold water, was the last time Erica touched anyone. Brynna didn't push Erica, she didn't hold her under the water, but she was just as guilty as if she had.

Brynna stayed in bed, staring at the ceiling, for two full days. When she slept, it was fitful and unsettling, and when she left her room, she was a walking corpse, expressionless, emotionless, dragging her feet toward the refrigerator or the kitchen sink. Her parents gave her a wide berth, but between her restless catnaps, Brynna began to notice that things were missing in her bedroom or bathroom: the nail polish remover that was there yesterday was gone. The three tabs of baby aspirin she was allowed to have, gone. A metal nail file, an ancient jump rope, her Daisy razors. Even the glass was gone from her picture frames.

My parents think I'm going to kill myself, Brynna thought, pushing her head into her pillow that was already beginning to smell sour and old. The thought brought no great emotion to her; she couldn't decide whether she was angry or intrigued, horrified or warmed.

She simply rolled over again and squeezed her eyes shut against the few bars of diffused light that still found their way through the blinds and did her best not to think about Erica.

When she opened her eyes on Sunday morning, she was able to shower and head down the stairs. She was even able to push around her half-mushy cereal and swallow a few bites. Erica's body—*her remains,* she kept correcting herself—still weighed heavy on her mind, but there was something else there too, something she was missing. She couldn't put her finger on what it was until late in the day when she crawled back in bed and pulled her tablet to her lap.

She had an inbox full of emails from Evan and Teddy and Lauren—there was even one or two from Darcy asking why she wasn't in school on Friday or why she wasn't answering their calls. It wasn't until a tweet from Evan popped up that Brynna realized what was eluding her: "Erica" had left her alone for three whole days.

Since the day Brynna had learned that Erica really was dead.

White-hot heat shot down Brynna's spine. Erica was dead, it was confirmed, and suddenly, the harassment stopped. Had she been alive just three days ago?

"No," Brynna muttered to herself, sweat making her T-shirt stick to her back. Her father said that Erica had been found—and here the sick roiled in her stomach again—in pieces. They didn't find Erica, they didn't find her body—they found her *bones.* Brynna's heart beat in her throat.

"Dad, Dad!" She sprinted down the stairs, breathing heavily when she threw open the door to his office. He froze, standing with his hand wrapped around a cut-glass highball glass, an inch of brown liquor at the bottom. Brynna's eyes went directly to it. His eyes followed hers. Her whole body clenched and thirsted. The glass, the bottle, could make all of this so much less real. The knife-sharp edges of memory, or reality, could be blurred out or forgotten completely. Maybe not forever, but even a few minutes would do.

Then she remembered why she was there.

"Dad, how did they know it was Erica that they found?"

He set the glass down, pushing it behind a framed picture, so it would be out of her line of sight, she guessed. "I told you, Bryn, they did something with forensics, I guess. They were able to match her."

"You guess? Are you sure? Or did they just assume the body was Erica's? Did it look like a teenage girl, so they figured it must be?" Brynna could feel the flush in her cheeks.

"No, honey. They wouldn't do that to the Shaws. They must be sure it's her." He sat down behind his desk. "Where is all this coming from?"

"She was alive, Dad, I know she was. She was here in Crescent City just a couple days ago—"

He shook his head. "She had been dead for months. There was no doubt about that."

Her father spoke with the kind of certainty that blanketed her entire body in a heavy, dark cloud. Because if Erica truly had been dead for months, then someone else was sending her those notes.

Brynna bristled. Now that Erica was gone, would her stalker go too?

ELEVEN

Brynna yawned as her mother turned the car into Dr. Rother's parking lot that Monday morning. She glared at the numbers on the dashboard clock—7:12 a.m.—and groaned.

"Couldn't we have done this after school?"

"Dr. Rother didn't have any openings after school, and your father and I both thought it was important for you and her to talk after..." Her voice dropped off. "Either way, we didn't think it was appropriate for you to miss any more school. Dr. Rother is really doing us a favor taking you before class."

Brynna hated the way her parents were suddenly presenting a united front, as though as long as she stayed screwed up, they'd hold together their screwed-up relationship so everyone could be nuts together. It wasn't exactly the picture of familial perfection she wanted. But the one thing she wanted less was to sit in Dr. Rother's office for the next fifty minutes and talk about Erica.

As her mother slammed the car door, Brynna's gaze wandered over to the coffeehouse where she had seen Erica slip in. It was as bright today as it had been that day, and the colors of the house and its patrons seemed to throb in the sunlight. It *had* been Erica. She hadn't made her up. Her stomach roiled. *Had she?*

"You coming, hon?"

Dr. Rother met them in the foyer where the right-out-of-high-school-looking receptionist usually greeted Brynna and her mother. Brynna never made eye contact with the girl, certain that when she disappeared behind Dr. Rother's door, the girl would press her ear against it, listening, thanking god she wasn't as messed up as Brynna was.

"I'm the first one here today," Dr. Rother said by way of apology, "so if you'll give me just a sec, we can begin." She fiddled around the stark-looking room—which could have been the waiting room of a dentist, an accountant, a lawyer, or a shrink, so generic were the beige paint, pressboard furniture, and itchy couches—while Brynna wedged herself against the arm of the couch and picked up an ancient-looking copy of *Seventeen* magazine. She didn't open the magazine, instead watching while Dr. Rother flipped on the coffee maker and her mother made benign conversation with the doctor, as though her daughter weren't suffering from paranoid delusions, severe depression, and/or a possible stalker.

"Okay, Bryn," Dr. Rother said with far too much cheeriness. "I'm ready for you."

Brynna and the doctor took their usual places across from each other, and Dr. Rother pulled out a new sheet of paper while Brynna went around studying every nuance in the room, just as she did during every session.

"Your parents are quite concerned about you."

Brynna shrugged, averting her gaze.

"They told me that Erica's body has been found."

Dr. Rother's words needled a tiny, cold opening in the blackness of Brynna's mind that she refused to acknowledge.

"How did that make you feel, Brynna?"

She wanted to laugh at the stereotypical psychiatrist question, how it made it sound like Brynna and the doctor were in some poorly written play that would have three acts, a dark moment (this one), and an ending where the crowd would applaud. There didn't seem to be an ending to what Brynna was going through.

"What do you want me to say?"

Dr. Rother straightened in her chair. "I want you to tell me how you're feeling. Have your feelings changed significantly now that we know Erica is deceased?"

Brynna pressed her fingernail into the wood grain of her chair. "You told me I had to accept that she was dead a long time ago."

"But you never did."

She refused to react.

"So now that the proof is irrefutable—"

"Irrefutable? They found remains. It wasn't even a body. It wasn't even Erica's body." She pressed her fingernail harder, relishing the sting of pain as the nail bent. She focused hard on the pain, on the chalky white mark that spread across her peachy nail.

"They've tested it, Brynna. It is Erica. Your mother told me there is going to be a memorial."

Brynna's chest tightened. All at once, the cloying smell of those lilies hit her nostrils and turned her stomach, and she could feel the stifling heat of the mortuary. "We already had a memorial for Erica."

"I guess at this one they're planning to inter her remains. Your mother said you were thinking of going."

Truthfully, Brynna had walked into the kitchen while her mother sat at the counter, her cell phone pressed to her ear. She was sitting stark silent and still, which was odd for the woman who routinely multitasked, and Brynna had paused in the near darkness of the hallway.

"I'm so sorry, Melanie," her mother had said. "I know this can't be easy for you."

Brynna felt the burn in her cheeks when she heard the name Melanie—Melanie Shaw was Erica's mother's name.

"Of course we'll be there."

There was a beat of silence and Brynna watched as her mother pulled a pencil and a piece of paper from the junk drawer and very carefully, very precisely wrote something down.

"I know Brynna will want to say a proper good-bye to Erica."

Brynna turned to leave as her mother hung up the phone. "Bryn? Is that you?"

She turned slowly as her mother slid off the barstool and came toward her. "That was Mrs. Shaw." She looked at her daughter as though she didn't know whether to smile or cry. "There's going to be a memorial for Erica. Small, graveside. Just family and close friends." She brushed a hand through Brynna's hair. "I told Melanie that we would be there. It'll be nice for you to say good-bye."

The memory flitted through Brynna's head, and she shifted in the chair she was sitting in, pressing her shoes against the gray industrial carpet in Dr. Rother's office.

They were quiet for a long while. Brynna stared down at her finger on the chair arm, studied the way the wood grain ran. She could feel Dr. Rother's eyes intent on her, a silent challenge.

Finally, "It should have been me that died."

Dr. Rother looked at her over the top of her legal pad and calmly set down her pen. Brynna absently wondered if the doctor had learned that in shrink school: when a patient says they should have died, set down your pen and look interested—even if you agree with them.

"Did finding Erica's body make you think that?"

Brynna wagged her head. "I've always thought that."

"And why do you think that, Brynna?"

Brynna hated the breathy way Dr. Rother's voice sounded.

"It just would have been better. Erica—Erica was better at—at everything. She was the better student, the better swimmer. She probably wouldn't have gotten fucked up." Brynna looked up from her jeans, feeling the creep of pink on her cheeks. "Sorry. Erica probably wouldn't have gotten messed up on drugs if I died."

"First of all, let's not go assuming what Erica would have done if the situation were reversed." Now the doctor put her notebook down too and leaned back in her chair, giving Brynna her "we're about to make a breakthrough" stare. "And second of all, about Erica being better than you at everything. Do you see what you're doing there?"

Brynna hated this part—the part where she was supposed to stumble on some brilliant realization and break down in tears or skip out of here, cured.

"No," she said with a slight grumble.

"You're idolizing her."

"So?"

"So, was Erica really better than you were scholastically? Didn't you say that you used to help her study?"

"Yeah, but—"

"And you were both on the swim team, were you not?"

Brynna raised an eyebrow, unwilling to speak.

"Was she really better than you, or did she simply have different strengths?"

Brynna looked over Dr. Rother's shoulder, staring out at the perfectly suburban scene beyond: a parked SUV, one of the thousands out there, gleaming in the sun; a woman dressed in head-to-toe Lululemon, pushing a jogging stroller; a random leaf rolling by as if on cue.

"It's perfectly natural, Brynna. No one wants to speak ill of the dead—have you heard that expression before? 'I don't want to speak ill of the dead'?"

Brynna rolled her eyes and wished the clock would move faster. "Yes, I've heard it."

"Well, people tend to go overboard in the opposite direction. Someone who died, especially if he died tragically or suddenly, becomes a great humanitarian. He'll be eulogized as a loving husband and father, even if he was a cheat and a jerk."

Brynna crossed her arms in front of her chest. "So what does this have to do with me and Erica?"

"Don't you see? You're doing the same thing with Erica."

White-hot anger split through Brynna. "Erica *was* a great person. She was awesome."

"I'm not saying that she wasn't. All I'm saying is that even in her passing, you have to see her for who she was. She wasn't better than you. Even if she got better grades or really was a better swimmer, it doesn't mean that you deserved to die."

"Neither did she!" Brynna was crying now, her hands fisted so tightly that she could feel her nails digging little half moons into her palms. "Erica didn't deserve to die. She shouldn't have died!"

"No, Brynna, she shouldn't have. But it's okay for you to wish that Erica was still alive without wishing that you were dead."

Sure, Brynna thought, *but what do you do if someone* wants *you dead?*

• • •

"B. B? B! Brynna Marie!"

Brynna's head snapped up so quickly she flicked ketchup onto her shirt.

Evan grinned and Lauren and Darcy looked away, lightly snickering. Teddy handed her a napkin.

"How'd you know my middle name was Marie?"

Evan shrugged. "Every girl's middle name is Marie."

Darcy and Lauren nodded their agreement. "Lauren Marie," Darcy said, thumbing Lauren. "Darcy ANN Marie."

"Teddy?" Evan asked.

"Actually, mine's Andrew."

"Anyway, welcome back from planet wherever-the-hell-you've-been. We're making homecoming arrangements. You two in for a limo?"

Teddy said something to Evan while Brynna's eyes wandered to the graying light outside the cafeteria windows. It was as if the moment Erica had been found, the dark and cold crept in and was holding on. The sky was spitting thick raindrops when she left Dr. Rother's office that morning, and although it had cleared since then, the vile-looking clouds remained. Brynna shivered.

"Wow. She's so excited about homecoming, she shivers."

Brynna blinked, just in time to catch the hurt look in Teddy's eyes. "Oh, no, I'm sorry. I am really excited about homecoming. Seriously." She looked at the skeptical faces of her friends and let herself flit into the fantasy of dancing with Teddy under twinkle lights—even if they were going to be strung up from the basketball hoops in the gym. She pressed her palm into his and squeezed. "I am."

He grinned, his blue eyes sparkling, sparking a sweet warmth low in Brynna's belly. He brushed a kiss over her lips, light and feathery, and her heart skipped a beat that sent a delicious tremble throughout her. For the first time since she could remember, her body was reacting to something other than terror.

"This has all been lovely, but it's time for class," Lauren said, loudly piling her books on top of each other. She cut her eyes to Brynna, cool but not mean. "You coming?"

Brynna nodded quickly and pecked another kiss at Teddy then

gathered her own books. Evan's hand on her arm stopped her before she turned.

"Don't tell the enemy anything," he hissed with a serious look in his eyes.

Brynna glanced around the cafeteria, surprised. "Who's the enemy," she hissed back, "and what am I not supposed to say?"

Evan scooched forward. "It's killing Lauren that she doesn't know who I'm taking to the dance. I looooove torturing her. It's killing her even more that you know and she doesn't."

Brynna's mind raced. *Did Evan tell me he had a date?* "But I don't know who you're taking, do I?"

"No. I haven't asked anyone yet. But don't tell Lauren that. Pretend like you know." He released her hand and gave her the shove symbol, and Brynna rolled her eyes, jogging to catch up to Darcy and Lauren just before they slid into Mr. Fallbrook's class. He was lecturing about the book they were reading—*Lord of the Flies*, one of Brynna's favorites—but with each tick of the clock, her heartbeat was growing more and more erratic. P.E. was her next class, and it was the first day of the swimming unit.

It should have been easier for Brynna, now that she knew Erica was dead, but everything inside her still seized up when she thought about stepping back into that water. It wouldn't be dark this time, and she wouldn't be alone—*and Erica really was gone.* She knew all of these things intellectually, but that didn't stop her heart from slamming against her rib cage every time the clock ticked past another minute. It didn't stop the clamminess on her hands or prickling sense of something not right that walked down her spine.

Lauren slapped her book shut when the bell rang, leaning into Brynna and rolling her eyes. "Is it me or was that, like, absolute torture?"

Brynna started then quickly gathered her composure. "I read *Lord of the Flies* at my old school. I actually kind of liked it."

"The book is whatever. I'm talking about Mr. Fallbrook. Weird-o." She drew out the *O* in her high-pitched, singsongy voice. "I mean, who steps up to take the place of a teacher who was murdered?"

"I thought it was the Spanish teacher who was killed."

"It was, but the only other person who spoke Spanish was—is—Señora Hill, who used to teach this class. So she moved, and Norman Bates over there"—she jutted her chin in Mr. Fallbrook's direction—"stepped up to cover for Señor Muerto."

"I don't care. I'd let him stab me any day."

Brynna looked up to see Darcy strolling through the doorway before she nudged up against Lauren's desk.

"You're so morbidly horny," Lauren said, stacking her books on her binder.

"I can't help it." Darcy's eyes cut to Mr. Fallbrook as he looked down, talking to a student. "He's so hot. Those eyes! They're, like, wicked blue. Like they can see right through you." She shimmied, a perfectly pressed pout on her lips, one eyebrow cocked so she looked seductive.

Lauren glared at Darcy. "Stop that. You're going to freak out the new girl." She petted Brynna, and Brynna shrank back.

"It's been over two months. When do I stop being the new girl?"

Lauren grinned. "When there's a newer girl."

The trio walked down the hall, Lauren and Darcy nattering on about homecoming and strapless bras while Brynna's mind ticked on about the P.E. class they were on their way to.

The day before, the class had been subjected to a mind-numbing game of dodgeball that devolved into fifteen girls half-heartedly bouncing giant red balls in the general direction of the other fifteen girls who pretended to dodge out of the way but in super-slow motion.

Brynna preferred that.

She even made an actual attempt at aiming the ball once or twice, but the second Mrs. Markie began announcing that they would start practicing for the end-of-the-year swim test, Brynna's hands went clammy, and the red bouncy ball flopped to the floor and dribbled away from her.

This morning, she had dutifully packed a bathing suit that her mother had bought for her and resolved to at least attempt to enter the pool. If the swim test was the only way to get out of Hawthorne High, Brynna was going to do it.

"This is my chance to be normal," she muttered to herself.

"Did you say something, Bryn?" Darcy turned to look at her, her crystal eyes wide, and Brynna shifted her weight. Darcy had never been anything but nice to her, but there was something there, something Brynna couldn't put her finger on, that bothered her about the girl.

"No, just that I'm not totally looking forward to getting into the pool."

"Ugh, ditto that," the other girl said, yanking open the locker room door.

"Don't worry," Lauren joined. "The first day is the intro to water class. 'This is a pool. This is water. Water is wet.' Pretty basic stuff. I doubt we'll even get a toe wet."

A cool wash of relief poured over Brynna. *Intro to water,* she mused. *I can do that. I can save normal for another day...*

Brynna slid into her swimsuit, immediately pulling her oversized towel over her shoulders and holding it tight to her chest. Lauren looked at her and chuckled. "What's your problem, Chase? Afraid we're going to catch a glimpse of your hot bod and fall in love?"

"Just...cold," Brynna managed.

Lauren was in her Hawthorne-green swim team suit; Brynna had a half-dozen of the exact same suit, only hers were Lincoln High purple and gold. She shivered and switched her gaze to Darcy, who was adjusting the straps of her suit. It was a delicate pink with even paler pink polka dots and contrasting striped piping. With its frilly little skirted bottom, it would have made anyone else look like a freakishly tall six-year-old, but on Darcy, with her white-blond hair, sex kitten lips, and chest that made Brynna shrug into her towel, she looked like walking sex. Sweat pricked out all over Brynna, and she thought about Teddy, about what her sweet boyfriend could see in her when he'd spent nearly a year with Darcy and all her candy striper/centerfold glory. But the thought was fleeting as the girls began walking toward the outdoor pool.

Lauren held the door open, and Brynna worked to control her breathing, trying to grab on to something that Dr. Rother told her about facing challenges. She couldn't think of it, and her frustration was overtaking her dread.

TWELVE

When all the girls were suited up in their Hawthorne High regulated bathing suits—no bikinis, no monokinis, no tankinis, or "inis" of any kind—Mrs. Markie lined them up against the far wall of the outdoor pool. Brynna was secretly relieved that the P.E. teacher had chosen to teach the class at this pool rather than the indoor one; the indoor one, Brynna thought, felt far too much like a coffin.

Mrs. Markie strolled in front of them, her tanned, freckled skin loose where the industrial-sized straps of her army-green bathing suit cut across her shoulders. She was wearing the suit with a pair of knee-length khaki shorts and her ever-present whistle. Her toes bled over the top of a pair of blue-and-white strappy foam sandals, "Hawaii" scrawled over the white part in a funky brush script. The ensemble gave her the look of a geriatric camp counselor. Brynna was so busy taking in Mrs. Markie that she failed to hear the teacher directing her students to the edge of the pool.

The shrill sound of the whistle shook Brynna out of her reverie. "In line, Chase!" Mrs. Markie barked.

Brynna didn't move, watching while the girls filed into four rows at the edge of the pool. One girl, who wasn't suited up, came out of the locker room and sat on a bench with a notebook.

"How come she doesn't have to swim?" Brynna asked Mrs. Markie.

Mrs. Markie dropped the silver whistle from her lips and looked disgustedly at the girl on the bench. "She can't swim. Can you swim, Chase?"

Brynna nodded blankly. "Does she still have to take the test?"

The teacher answered Brynna with a quick burst from the whistle. "Mind your own business and get in line."

Brynna slowly made her way to the lines of girls, stopping to suck in her breath when the four girls at the head of each line simultaneously jumped into the water and swam the short way across the pool.

"What happened to 'Intro to water day'?" she breathed as her heart rate started to ratchet up.

She watched, stunned, as the girls cut through the water and climbed out of the pool on the other side just as the next four jumped.

"What is this supposed to teach us, exactly?" Brynna asked Lauren, who was standing in front of her.

Lauren shrugged. "That if you fall in the pool, you can climb out, I guess. I know the trainer came over and made our dog do the same thing." She turned all the way around to face Brynna. "Scared?"

"No." Brynna forced a chuckle. "Why would you say that? I mean, I can swim."

"Good," she said, turning back around. "Because if you can't, they make you take the beginning class with the middle schoolers."

Brynna looked toward the girl on the bleachers, mercifully clothed. Her stomach lurched, a fist of anxiety tightening in her gut. She raised her hand.

"Um, Mrs. Markie, I'm not feeling so well."

Mrs. Markie took her time coming around the pool, using her whistle every five feet before stopping to yell at someone in the water, someone getting out of the water, or someone on the way into the water, before she approached Brynna.

"What's that now?"

Brynna pressed her palm against her stomach. "I don't think I should swim today. I feel like I'm going to throw up."

Mrs. Markie pressed the back of her hand against Brynna's forehead. "You don't feel hot."

"Maybe it was something I ate."

She knew exactly what it was but wasn't about to announce that she was afraid. According to Brynna's mother, Mrs. Markie should have known about her fear. She had, after all, granted Brynna permission to "practice" in the indoor pool, but now her slate-gray eyes looked hard, her lips pressed into a thin line, edges pulling downward.

Brynna glanced away from Mrs. Markie and her interrogating eyes and instead looked down, seeing the droplets of water that splashed up after the girls jumped. It speckled the concrete underneath her, and rivulets of water rushed toward her, pooling around her bare feet. "I don't think I should go in."

Brynna could hear her classmates' arms pounding through the water. The sound of the water frothing with their kicks, with their wriggling bodies, made her think of Erica, and her stomach really did sour, bile itching at the back of her neck.

"You're not trying to get out of class, are you, Chase?"

Brynna shook her head, and Lauren leaned into her. "You were fine five minutes ago," she murmured.

Darcy hit the water next, and fire shot up the back of Brynna's neck as she watched the blond girl suspended in midair before her pointed toes cracked the undulating surface of the water. She was transfixed, horrified as the water swallowed Darcy up—her strong, tanned legs first, then over her belly, her arms, her shoulders, and finally, her blond head engulfed, disappearing under.

"Erica!" The blood-curdling scream ripped through the concrete enclosure, and Brynna looked around, stunned. There was water on her face and she was moving, her thighs burning as she propelled herself forward. She felt her fingertips break the water, and then her face was under. Her eyes sprang open and she heard the repeated thud of limbs slapping water, and then, there was Erica.

Brynna could see Erica's painted toes barely scraping the bottom of the pool. She could see her elegant arms pawing at the water as she struggled to stay afloat. She was more compact than Brynna remembered, but it was easier to toss an arm around her, push Erica to her back, and then swim with her toward the shallow end.

She had rescued her. Erica would survive.

"What are you doing? What are you doing?"

Brynna could barely hear the gurgled words for the sound of the waves and the odd chirping sound cutting through the night. She opened her eyes and the sunlight blinded her, stopping her for a beat while Erica struggled against her, finally breaking her hold and getting away.

"Chase! What the heck was that?" Mrs. Markie barked.

Brynna blinked, her feet settling on the smooth bottom of the pool.

Then her heart started to go. A single beat, and then a single beat more. Faster, faster. Brynna was standing in water up to her elbows, and there were people all around her, lining the square edges of the pool, eyes wide, mouths opened. Her stomach started to churn, and the panic shot through her, chilling her body even though the water temperature was warm.

"Get out, Chase."

Brynna barely heard the words, but her feet were rooted in place. Her body was a thousand pounds and solid steel. She tried to force something to work, something to move, but nothing did.

She was terrified.

All around her, the water waved and slapped.

Erica?

Her vision started to blur.

"Brynna!"

She vaguely recognized that voice. *Erica? Ella?*

Somewhere, there was a sucking sound as a body entered the water.

Brynna's teeth started to chatter, and the clouds, thick and gray, snaked across the sun. The pool was enveloped with a sinister gray.

"Brynna?" That voice was close to her now, at her left ear, and Brynna wanted to acknowledge it—but not as much as she wanted to sink back into the water. She felt the lap of the water go over her arms, then over her shoulders. It would be so easy, so comfortable. Then she could be with Erica. She could apologize. She could say it was her fault. She could sleep…

The water engulfed her like soft, enveloping arms. She felt it on her lips, on her nose. Her lungs burned at first, but it was so peaceful under the water that she didn't struggle. All sound was muffled as the water plugged her ears, and the world above her wobbled outside of the water and was moving so far away, so fast.

"Come on, Brynna!"

Lauren's arms darted out instinctively to cradle Brynna, and Brynna lay still, stiff in the water, unable to move. She watched the clouds in the sky as she slid out from underneath them, Lauren's legs kicking gracefully beneath her. By the time they reached the edge of the pool, there were people to help scoop Brynna from the water as they commanded her to move, but she couldn't, not even an eyelash, not even a single inch. Nothing worked, and once again, she had lost Erica.

At some point, Brynna slipped back into her clothes and someone called her mother. She remembered everyone being silent, everyone watching as she hiked up her shoulder bag. In the locker room, Lauren linked arms with Brynna, ready to steer her toward the hall. Her lips felt numb.

"I just freaked out."

She felt Lauren squeeze her arm. "It's okay. Do you want to talk about it? Talk about what—"

Brynna wagged her head, the stink of chlorine in her hair making her nauseous. "Do you think Darcy hates me?"

"I don't hate you, B," came a voice from the back of the locker room. "You can tell us what's going on."

Brynna looked at the faces of her new friends, both drawn, both concerned. She wanted to talk—but what could she say? *My best friend is dead, really dead, because of me. I thought she was alive, was after me, but it was all in my head. I saw her in the pool today, but it was all in my head…*

She pressed her palms to her ears as if she could quiet the chatter that kept going, the constant stream that told her she was crazy, crazy, crazy, and broken, that she would never be fixed, that she would always pay. Her own mind was her enemy, splashing up pictures of Erica, bringing up that moment, that night, the dare.

"I don't know," she said thinly. "I just—I thought Darcy was someone else." It felt like a betrayal to Erica, but it was all Brynna could say to keep herself afloat.

Her mother arrived with that same pinched look that Brynna knew from before—the one that was constantly worried, constantly blaming herself for the things her crazy daughter did. Brynna wanted to reach out and pat her shoulder, to tell her mother that none of it was her fault, but she couldn't. Her limbs felt stiff and immobile and she rested her head against the cool glass of the passenger window as her mother drove her home in silence.

When they reached the house, Brynna made a direct line for the door and from there toward the stairs, but her mother stopped her, her hand tight on Brynna's.

"Honey, was this about Erica?"

A maniacal giggle gurgled up and Brynna fought it back. "Of

course it was about Erica," she wanted to scream. "Everything is always going to be about Erica." But instead she stayed silent.

Her mother rubbed her hand. "That's over now, Bryn. Erica is going to be laid to rest. She's at peace."

She smiled as though she actually believed it, and Brynna nodded then shook her hand free and headed up the stairs. She washed the chlorine stink out of her hair then slipped into her bed, pulling the comforter up over her head. She wanted the darkness. She wanted to sleep. She wanted to be wherever Erica was if only so that Erica would stop coming after her, would stop making her feel so goddamn crazy.

Even if that meant she had to die.

Brynna kicked off the covers and went to her bathroom, yanking open the medicine cabinet. She pawed through everything in there—some old makeup, a few boxes of Bioré pore strips, and some hair gel—but there was nothing there that would soothe her. She stepped into the hallway, hearing her mother popping off plastic take-out lids. Brynna crossed the threshold into her parents' room and went directly to their medicine cabinets.

Her mother's was stripped clean other than a box of hair dye and some Tums; her father's had even less.

"There's got to be..." she muttered under her breath while pain pounded a steady drumbeat against her skull. Brynna went through the bathroom drawers and found exactly two aspirin in a tiny pillbox. She popped them in her mouth and chewed, liking the bitter taste of the chalky things as they splintered under her molars. She dug in the same drawer and came out with a bottle of

Nyquil, the safety seam already broken. The warning on the bottle said everything Brynna wanted: extreme drowsiness.

She could sleep.

If she could sleep, she couldn't feel Erica. She couldn't feel crazy. She couldn't feel anything at all. She twisted open the cap, tilted her head back, and drank every last bit.

• • •

"Brynna! Brynna! B!"

A boy was saying her name. He was touching her too, his fingers pressing hot spots onto her bare shoulders. She smiled at him and tried to speak, but her tongue was stuck up against the roof of her mouth and it was so heavy, too heavy. She didn't need to speak though, because he saw her and she could see him too. Sandy hair, bright eyes, fuzzy all around the edges.

"Brynna, can you hear me?"

There was a shriek, like seagulls, and the sun was too warm, making Brynna break out into a damp, cool sweat, but she nodded her head because she could hear him. Her head felt heavy too. Heavy and oversized and nodding, it took monumental effort and shot another round of heat, another round of beaded sweat at her hairline and above her upper lip. She wondered who the boy was.

She told him she was going to close her eyes. She heard her own voice even though she couldn't feel her lips move, and she knew, somehow, that the boy agreed with her and would keep her safe. She told him her stomach hurt. He told her it would be okay.

THIRTEEN

It was the buzzing that woke Brynna up. It was constant and excessive, and Brynna couldn't tell if it was inside her head or outside. Inside, she guessed, because her head ached like nothing else had before, a constant, sickening pulse that shot nauseating waves to her gut.

"Ugh," she moaned. "Ughhh..." Her body felt foreign and restrained. Something pinched at her arm, and her hand—just one of them though—was ice cold. It made her fingertips hurt.

"Brynna?"

Her mother was at the side of her bed, and Brynna liked the cool feel as she pressed her palm against Brynna's cheek. "Oh, thank god, Brynna."

"She's awake?"

Brynna finally pulled her eyes open, but it was like blinking through a thick coating of Elmer's glue.

"Mom? Dad?" Her parents were blurry blobs in front of her. They swirled and straightened and then the details came into view. Her mother's face, drawn, pale. Her father, his cheeks ruddy and purplish, his eyes glazed.

"Don't try and move. Don't try and do anything."

Brynna shifted in her bed and then looked around. "Am I—is this the hospital?"

"Where the hell else did you expect to end up?"

"Adam, stop!"

Brynna watched her mother bat at her father and then block him from her view. "Brynna, honey, if you were having problems, you could tell us. If you were so unhappy."

"I don't understand—why—" Brynna paused, the whole ordeal flooding back to her.

"You drank a whole bottle of Nyquil, Bryn. And you took pills."

"And whose fault is that, Adam? Why were those even in the house? You know she's an addict. We don't keep temptation in the house!"

Brynna broke out in a cold sweat, her stomach twisting in knots. "Stop! Stop it you, guys! Please!"

Her parents turned as if they just realized she was in the room. Brynna opened her mouth and then closed it when there was a knock at the door. A nurse poked her head in, smiled warmly at Brynna and said, "Your friend is here to see you."

"One second, please."

"It was an accident," Brynna whispered, feeling tears at the edges of her eyes. "I didn't mean to. It was an accident."

Her father sighed but looked resigned. Her mother wouldn't look at her at all.

"We'll talk about this with Dr. Rother later," was all her mother said as they followed the nurse out the door.

"I didn't mean to interrupt—" Brynna heard from the hallway.

She perked up, surprised as the little blond came into her room. Darcy's pale features looked even more washed out under the harsh fluorescent lights. She shifted the miniature rose she was holding from one hand to the other before she placed it on Brynna's nightstand. Brynna instinctively pulled her blanket up to her chin, trying to hide she didn't know what, wondering how much Darcy knew.

"Hey, Darcy," she said.

"If it blooms, they're supposed to be yellow," Darcy said, gesturing to the plant. "You know, the color of friendship or whatever. And the balloon is cheesy but it came with."

Brynna glanced at the mini Mylar balloon, a *Blue's Clues* knockoff barking "Being Sick is Ruff!" She broke into a soft smile.

"It's great, thanks."

"So, I'm sorry about the pool."

Brynna blinked. "The pool? I was the one who dive-bombed you."

"No. I know you were just trying to help…because you thought I was drowning or whatever. I wasn't, but that was nice of you. So thanks."

Brynna felt the blood rush to her cheeks and was certain that her vitals would pick up the spike in her blood pressure. She had plunged into the pool to rescue a perfectly adequate swimmer, and then she went catatonic in the shallow end.

"I guess you think I'm kind of a freak, huh?" She played with the satin edging on the pale yellow blanket.

"It doesn't matter what I think."

The girls each studied opposite walls for a beat before Darcy, without turning, spoke. "I know you were there that night."

Brynna held her breath, her eyes wide and fastening to Darcy's profile.

"I know what happened to you."

Brynna's lips felt like they wouldn't work, and this time it wasn't because of the Nyquil. "Wh—what are you talking about, Darcy?"

Darcy turned to face her. "At Point Lobos. The night your friend died. I know that you were there."

Brynna felt her mouth fall open.

"Don't worry." Darcy rushed up close. "I'm not going to say anything about it. It's just that your name sounded familiar. My dad is a photojournalist. He was there that whole month. I help him develop his pictures, and I saw—I remember you."

Brynna felt a chill that had nothing to do with the weather. "What?"

"My dad told me what happened. That a girl, about my age, jumped off the pier and didn't come back up. He told me that girl did it with a friend but she survived." Darcy's eyes flashed with something, and Brynna didn't know if she should feel relieved that someone knew her secret or terrified that someone was going to call her a murderer.

"I didn't recognize you at first. You changed your hair color and your cut." Darcy absently brushed her fingers through her own thin blond hair. "And I knew I recognized you but I just couldn't place you. Until today."

Brynna's saliva soured and she swallowed it down, her stomach feeling hollow from when they pumped it and desperately achy. If she had the strength—and wasn't hooked up to all the buzzing, beeping machines—she would run out of the room, straight past Darcy and her parents pointing fingers at each other, straight back to the pier at Point Lobos. She would crash into the water and welcome the riptide when its fingers wrapped around her and pulled her under, tumbling her along in a pitch-black abyss.

"You said her name." Darcy's eyes looked dreamy. "Erica, right? It was Erica."

Everything inside of Brynna was pulsing, moving, throbbing. She thought about the tweet, about Erica in the coffeehouse. Could Darcy be responsible?

"You jumped in without a second thought, thinking I was her."

"I—I—"

"You must have really loved her. Erica."

"I did. I do. She's my best friend."

"So why did you come here?"

Brynna's blood pressure stared to come down. She started to feel a modicum of calm as Darcy sat in the visitor's chair by Brynna's bedside.

Brynna licked her lips, pressing her top teeth against her bottom lip. "My parents wanted me to leave. I got—I was—it was really hard for me after Erica." Her eyes flicked to Darcy's, trying to read them, but Darcy's still held that glossy, dreamy look. "It wasn't like I wanted to go."

Darcy dragged her long, elegant fingers up the length of the chair's armrest, her head cocked as she listened to Brynna.

"It must have been hard for you."

"Yeah."

"Leaving her behind like that."

Brynna's attention snapped like a broken rubber band. "What did you say?"

"Knock knock!" The overly cheery nurse poked her head through Brynna's door a millisecond after she knocked. "Visiting hours are over, honey," she said to Darcy.

Darcy hopped up while Brynna tried to process the last fifteen seconds. "What do you mean by—"

But Darcy had already left with a halfhearted good-bye while the nurse poked around Brynna, trying to fluff up her pillow. When the nurse shut the door, Brynna was left with the faint smell of the miniature rose and Darcy's last words turning over and over in her mind: "*It must have been hard for you...leaving her behind like that.*"

• • •

Four days passed uneventfully, but Brynna still found it hard to breathe. She wanted to think that "Erica" had gotten tired of her or had moved on to someone else, but she couldn't quite believe that. Her parents were keeping a tight leash on her, dropping her at school, picking her up the minute the bell rang, and surreptitiously sniffing at her hair and clothing for telltale cigarette smoke or general drug odor when they thought she wasn't paying attention. She had to present her backpack and purse upon coming and going and grit her teeth while her father pawed through it, his own breath a noxious combination of smoky scotch and Crest that she wasn't supposed to notice.

On the fifth day, Brynna dumped her backpack at the usual checkpoint, but her parents still circled around her like nervous sharks, unsure if they were predator or prey.

"What?" Brynna asked, her head snapping first to her father then her mother.

"Come into the living room, please." Her mother sounded strangely formal and even seemed to walk with a more careful step. Brynna looked over her shoulder as her father followed behind.

"What's going on?"

Her mother stepped aside with what would have been a *tah-dah!* if the item on the table were something that Brynna should have been excited about. But all it did was make her stomach sink and resigned her to knowing that no matter what she did, no matter what was happening, she would always be a drug addict and her parents would never stop second-guessing, never stop wondering how they could have protected her better.

"You're giving me a drug test?"

Her father edged in front of Brynna and started yanking open the little cardboard box on the kitchen table. He turned and presented her the "sample" cup, and Brynna shrank back, remembering those first humiliating days at Woodbriar Rehabilitation Center.

Brynna woke up and stepped out of bed. There really was no reason to get dressed, although the nurses here at "Hugs Not Drugs," as some of the other patients called it, encouraged them to get back to their daily routine—the parts of it that didn't include getting drunk or high—as much as possible.

She shimmied into a hospital-approved robe, startlingly white, like everything else in the place, and was met in the doorway by Marcus, the orderly. He was two whole heads taller than Brynna and had forearms like giant hams. Faded tattoos were barely visible on his dark skin, and he looked every bit like he could crush you with a stare. Marcus was linebacker big and bald, and had the softest, sweetest voice Brynna had ever heard. He was getting off duty when she came in last night, but he was the one who put her instantly at ease. Louise, the night warden, was sour and pinched, and for every one of Marcus's soft, doughy folds, she was angled and sharp, wearing her disdain for her charges as plainly as she wore her uniform.

"Hey, Marcus," Brynna said softly.

His face broke into a wide, easy grin. "How'd the first night go, Sleeping Beauty?"

Truthfully, Brynna wasn't sure she'd slept at all. She remembered staring at the industrial ceiling above her, watching the way the raindrops cast murky, gray-blue shadows against the ceiling tiles.

"Okay, I guess." She pointed to the ladies' room across the hall. "I've got to go to the bathroom."

"No problem." Marcus turned around and fiddled in his cart, then Brynna heard him mumble something into the miniature walkie-talkie that all the Woodbriar nurses had clipped to their shoulders.

Brynna took a step into the hallway, and he held up one meaty palm to stop her. "Escort's not here yet. And you need this."

She looked down incredulously as Marcus placed a little plastic cup in her hand. Heat shot through her, and her mouth went dry as she blinked at the man in front of her.

Marcus gestured toward the cup. "You know the rules. Every morning."

Brynna tensed at the thought of locking herself in the bathroom, peeing into that stupid cup, and—what? Handing a full cup of urine to Marcus? Humiliation hummed through her body, and she wanted to sink into the shiny white laminate underneath her. A woman Brynna didn't recognize came strolling down the hall with a neon-green bungee keychain wrapped around her wrist. She paused in front of the women's restroom, sunk her key in the lock, and opened the door a foot. "You coming?"

Brynna looked at the specimen cup in her hand. She looked at Marcus with his eyes that suddenly didn't look so soft anymore. She looked at the woman, her "escort," guarding the threshold to the bathroom.

And she wondered how it was that she had gotten herself here.

Brynna took the cup from her father's hand. All she ever wanted at Woodbriar was to come home. But now home was just like rehab.

"You've been home from the hospital for over a week now…"

"And I've seen Dr. Rother almost every day. I've done everything I'm supposed to be doing. I'm even back at school."

"We just want to make sure this isn't all too much for you."

Brynna pointed toward the drug test. "And that's your way of doing it? How about just asking, 'Hey, Bryn, are you doing okay'?"

Her father cleared his throat while her mother shifted her weight. "Brynna," she said, "we're all in new territory here. There isn't exactly a handbook on how to help you. We're doing the best we can. We just want to make sure you're safe."

Her mother's words grated on Brynna's teeth.

"Fine. Do you want to come in and watch me pee too?" she asked.

"Brynna, we're doing this for your own good. We all know that sobriety is a process—"

Heat seared Brynna's insides. "You can stop quoting the posters, Mom. I remember what every one of them said."

Every room at Woodbriar was festooned with framed posters with calming photographs—a cupped hand collecting drops of water, a rainbow in front of a pale orange sunset—and each poster bore some kind of twelve-steppy message that made the Woodbriar residents—at least the ones that Brynna knew—sick to their stomachs.

"Do not talk to your mother like that, young lady." Her father scoffed. "Now go."

Brynna rolled her eyes, annoyed but stung, as she went into the bathroom. Ten minutes later, all the test tabs turned their innocent colors—amphetamines (blue), *negative*; barbiturates (pink), *negative*; benzodiazepines (green), *negative.* Her mother had gotten the super-test-for-everything pack, so Brynna had to stand there in the kitchen, growing angrier by the second as her father ticked off the other eight drugs she was *not* doing.

"Okay," her father said with a resigned sigh.

Brynna snaked her arms in front of her chest. "At Woodbriar, I'd get an hour of free time when I tested negative."

"Brynna, drug testing was part of your plea bargain," her mother said.

"From the court. Not from my own parents. But thanks for the vote of confidence."

FOURTEEN

Brynna was making an angry beeline for the stairs when her cell phone chirped loudly. Her father snatched up Brynna's purse from the kitchen table where it had been searched and held it out to her.

Brynna skulked back and answered her phone, once again turning her back on her parents. "'Lo?"

"We're ten minutes away."

Evan.

"Ten minutes away from what?"

"From your house, dork."

Brynna rested a foot on the bottom stair. "Why are you coming to my house?"

"Homecoming shopping. Hello? We talked about it, like, five minutes ago."

Brynna did a mental head slap. "Oh, right. Homecoming shopping. Look, Ev, I'm just not feeling very—"

Brynna felt her mother come up behind her and lay a gentle hand on her shoulder. "Go," she mouthed, pressing a credit card into Brynna's palm.

"Hold on." She pulled the phone from her ear and glared at her mother. She was spitting mad, but the look of apology and desperation in her mother's eyes shut her up directly. Brynna sighed and pushed the phone to her ear. "Okay, just honk when you get here."

She hung up the phone to see that her mother had disappeared back into the kitchen. Both her parents were seated at the dining table, silent, a strange picture waiting to begin.

• • •

Evan pulled up in Brynna's driveway and gave a short honk. Brynna, still not entirely sure—still not entirely thrilled—hiked up her shoulder bag.

"Just get yourself something fun, hon. You deserve it." The apology still hung heavy in her mother's eyes, and Brynna ached for her, but the wisp of anger was still there.

"Sure, Mom."

She ran out the front door and slipped into the front seat of Evan's car, poking her nose into the backseat. "Just the two of us? I thought this was a gang homecoming takedown?"

Evan shrugged his shoulders as he backed out the sloped drive. "Lauren and Darcy are taking their own car because Lauren has swim team practice or something."

"They do night practices at Hawthorne?"

"We've got the indoor pool."

Brynna didn't want to swim. She didn't want to think of the pool, but somewhere, way back in her head, she felt a little dig of jealousy that Lauren could jump in the pool so easily, could cut through the lanes without turning into a spastic mess. More than the drinking or the drugs, the fact that Brynna couldn't handle *water* made her feel crazy.

They spent the rest of the drive chatting about nothing, and by the time Evan guided the car into the mall parking lot, Brynna was actually feeling excited about the prospect of bad food-court food and homecoming shopping.

They found Lauren and Darcy snarfing down tacos at a corner booth, Lauren with a stack in front of her, Darcy moving much more daintily.

"Sit," Lauren said, mouth full of taco. She mumbled something else unintelligible and Darcy translated.

"She said that she is wearing green, so that's off the table. I'm going pink, so Bryn, you've got the rest of the color wheel to choose from."

Brynna laughed. "Really? None of us can wear the same color dress? Since when did we turn into a posse of mean girls?"

"It's not about being mean," Darcy said a little coldly. "It's about being polite."

Brynna's eyebrows went up, but she knew better than to challenge a girl about prom wear. "No green, no pink. Noted."

Once the girls finished their tacos, they made a beeline for Formal Invite, Brynna and Evan taking up the rear.

"I really don't want to do this," Brynna moaned.

Evan stopped to stare at her full in the face. "Wait. Sixteen-year-old girl, credit card, no stated spending limit." He pressed the back of his hand to her forehead. "You must be sick."

"Hey." Brynna ducked away from him. "Stereotypes. I've just

never been the homecoming type. And you—aren't guys supposed to hate this kind of thing?"

Evan mimicked Brynna's expression and stance. "Hey! Stereotypes!"

The pair couldn't have been more than two minutes behind Lauren and Darcy, but by the time Evan and Brynna walked into the door, each girl was already loaded down with an armful of selections.

"They don't waste any time, do they?" Brynna asked.

"That's only round one."

Brynna and Evan started pawing through a rack of rainbow dresses, each more tulle-y or lacy than the next.

"What do you think about this?" Brynna asked, holding a slightly less foofy garment in front of her.

Evan wrinkled his nose. "One shoulder dresses make everyone look like Tarzan. Besides, I don't think that pink is your color." He turned around to a second rack, pawing through a sea of blues that bled into wild turquoise.

"This!" He yanked out a dress and held it out to her, imminently proud. The deep blue dress had thin spaghetti straps and a ruched bodice. It flared out gently, unlike the masses of cupcake dresses they had previously seen. The delicate fabric was scattered with tiny beads that sparkled each time the dress moved. It was gorgeous, but it horrified Brynna.

"Shouldn't we wait to buy dresses until we actually have a date for the Winter Formal?"

"Of course not," Erica said with a frown. "I read this article about this woman who was single but she wanted to get married super bad.

She bought a wedding dress and voila! The universe kicked out a man and she was married within a year. It's all in the power of positive thinking, you know? Put it out to the universe."

"That sounds really pathetic," Brynna scoffed.

"Stop being so negative," Erica said through the dressing room door.

"Ugh." Brynna turned back to her reflection in the mirror. "I hate the way my shoulders look in spaghetti straps. I look like a linebacker."

"Negative, negative," Erica sang. "Okay. One, two, three, open the door!"

Both girls threw open their dressing room doors and appraised each other. Erica was hiding her ridiculous grin behind her hand, but Brynna's mouth dropped wide open.

Erica looked amazing.

The delicate straps on the dress she was wearing showed off her tanned, strong shoulders. The ruching along the side accentuated her hourglass figure, and the deep blue fabric with its multitude of sparkles made Erica's brown eyes look that much darker, that much more mysterious.

"This is my dress," she breathed.

"No." Brynna took a step backward. "No," she said again. "I hate that dress."

Her heart was beating, and she tried to suck in those slow, Dr. Rother-assigned deep breaths, but her mind was tumbling.

Get a hold of yourself, Brynna. It's a different dress. Lots of stores probably had that dress.

"Okay," Evan said, shoving the offending dress back into the rack. "You can just say you hate my taste. You don't have to go catatonic."

"I'm sorry. I just—that's just not my style." She grabbed the closest dress she could find. "This. This is more my style."

"Oh, Bryn, that's going to look awesome on you." Lauren stepped out of the racks with a dress slung over one arm. She fingered the edge of the dress Brynna was holding, and Brynna looked down at it herself. It was white with a single strap and a gauzy bust line. A row of delicate rhinestones lined the bodice, catching the light just enough to reflect back a tasteful sparkle. There was ruching at the waist, and then the dress flared out with a full skirt. She blinked, surprised at how simple and lovely it was.

"You have to try it on!"

Erica's dress was forgotten as Lauren and Darcy rushed Brynna to the dressing room. They holed up in the adjoining two, commentating through each step of their trying-on process.

"This thing makes me look like a Vegas show girl—in the worst possible way," Darcy moaned.

"Is my butt really that big, or is that just sequin distortion? Please say it's sequin distortion," Lauren responded.

"I don't know," Evan called from his spot outside of the rooms, "but I'd vote for giant ass over fabric failure."

Brynna removed her clothes hastily, slipping the cool fabric of the dress over her head. Immediately, she felt the satin slide down over her chest, felt the way the bodice hugged her curves as the filmy skirt flittered just above her knees.

"Oh, Bryn, that's amazing on you!"

Lauren hung over the side of Brynna's dressing room, eyes wide. Darcy popped up on the other side, her shoulders engulfed by an obscene ruffle of pink.

"That's amazing! If I didn't already have my dress, I'd buy that one." Darcy made a motion for Brynna to spin and she obliged. "It's really gorgeous!"

Brynna slunk out of the dress, hurriedly slipped into her own clothes, and met Evan at the counter. Darcy and Lauren had already discarded their failure frocks and were poking at a display of sparkly jewelry.

"I think I'm going to get this one."

"Lauren." Darcy pointed to her watch. "If you want me to drive you to practice…"

Lauren swung her head to Evan. "You're going to pick me up at eight, right?"

"Duh."

"Great." She shoved the dress she was holding into Evan's arms. "Tell Mom I said thanks. And find me some shoes!"

Brynna and Evan could hear Darcy and Lauren giggling until they were out of the store and had blended into the throngs of mall people outside.

"Do you not want to go to homecoming with Teddy?" Evan asked, stepping closer.

"Why would you say that? I like Teddy. I want to go with him."

"Well, and I'm no expert, but I thought girls were supposed to be all excited and flittery about their homecoming dresses. Not grab the first one off the rack and be done with it."

Brynna tried to remember the words to the song playing on the store's sound system—anything to take her mind off Erica and that stupid dress, anything to cover up the thundering sound of blood rushing through her ears.

"I'm not most girls," Brynna said with a smile she hoped would look convincing. "And this wasn't the first dress I pulled off the rack. It was the third."

By the time Brynna returned home, she was almost excited. She had spent an afternoon just like a real teenage girl—a real teenager who wasn't crazy, wasn't likely to go on drugs at any given moment, and who was not responsible for something heinous. She was jumpy still, but the idea of spinning with Teddy in the filmy white dress was enough to bolster her spirit and make her excited.

"You got a dress!" Brynna's mother clasped her hands in front of her chest as Brynna entered the living room, the long garment bag trailing behind her.

"Actually, I decided to go with a tasteful pantsuit."

"What?" Her mother's mouth dropped open, panic in her eyes.

"I'm kidding, Mom. I got a dress. It's girly and everything."

"Well, come on, I want to see it!"

Brynna was contracting some of her mom's giddiness, and she worked to untie the knotted plastic at the bottom of the bag, eager to see what her mother would think.

"No, no, not like that! Go in the bathroom and make an appearance." Her mother pointed to the bathroom door, and Brynna offered her the expected teenage groan face.

"Oh, come on!" her mother went on. "Give me this. Your dad is on his way to the airport and you're my little girl. Indulge your mama."

Brynna rolled her eyes but was secretly happy to sweep out into the living room in the gown.

"Okay." She trudged into the bathroom and hung the dress on the back of the door, feeling a tiny, unexpected flutter of butterfly wings in her stomach. She finished undoing the bottom knot and pushed the plastic up over the gown.

A thousand pinpricks jabbed at her skin. Her breath caught in her throat. Brynna went for the doorknob, desperately trying to turn it, desperately trying to get out of the bathroom.

She looked at the dress, the blue spaghetti strap, ruched dress that Erica was going to wear, hung up on the bathroom door, and fingers of terror grabbed at her, pulsed for her.

"No, no!" Brynna pounded against the door. "No!"

"Brynna, what's wrong? What's going on?"

It's just a dress, Bryn, just a dress. It was at the store; it could have been a mistake.

Even as she tried to talk herself through the fist of panic that tightened in her gut, Brynna knew it was wrong. She saw the woman at the counter. She saw her slip the white dress into Brynna's bag. She watched as the woman tied the bottom—"extra tight, because if it opens up, this thing is going to get dirty fast."

Brynna pulled open the door and her mother stood there, flushed.

"What's going—" She turned toward the dress, her eyes immediately lighting up. "Oh, Bryn, that's beautiful!" She snatched the dress from the back of the door and attempted to press it up against Brynna, but she snaked back as if the dress were solid poison.

"That's not the dress I bought," she mumbled. "That's the wrong dress."

Her mother held it at arm's length. "It's a pretty beautiful wrong dress."

"That's not mine," Brynna snapped. "It's not for me."

"Well, we can't get back to the mall tonight—it's already closed." She pressed the dress toward her daughter. "Try it on—just once. For me?"

Brynna shook her head, the lap of water reverberating in her head. Her mind showed a constant slideshow of Erica, first in the dress, then in the pool, and then in the ocean until she was gone.

Brynna started to tremble. She wanted to tell her mother that this was Erica's dress—not Brynna's, not the one Brynna picked out—but she knew how it sounded: crazy. If she told her mother that she even *saw* the saleslady put a different dress in her bag and that Erica must have switched them, she would sound like she had lost it.

She bit her lip. She couldn't let her mother think she was going crazy, especially since Brynna herself wasn't sure that she wasn't.

"Okay, okay, no dress." Her mother tossed it aside and gathered Brynna in her arms. "It's not that big of a deal, okay? We'll take it back tomorrow," she said too brightly. "Or I could take it back and I'll just get the one that you wanted. What color did you say it was?"

Brynna swallowed, her stomach turning over and over on itself. She tried to process the words her mother was saying, tried to remember the color of the dress she had actually picked. She saw white in her mind's eye, but when she tried to recall the image, the white turned into foam on the waves as they broke over her legs, and Erica was already gone.

FIFTEEN

A tittering chatter was reverberating through the Hawthorne High students when Brynna stepped on campus the following morning. Immediately, unease pricked out all over her, and she shrank back into her hoodie. The weather had made a quick shift from mostly blue to all gray over the last night, and the manic shift caught half the students still hanging on to cut-off shorts and tank tops, while the other half cuddled into chunky sweaters and knee-high boots.

Brynna liked the fall. She relished the gray, the constant spit of moisture in the air. Nobody thought of the ocean in the fall. It was all toasty cocoa and holiday shopping, and Brynna could blend in with it all. She started down the hall, her heart thundering with every step. It had already been a week. Why did people still care? How much did people know? People were shifting, turning to look at her, and Brynna was vaulted back to those first days, returning to Lincoln without Erica.

Everyone is blaming me, everyone is judging me.

Her ears strained, listening to the familiar refrains "total druggie," "overdosed," "suicidal," "crazy," and Brynna tried to steel herself against it. When she saw Lauren cutting through the crowd, a lightness went through her. Lauren knew what happened; Lauren didn't judge her. Lauren was her friend.

She stopped in front of Brynna, her dark eyes glazed in fury. "I can't believe you."

A crowd of students chattering around them went immediately silent, all eyes turning toward Lauren and Brynna.

Brynna blinked, genuinely shocked. "What are you talking about?"

Lauren's eyes narrowed to dagger-thin slits, and every inch of her oozed hate. "How could you do that to my brother?"

Her voice cracked on the last word and something peaked in Brynna. "What are you talking about? What's wrong with Evan? Is he okay?"

Lauren rolled her eyes and huffed at Brynna.

Darcy walked up alongside, and Brynna turned to her, her eyes imploring. "Darcy, please tell me what is going on. I have no idea. What's wrong with Evan?"

A sputter of laughter came from down the hall then the unmistakable sound of a body crashing against metal as someone was shoved up against a locker. Brynna craned her neck to see. "What's going on?"

"Fag!" The word cut down the hall and cut Brynna in two. It was Meatball—the letter-jacketed thug that Brynna had met her first day of school—and his gang, and they were striding forward, cutting through the kids, yanking the papers that were taped to the fronts of nearly every locker.

"What are those?"

She could see the hard press of Lauren's jaw as she gritted her teeth. Her eyes were beginning to water, tears building up on her lower lashes. Darcy leaned over and carefully removed one of the full-color flyers, handing it to Brynna. She held on to the edge, shooting a look of pure disgust at her.

"Oh my god," Brynna breathed. "Who did this?"

It was a mock-up of a magazine cover, and someone had photoshopped Evan's face onto the body on the cover. He was surrounded by meaty men in underwear looking up longingly at him, pawing across his chest. The title of the magazine was written in with a thick black marker: *Today's Gay.* There was a fat black arrow pointing to Evan, and a myriad of horrible slogans written around him.

"This is awful. Who would do this? Who did this?"

The last thing Brynna remembered was looking from Lauren to Darcy, whose eyes were wide, blank orbs, before she felt Lauren's hands on her collarbones. Her balance was thrown off as Lauren lunged, and Brynna stumbled over her own feet, her leg crumpling as she fell to the ground. Her elbow struck first and then her hip as she gripped Lauren's fingers, trying to rip them from her shirt.

"You told the whole fucking school he was gay! He trusted you!"

Lauren was yelling and huffing, and Brynna was trying to process the spiderweb of pain shattering her elbow, Lauren's fingers digging into her flesh, the throb of students chanting "fight, fight, fight!" around them.

"I didn't say anything. I didn't do that," Brynna tried to manage, tried to roll Lauren from her, but the girl was bigger and her thighs were clamped hard around Brynna's waist. She winced when she felt Lauren's nails dragging across her face.

Someone stepped on her hair.

The chant had gone from a throbbing, single-voiced rhythm to screeches and yells.

"What the heck is going on here?"

And then it was over.

Brynna was still lying on the linoleum floor, breathing hard, when Mr. Fallbrook yanked Lauren off her. The surrounding students scattered like roaches in light. The only two faces that remained, looking down at her with a combination of pity and hate, were Darcy and Teddy's.

"Where's Evan?" Brynna winced at the fresh blood that flooded her mouth from a cut lip but climbed to her feet anyway.

"Leave him alone, Brynna," Darcy said, her voice soft.

"Either someone tells me what happened here, or we're all going to the principal's office." Mr. Fallbrook's eyes were hard, sharp pinpricks as he looked from Brynna to Lauren and back again.

"It was her," Lauren said with a low snarl. "Ask her what happened."

Mr. Fallbrook held one of the hateful flyers in his hand. "Did you make this, Brynna? This goes beyond bullying. This is a hate crime."

Brynna stepped forward, her cheeks flushed, her palms feeling raw from where they rubbed against the concrete. "I didn't do it." She looked toward Lauren. "I didn't make that. I would never make something like that."

Lauren looked at her, her face a mask of white-hot rage.

"And you two? Why were you fighting?"

Brynna cleared her throat and took a tiny step forward, glancing back at Lauren, then back to Mr. Fallbrook. "It was a misunderstanding. Please don't punish Lauren, Mr. Fallbrook. It was my fault."

Mr. Fallbrook sucked in a long breath as he looked from Brynna to Lauren. "Is this true?"

It looked like it took all of Lauren's strength but she nodded curtly. "Everything's fine," she said, teeth gritted.

The bell rang and Mr. Fallbrook set them loose. Brynna spun on her heel and headed for Evan's locker. He was there, piling books in his bag. He froze when he saw her, the same hateful look that Lauren had washing over his features.

"What do you want?"

"Evan, please," Brynna said. "I have no idea what happened. I just walked on campus and Lauren came after me. She attacked me."

Evan's lips actually cocked up in a smirk, and Brynna could feel the lump growing in her throat. "Evan?"

He slammed his locker shut and stood in front of her, legs akimbo like he was getting ready to fight as well. "What did you expect, Brynna? That everyone was going to throw me a parade or something?"

"Evan, you can't believe that I would make these things." She snatched them off the lockers around them, crumpling them into a ball.

"Yeah, Brynna, you go gather up all the print ones. I've still got this one for my scrapbook." He whipped out his tablet and thrust it at her, the Hawthorne High webpage popping up, boasting a big, grinning picture of Evan. Written across the shot in a jabbing, angry red scrawl were the words "Guess who's gay?"

"That's awful. You think I did—?"

"Who else, Brynna? I told you. Just *you*."

"It's not like it wasn't obvious," Brynna spat back.

Evan stared at her, his whole face contorted in pain, surprise, and biting anger.

"It doesn't matter," he said in a low, even voice. "I told you."

"Evan, why would I do this to you? What would I have to gain? Seriously." She reached out for him, but he shrugged her hand off violently.

"I don't know why you would do this, Brynna. I'm beginning to think I never even really knew you at all." Evan spun, his back to her.

"I didn't tell anyone, Ev. And what's the problem anyway? Being gay is no big deal. It shouldn't even have been a secret in the first place."

Now Evan spun back toward Brynna, his every feature alive with fire. Anger rolled off him in waves. "That's not your decision to make. Being gay might not be a big deal to you, but it is to me. It doesn't matter if people 'figured it out' on their own. I needed to be the one, Brynna. I needed to be the one to tell people, not you!"

He turned and stomped down the hall, but Brynna couldn't move. She could hear the reverberating sound of his footsteps fading as he walked away from her and finally disappeared around a corner.

She knew she should move, but her feet were rooted to the glossy hallway tiles. Her body felt heavy, and her blood seemed to thrum, to pulse over the ache in the jagged skin of her torn palms, and she could taste it at the corners of her mouth. Faint. Metallic. It made her stomach ache and filled her nostrils with that fresh meat smell.

She swallowed down bile.

She felt the sting of Evan's words on her cheeks as if he'd slapped her, and for once, she didn't want to numb the pain. She let Evan's anger sink into her.

It didn't take long for the news of Brynna's betrayal to overtake the news that Evan was gay. Immediately, she was a pariah, and classmates who'd never noticed her before were glaring, staring, studying her, and whispering. They avoided her when she walked. They left the bathroom when she entered. Their malevolence traveled in a thick cloud wherever they went, but Brynna didn't mind it. It felt better for people to be angry with her than it did for them to avert their gazes only to glance back with pity in their eyes when they thought she wasn't looking.

There was no follow-up from Erica either.

Brynna waited, holding her breath each time her tablet chimed, each time she logged into her email. She hadn't told anyone about Evan, and no one else had taken responsibility. It had to be Erica.

But Erica is dead. The refrain kept ringing in her head.

• • •

After the final bell, Brynna sped down the hall, head down, watching her sneakers against the scuffed hallway's linoleum. She spun when someone wound their arm in hers, and when she looked up, Teddy was there. Her heart stopped mid-beat, and she waited for him to say something, for his expression to crack and give her the tiniest clue as to what he was thinking, what he was feeling. Instead, he tugged her down the hall silently then ushered her into the empty choir room.

"Hey," she said softly.

Teddy sat on a desk, his eyes locked on hers. "Hey."

They were silent for a beat before Teddy went on. "What's going on, Bryn?"

"I didn't—I didn't out Evan, I swear."

"You don't have to convince me. I know you wouldn't do something like that. Besides, it's not exactly like it was the secret of the century. So, since you didn't do it, do you have any idea who did?"

Brynna pinched the bridge of her nose. "Meatball?"

She knew it wasn't Meatball, but she threw it out there anyway, hoping to see what—if anything—Teddy knew.

He shook his head. "Doubtful. Meatball likes to torture Evan in person. And besides, have you seen the meat hooks on that guy? I don't think he types so much as just mashes a bunch of keys together." Teddy mimed apelike hands mashing at a keyboard, and Brynna smiled in spite of herself.

The whole school was mere feet away, but Brynna felt comfortable in the room with Teddy. He was warm and concerned, and when he smiled, everything bad about Brynna's life melted away.

She wanted to smile as easily as he did. She slid up on the desk next to him. "You know how in movies the person always says, 'now you have to promise me you won't think I'm crazy' before they tell the other person something crazy?"

Teddy nodded, but his eyebrows were raised. "Yes..."

"I'm not even going to say that because you're going to think I'm crazy regardless."

He smiled and gestured for her to go on.

Brynna sucked air through her teeth, her stomach burning, heart thudding in her chest. "I think someone from my old school might be after me."

Teddy's relaxed expression went to concern. His lips tightened, and his eyes widened. "What do you mean, 'after' you?"

"I think someone is trying to hurt me. Or scare me at least." She swallowed, kicking her legs underneath the table. "I think that person wrote the headline about Evan. I think that person was in the pool with me the night that you found me."

"The night you wouldn't let me go to the police."

She nodded slightly, watching her legs swaying under the table. "Yeah."

"Brynna, you could be in real danger. You need to tell someone. We need to tell someone."

Her lower lip started to tremble, and the classroom swirled in front of her. "I can't go to the police. I'm chasing a ghost, Teddy."

Teddy pulled Brynna to him, and she cried into the crook of his neck. He stroked her hair softly, and she cried out the tension of the last few hours, weeks, months.

"It's going to be okay, Brynna," he murmured softly. "It's going to be okay. We'll go to the police or your parents."

Brynna breathed in the clean soap scent of Teddy's soft skin. "Can we just stay here, like this, for a while?"

Teddy nodded, resting his chin against her head.

Brynna prayed that they could stay that way forever.

• • •

When Brynna got home that Friday, all she wanted to do was sleep, to spend the entire weekend underneath her covers, waiting for time to pass.

It was Saturday afternoon, and Brynna was flopped on her stomach in her room, reading, when she heard the echo of the doorbell. She paused, holding in a breath, when she heard the murmured conversation of both her parents and a guest. Interest piqued, she peeled out of bed and pinched the shade up an inch, her stomach falling into her shoes.

"Honey," her mother said, rapping on the door before poking her head in.

"Teddy's here."

"Right." Her mother's smile faltered. "You didn't tell us the dance was this weekend." She looked Brynna up and down. "Did you forget?"

Truthfully, Brynna had. But she also had no reason to think about it, since her friends weren't speaking to her. "Why is Teddy here?"

"I'm assuming to pick you up for your date. He's wearing a tuxedo and he has a corsage and everything."

Brynna could see that absolute joy in her mother's eyes, and guilt stabbed at her. *She probably thinks I'm all better,* Brynna thought sadly. *She probably thinks I'm normal again.*

"Can you send Teddy up here, just for a second?"

Her mother raised a brow but nodded, and a few seconds later, Teddy was standing in her doorway.

He looked handsome, his rented suit midnight black and pressed to razor-sharp edges. His hair was pushed back—enough to look like he'd made an effort, but not so much that he looked like he was trying—and Brynna grinned without meaning to.

"What are you doing here?"

Teddy held up the corsage. "Uh, going to homecoming, I thought."

"You still want to go with me?"

He glanced down at the carpet and kicked softly. "You told me you didn't make those flyers and I believe you. You told me that it wasn't you who outed Evan and I believe you." He dropped his voice. "I can't believe that you won't let me go to the police about the person you think is stalking you…"

Brynna pumped her head, hoping to drop the subject.

"So are we going or not?" Teddy asked.

"Let me just get dressed."

Teddy went back downstairs while Brynna raced into the shower, giddiness flipping her stomach. She didn't pause to think about Erica, to breathe deeply through the belting water. She didn't think about anything but Teddy and her and homecoming, until she went for the garment bag in her closet, unzipped it, and stopped.

It was still Erica's dress.

In all the fuss, her mother hadn't returned it. Brynna hadn't thought about it.

There was nothing else in her closet except hoodies and jeans, so Brynna slid the dress from the bag and closed her eyes.

"I'm sorry, Erica," she muttered. "I'm so, so sorry."

She stepped into the blue dress, the mounds of frothy fabric swirling around her. The bodice—tight, sparkly—fit her exactly the way all of Erica's other dresses fit her—slightly tight across the bust, a few inches shorter than she was comfortable with. She blew out a shaky breath, feeling heat surge through her. This wasn't just like Erica's dress. It *was* Erica's dress.

Brynna's parents took the requisite paparazzi photos of Teddy and her, and Brynna tried to feel comfortable in Erica's dress. Teddy complimented her, and all she could do was smile thinly and nod, thinking of Erica, thinking of the way she held the dress in front of her and twirled.

"It's incredible, right? It's, like, the color of the ocean."

They were in Erica's room with the lights on and the radio softly playing. Brynna's hair was in a sloppy ponytail, and one eye was dressed with a sparkly, smoky eye shadow while the other waited for the next look Erica wanted to practice. All at once, Erica stopped dancing and Brynna felt her hackles go up, her skin tightening.

"Did you hear that?" she asked Erica.

Erica went to the window, squinting into the blackness outside. She yanked the cord and the blinds came crashing down. "It's probably my creepy stepbrother. He's been lurking around."

Brynna stared, wide-eyed. "Christopher? Isn't he, like, twenty-five?"

Erica nodded. "Something like that. And he's not supposed to be within eight hundred feet of here."

"What are you talking about?"

"He's got some crazy obsession, Brynnie." Erica pushed her hair back over her shoulder and twirled again in the mirror. "So, how do I look?"

A shock wave zipped through Brynna and she straightened. She had forgotten that night, buried it back under memories of the beach, that night, the dare.

Erica had a stepbrother.

"Are you okay, Bryn?"

Teddy cocked his head to look at her, his ice-blue eyes catching the streetlights in the darkened car. She studied him, suspicion crashing over her as she scrutinized.

No, Brynna thought to herself. *That's ridiculous—unless Teddy was almost thirty, pretending to be a kid.*

"It's nothing," she said hastily, shaking her head. "I'm just looking forward to going to the dance."

The Hawthorne High School parking lot was packed, but Teddy found a spot near the back. He killed the engine and the car fell into silence. Brynna went for the door, but he stopped her with a hand on her forearm.

"Wait."

The soft touch and gentle tone of Teddy's voice should have made Brynna swoon, but instead, her blood ran cold, every cell on high alert. She stared longingly at the blue-black concrete outside of the passenger-side window and slowly turned to Teddy, pressing her palms together so he wouldn't see her hands shaking.

Not Teddy! She instructed herself. *Act normal!*

"What?"

Teddy's lips pressed up into that half smile that Brynna used to find so endearing, but in the darkness of the car and with her blood pulsing in her ears, she suddenly found off-putting.

Still smiling, he undid his seat belt and twisted around in his seat, fumbling with something behind his chair. Brynna's heart started to pound, and she cut her eyes back to the car door.

"This." Teddy righted himself in his seat and presented Brynna the coffin-shaped plastic box he had carried into her house. A tiny white spray of baby roses and electric green fern was nestled in iridescent shredded paper in the back of the box, and Brynna grinned, feeling sheepish. He popped open the box and slid the corsage over Brynna's wrist.

"Sorry," he said as he straightened it. "I thought you said you were going to wear a white dress."

Brynna glanced down at the corsage and grinned at Teddy, pecking a quick kiss on his lips.

"Now we're ready to dance!"

• • •

The Hawthorne High School gym was draped with tulle and twinkle lights, and rented silk plants spilled between fake pillars and spires. The look would have been magical if suspicion and fear weren't still thrumming through Brynna's veins.

She tried to brush everything off and just be happy for the moment, but she heard every sound, every person creeping through the darkened gym. Were they watching her?

"Are you cold or something?" Teddy asked after they'd finished their first slow dance.

"Why would you say that?"

He ran the back of his fingers over Brynna's bare arms, the touch so soft and sensual that Brynna forgot what she was supposed to be afraid of. "You have goose bumps." He held her a tiny bit closer. "And you've been shaking."

Teddy clasped his hands behind Brynna's back and pulled her toward him, her chest crushing up against his. She couldn't move, but she liked the feeling of being cared for, that someone was holding her near enough that nothing bad could happen. For just a millisecond, she was able to let her guard down, to melt into Teddy's warmth, to listen to the powerful, steady beat of his heart against her.

"This is nice," she murmured.

She felt him nod then rest his chin on the top of her head. "You don't have to be afraid, Bryn. I'm never going to hurt you."

Brynna wished she could believe that, but his saying it stiffened her spine again and she was filled with ice. She broke the embrace and stepped away. "I'm going—I think I'm going to get some punch now."

She left Teddy standing, dumbfounded, in the middle of the dance floor while she went to the refreshment table, swishing a paper cup through the bowl of ice-cold punch. She took a big glug, and the second the liquid passed her lips and went coursing down her throat, she knew exactly what it was: spiked.

The alcohol hit her stomach with an enveloping warmth, and Brynna tipped the cup again, finishing it in a second gulp. She glanced across the gym to where Teddy was standing, watching her, hands in pockets. He turned when Darcy approached him. She dipped her cup in a second time and finished that serving, focusing her eyes on the swirls of light in front of her. She took a step and smiled as she felt the booze work its way through her system—nothing really, just a comforting little blur as she stepped.

She spied Evan in the corner and paused, sucking in a breath. Their eyes locked, and his were cold and dark. Every time Brynna turned, someone else was turning their back to her. She slugged her cup through the punch again and closed her eyes.

When she opened them, Erica was sliding out of the gym, her dress—the exact same one that Brynna was wearing—shimmering under the disco lights.

SIXTEEN

"No," Brynna murmured to herself. "Erica is dead."

But the crash of the door crashed Brynna to reality and she dropped her empty cup, shoving past the couples on the dance floor, making her way toward the door.

"Bryn, wait!"

She vaguely heard Teddy call to her, vaguely felt his fingertips brush across her bare skin.

She needed to find Erica.

She was groping blindly through the darkened hall, unsure which direction Erica had gone but somehow certain too. Something drove her forward, and she stumbled over her own feet, mumbling.

"Erica, please come back!"

Brynna's words were slurring and her tongue felt heavy in her mouth. Her whole body broke into a cold sweat, the stiff fabric of the dress itching against her moist skin. Behind her, she heard the double doors smack shut as Teddy came into the hallway, calling out for her again.

"Brynna!"

The edges of his words were blurred and seemed to bounce off the locker-lined walls around her. Brynna stumbled and blinked, trying to bring the hallways into focus, but the linoleum, the lockers, the cheerleader-made GO! FIGHT! WIN! posters swirled and fish-eyed around her. Her head felt like it was in a vise grip, and everything around her seemed bigger, brighter, and sharper. She could smell the scent of seawater on the air. She pushed forward and, catching her heel, crashed to her knees in the hall. The faint glimmer from the emergency lights caught it before Brynna did: the faint, wet outline of a footprint.

Brynna pressed herself to her feet, hearing the tear of her skirt as she stepped on the hem. She hunched and squinted, following the line of footprints.

Her head was pounding a painful rhythm now, and her stomach was doubling in on itself. Her limbs ached, and the sweat was dribbling from her forehead, stinging her eyes. But she couldn't stop. She had to follow every footstep. She had to find Erica.

She rounded the corner and slowed as the enormous double doors that closed off the indoor pool swam in front of her. She reached her hands forward and pressed on until she gripped the handles, feeling a horrifying tremor shoot through her when the doors didn't move. They were locked.

She could feel her temperature ratchet up, and she knew that something was desperately wrong. She went to the window and cupped her hands, her stomach going to liquid.

The light was on in the Olympic-sized pool, a watery yellow spreading down the length of the gently lapping water. It glistened on the edges of a girl, creating fairylike sparkles on her long, black hair as it fanned around her head while she floated facedown in the water.

"Erica!"

Brynna pounded on the glass and yanked on the doors but nothing happened. The girl still floated effortlessly, her body buoyant, her limbs pale-colored under the water. When Brynna leaned in harder, she noticed that Erica was wearing a dress—a green dress with ruching and pick-ups, and the glinting color underneath her black tresses was a bright, cherry red.

"Lauren!"

"Brynna!" Teddy rounded the corner and stopped short, his eyes wide as she struggled against the door, pounding, desperate.

"Teddy, it's Lauren! She's in there! She's in the pool!" Brynna tried to form the words but it took effort. Her mouth felt numb and her head felt tight. Teddy's image wobbled, and she spread her feet to try to steady herself. When she blinked, Darcy was there too, and Evan.

"Lauren?"

Lauren walked around the corner then, her face screwed up in confusion as she took Brynna in.

Brynna took a step backward and pressed her palm to her forehead. "I don't—I don't—"

She glanced back through the windows toward the indoor pool and gripped the door. It was black beyond the window. There were no lights, no pool, no glistening body floating peacefully. It was just...blackness.

"I think I need to sit down now."

Teddy rushed to her side just in time for Brynna's knees to wobble then finally give out. She sat down hard on the cool linoleum and heard someone chuckle in front of her. When she looked up, most of her class was in front of her, gathered just beyond Darcy and Lauren and Evan who were giving her disgusted looks.

"Dude, that girl is trashed!" someone muttered.

"Wasted!" someone agreed.

"No." Brynna shook her head, pressing her palms against her temples. "I didn't drink. I don't drink anymore."

"You don't have to lie, Brynna," Darcy said, her white satin shoes just inches from Brynna.

"No."

"Excuse me, excuse me."

Brynna looked up when Mr. Fallbrook pushed through the stream of students. They split, making way for him, and he crouched down in front of Brynna. She stared at his hand splayed on his knee, at the fat class ring that was on his finger. It mesmerized her.

"Are you okay, Brynna?"

Brynna felt Teddy's arm tighten around her, and though she wanted to answer, the darkness was closing in. Shadows nipped at her periphery, and the sounds of students backing up and disappearing was fading too.

"She's fine, Mr. F. Please?"

An exchange took place but Brynna couldn't follow it. Her eyes felt so heavy and everything was taking such effort. Just breathing, blinking—it was exhausting. She rested her head against Teddy's shoulder and gripped the lapels of his jacket.

"Teddy," she said, her lips feeling dry and chapped. "Teddy, I want to go home now."

She felt someone else reach out for her, and when she looked, she was able to make out Mr. Fallbrook's face. He was looking back and forth with a slightly panicked grimace, and voices buzzed around her, slowed, stretched out, like her iPod on its last battery leg.

Out of nowhere, a wave of terror shot through Brynna and she rolled onto her knees.

"Lauren?"

Lauren knelt in front of her and Brynna tried to focus. "You were in the water," she said in a heavy whisper. "I saw you in the water."

"No, Brynna, I wasn't." Lauren drew nearer, her lips against Brynna's ear. "Brynna, what happened to you? What are you on?"

"I think I should call her parents." Mr. Fallbrook's stern voice was unusually focused, and Brynna looked toward it.

"Please, Mr. F, she's okay. She just had a little too much to drink."

"The punch," Brynna mumbled. "There was something in the punch."

Her head continued the drumbeat, and stars shot bright light in front of her eyes. "Booze and something else."

"She doesn't look—"

"Olivia Shea is throwing up in the gym."

Brynna looked toward the voice and started. "Evan?"

He looked down at her, something in his eyes. Mr. Fallbrook paused then leaned into Teddy and Brynna. "You two wait here. I'll be right back."

The second Mr. Fallbrook disappeared around the corner,

Brynna felt her head and shoulders being swept up and her stiff legs being lifted. Her head flopped to the side and she looked at Evan.

"You're helping me?" she asked, using everything she had left to move her lips.

Evan didn't answer, but he didn't move his hand from her calf where it was resting.

• • •

The room was dark when Brynna opened her eyes. She was uncomfortable, pinned down by a heavy duvet and blankets, her body aching with even the most miniscule of movements. She blinked and tried to make out shapes in the darkness, finally pushing herself up to sitting. She sucked in a nervous breath and pressed her hands up against her chest when she realized she was wearing a strappy tank top she didn't recognize. Suddenly, the light flicked on and she blinked repeatedly, pressing a palm in front of her face to block out the light.

"Brynna?"

Darcy was in front of her in a pair of extra-baggy flannel pajama bottoms and a tank that matched Brynna's. Her homecoming makeup was still on and her sparkly, smoky doe eyes looked out of place with her muted lips and sloppy hairdo.

"Where am I?"

"You're at my place. Evan, Lauren, and Teddy are downstairs. We didn't want to take you home—we didn't want you to get in trouble."

"You didn't? Why? I—I thought you all hated me."

Darcy let out a deep breath. "It took some convincing to get Evan and Lauren to come around. Teddy said you swore you didn't do it. And besides, you looked so pitiful tonight…"

"The punch." Brynna's throat was achingly dry and her words were hoarse. Darcy came to the bedside and opened a bottle of water, handing it to Brynna.

"It was Meatball."

Brynna drank half the bottle. "Meatball?"

"He spiked the punch. A whole weird concoction of stuff—booze, drugs. Fallbrook called the police."

"Did he call my parents too?"

Darcy shook her head, her arms threaded in front of her chest. "Evan texted them. They know you're here."

Brynna paused, playing with the cap from her bottle. "Did you tell them about Erica?"

Darcy sat softly on the edge of the bed and smoothed the duvet over Brynna's feet. "I didn't tell them anything, Bryn. There's nothing to tell."

Brynna nodded, her eyes locking on Darcy's. She wanted to believe her friend, but there was something dark, something nagging on the periphery. Something that Brynna knew she should pay attention to, but the fog of the dance, the punch, was too much, and she couldn't make it out.

"Thanks," she said simply. "For everything."

When Brynna went home, her parents were seated at the kitchen table, her dad silently reading a newspaper, her mom in her funky bifocals, sketching absently on the edge of her napkin.

Her father looked up first, and for a split second, the world hung, suspended. Brynna waited for the drug test to be slid across the table or for her packed suitcase to be handed to her as they took her back to Woodbriar. Her stomach lurched though there was nothing in it; she had been throwing up all morning at Darcy's house. Her lips were cracked and parched and her throat was bone dry.

"So," her father said, setting down his newspaper. "How was it?"

Brynna blinked, waiting for the snarl.

"The dance?" she asked meekly.

Her mother dropped her pencil and pushed out the empty chair next to her. "Well, come on, don't keep us in suspense!"

"Your mother and I were very happy to receive your text. Thank you for being so responsible, hon."

Brynna touched her cell phone in her pocket and slid into the chair her mother offered. Under the table, she searched her text log to see a text she never sent:

Going to spend the night at Darcy's house. You have her parents' number if you want to check with them. That OK?

Her hackles went up and she pressed her fingers to her forehead. Was she so messed up she forgot she sent the text? *No*, she thought. *Evan. Darcy said he sent the text.* The night came back to her in painful blips and pieces.

"Bryn?"

"Sorry," she yawned. "I'm just tired. Darcy and I stayed up talking half the night."

"Well, you've got a couple hours before we have to go if you want to take a little cat nap."

Brynna stiffened. "Where are we going?"

Her parents exchanged a glance, and the hint of joviality was gone. "Today is Erica's memorial, sweetheart. Did you forget?"

Brynna fought a grimace. "No, I didn't forget."

• • •

Brynna stared into her closet, her fingers walking over her hangers as she looked at the same bunch of clothes over and over again. Her homecoming dress—or Erica's dress—was draped over the back of the chair. She glanced at it once before shoving it into the depths with a slight shudder.

What had happened at the dance?

She sat back on her bed and tried to replay the events: the dance itself, the first swig of punch. She remembered the bitter taste of the punch. She stood up again and started to pace, trying to put the flimsy, shadowy pieces together. There were other people at the table. Were they drinking? Who else saw Erica? Who else was there?

She remembered, vaguely, Meatball standing by the bowl when she took the first cup.

Was he trying to poison me?

Brynna gulped and pulled Meatball—whose real name was Steven Thomson—and his phone number up in the Hawthorne High registry. She dialed and counted the rings until Meatball answered, his voice groggy with sleep.

"Yeah?"

She cleared her throat. "Steven?"

"Who's this?" He sounded slightly more awake.

"It's Brynna. From school? From the dance?"

There was a long pause, and Brynna thought Meatball was going to hang up on her. Then, "Yeah? What do you want?"

"I know you spiked the punch last night."

He kind of did a snorty little laugh that made Brynna's skin crawl. "Yeah, I spiked it. The booze was my idea. The drugs—"

"So there were drugs."

"For you, yeah."

Cold steel shot through Brynna's whole body. "What do you mean, for me?"

"I was doing a favor. The money was good. You're fine. No harm, no foul, right? My man Teddy have a good time?"

Horror sickened Brynna's stomach as tears swelled before her eyes. "Teddy paid you to put something in my punch?"

"Look, whaddya want? You want another hit?"

"No, of course not. Teddy bought a hit from you and told you it was for me?"

"Nah, it wasn't Teddy, it was a chick. That other chick."

Brynna was reeling. *"...it was a chick."* Her lips trembled and she wrapped an arm around herself, trying to stop the tremor. "Did she have long black hair?"

"I'm not a freakin' hairdresser. Are you ordering or what?"

Brynna hung up the phone without answering.

Darcy drugged me, Brynna thought. She waited to be overcome with anger, but all she felt was a deep, aching betrayal. *Was Darcy responsible for everything else too? Were they all in on it?*

SEVENTEEN

"Bryn, we're leaving in ten," her father yelled from the downstairs landing.

She turned, still stunned, and scanned her closet again. *Darcy was there when we were dress shopping. She suggested I go to the locker room and change my clothes when I found the purple crepe paper.*

She felt sick and groped through her closet blindly, pulling out anything dark to reflect her mood. She finally selected a retro black dress with shiny gold buttons that Erica would have hated and pulled on a pair of black tights and black shoes. She yanked her hair back into a severe-looking bun and glanced at herself in the mirror. She looked like a cross between a schoolmarm and a ninja and the look wasn't flattering, but that was Brynna's point. She didn't want to be noticed. Not that she didn't want to be recognized—she didn't want to exist at all. She was back to being a loner, back to being punished. Brynna tucked her purse under her arm and grabbed her phone when her mother called.

Her parents were solemn-faced and stayed that way through most of the journey into Point Lobos. She knew when her father offered to pull over at a Starbucks that they were getting close, and Brynna's chest started to tighten. She glanced down at a discarded newspaper while she waited for her family's drinks, and her skin started to prick. A three-inch column on the bottom left corner had a black-and-white picture of Erica, head thrown back, grinning. Brynna knew that picture; it was from a water park they had gone to their freshman year. She tried not to read the headline but couldn't stop herself.

Point Lobos Teen's Remains to Be Interred Today

The next few lines gave a short blip about Erica and then directions to the memorial and where donations could be sent. Brynna's stomach churned and when they called her name, she dropped her latte into the trash.

She couldn't get the words out of her mind: remains. They weren't going to bury Erica; they were going to bury her *remains*.

Brynna handed her parents their coffees and clicked herself into the backseat while her father started the engine. Her mother leaned over the seatback and squeezed Brynna's hand, offering one of her mom looks—this one soft and apologetic.

"You know, if you don't want to do this, the Shaws will understand."

Brynna's mother had said that before they left too, and Brynna was beginning to wonder if the Shaws had called and said that they didn't want Brynna there. They didn't want the girl who survived—when their daughter didn't—to celebrate Erica's short life.

Brynna breathed deeply, feeling the butterflies flapping madly in her stomach. "I want to be there," she said, not sure if she meant it.

Her parents tried to make conversation as they passed the Point Lobos sign. They asked trivia questions and her dad sang badly to

Beyoncé, which should have mortified Brynna, but she was too busy studying every inch of the passing landscape to notice.

It seemed like something should be different now that Erica had been found. But nothing was. Chow Foo's heavy red and gold embossed doors still stood out among the clapboard shops and swinging glass doors; street signs still looked like they sprang out of the little piles of sand at their bases; tourists with chubby-cheeked toddlers still looked each way while crossing the street, dragging a string of Donald Duck rafts behind them. There was a line at the ice cream shop, and Brynna narrowed her eyes, recognizing a few kids from Lincoln High and wondering, with a growing heat, if one of them was playing with her, pretending to be Erica.

Her heart started to slam against her rib cage as her father steered the car through the big iron gates of the Point Lobos Cemetery. The place should have been calming with its gently sloping green hills and carefully manicured bushes with the last of the fall flowers, but Brynna was on edge, clenching her fists so hard that her nails dug little half moons into her palms.

Her father steered them to a tiny road that was suddenly lined with cars, and Brynna watched people walking from all directions. They spun as the car crept by, squinting to see inside. Brynna shrunk.

I shouldn't be here.

She sucked in deep breaths but it did nothing for the trembling.

Erica's death was an accident, she said to herself.

Everyone is looking at you.

The Shaws walked up at the same time the Chases did, and

Brynna was glad for that. All eyes went to Mrs. Shaw and hands went out to Mr. Shaw. Brynna was steering her parents toward a group of folding chairs half obscured by the weeping willow when she heard, "Oh, Brynna, you look so wonderful."

Brynna turned and blinked at Mrs. Shaw. She was an older version of Erica, her shoulder-length black hair more gray than Brynna remembered, but still with a mix of that stunning blue-black that Erica had. Staring at Mrs. Shaw was both comforting and unnerving, knowing what Erica would have looked like, knowing that sentence always ended with, "had she lived."

Brynna leaned into Mrs. Shaw's hug and held her tight, silently trying to convey her apologies.

"I like your dress," she said, nodding at Brynna's black sheath. "You know Erica would have hated it." Mrs. Shaw smiled and Brynna smiled back.

"Anything born before 1990," Brynna said, remembering Erica's distaste for anything vintage.

"You and your parents will come sit with us."

Mrs. Shaw pulled Brynna through the crowd, and the whispers started scratching at her skin.

"Can you believe Brynna's back?"

"I heard she went to jail."

"I heard she went crazy."

None of Dr. Rother's exercises could stave off the looks, the hands cupped over mouths and heads leaning in. Nothing that Dr. Rother taught her could quell the guilt and the sadness that welled up inside her.

Mrs. Shaw shuffled Brynna and her parents down the aisle then took a seat.

Brynna nodded and tucked her hands in her pockets as people took their seats. She started when she felt her phone vibrate. She glanced down, seeing the little tweeting bird. Her breath hitched and her stomach plummeted when she swiped the screen.

@EricaNShaw has a message for you!

Finger trembling, Brynna swiped the screen.

Lovely day for a memorial. What do you remember, Bryn?

Brynna gritted her teeth and pushed out the keyboard on her phone.

I know this is u, Darcy. I talked to Steve.

There was no response by the time the service started, and Brynna felt stung. She hoped that Darcy would at least acknowledge what she'd done, at least own up to what she put Brynna through.

Everyone assembled stood when the priest asked them to, and Brynna started when she saw the casket in front of her. She had noticed it when she and her family came to the site, of course, but now, with a priest at the head, flowers draped on top, and a smiling picture of Erica at the foot, it became real to Brynna, unmistakable evidence that Erica was never coming back.

A sob lodged in her chest, and she was not only overcome with guilt for being the one to survive, but for knowing that Erica had been out there, somewhere, all this time while Brynna was jumping at her own shadow, thinking horrible things about her best friend.

How could I have thought that she hated me?

Mrs. Shaw's hand found Brynna's. She squeezed, and the last several months crashed over Brynna in an aching wave and every inch of her was filled with sorrow. She sat back on one of the metal chairs, crying huge, body-wracking sobs over Erica.

When the memorial ended, someone began collecting chairs. Brynna watched Mr. Shaw slowly turning, his red-rimmed eyes scanning the horizon as though he were expecting Erica to come walking in from the woods.

When he turned to Brynna, he was pinching the bridge of his nose and sighing. "Christopher's not here," he said to his wife.

"We can at least thank God for that."

Brynna split away from the Shaws, from her own parents, standing on the edge of Erica's grave. The coffin had been lowered in, and off to her left, two workmen with shovels stood half-hidden in a clutch of trees, waiting to finish burying her. Brynna couldn't help but think they were like vultures, circling their prey.

"Honey?" Her father's touch was gentle on her shoulder. "We're going to get going over to the Shaws now."

Brynna nodded numbly, offering Erica a final good-bye in her head.

"I'll meet you out at the car. I'm going to stop by the ladies' room first."

People were leaving slowly, milling in clumps around the cemetery grounds, and Brynna tried to avoid them all. She wound around the stone pathways that cut through the grounds, keeping her eyes on the path rather than the headstones that surrounded her. She didn't want to think that they were leaving Erica there, among hundreds of people she didn't know.

The crowd had thinned considerably when she came out of the little chapel's restroom.

"Hello there."

Brynna gasped then grabbed her chest and finally looked up, a relieved smile on her face. "Mr. Fallbrook! Sorry, you scared me. What are you doing here?"

He cocked his head in something that looked like amusement, but there was a weird, almost sinister smile on his face.

"You don't know?"

Brynna fell in step with him, and they moved toward the parking lot. "I don't know what? Did you know Erica? I know you were at a different school before you came to Hawthorne."

He nodded, his smile still fixed. "I did know Erica. Rather well." He paused and Brynna waited for him to go on. He didn't.

"Um, from another school or something?"

"Not exactly. We were much closer than just a teacher and student."

Brynna glanced up, a dark pit forming low in her belly. "I—I don't understand."

"She was a very, very special girl, Erica." There was a slight, faraway look on Mr. Fallbrook's face, and Brynna's nerves started to hum.

"I—I don't think I know what you mean."

Mr. Fallbrook snapped toward Brynna. "You don't think she was special?"

"No, of course she was. She was my best friend. My best friend in the world. How did you say you two knew each other?"

A slow smile spread across his face. "We were very close. Like family."

The pieces started to fall into place, but Brynna had to shake off the fog that covered them.

"I know you too, Brynna. Really well."

Brynna swallowed, her fear growing. "You're—are you—her stepbrother?"

"Ding, ding, ding!"

The look on his face was chilling. His ice-blue eyes were shooting daggers. His handsome face morphed into a mask distorted in anger. Hate rolled off him in waves, and Brynna stepped backward, ready to run.

But Mr. Fallbrook already had her.

She twisted over her own feet as he flipped her so her back was firm against his chest. His one arm clapped both of hers down, his other hand tight against her mouth. She could taste the blood as her teeth dug into her cheeks each time he gripped her harder.

"You're going to stay very, very quiet, do you hear me, Brynna? As quiet as my sister is over there in that big pine box."

Christopher.

He jammed her against the door of his car, pinning her there with a knee to her back. He moved his hand from her mouth, but her scream died in the air when he pulled the glistening silver blade in front of her eyes, then held it against her neck. She could feel her skin give into the blade, could feel the hot itch start as her blood started to bubble.

"I'm just holding the knife here, Brynna. If you move, it's probably going to cut you. It's probably going to slit your throat. But it won't be my fault, will it? It'll be yours."

She felt him lasso her hands with a zip tie, then he pulled it so tightly she winced. The blade cut into another layer of skin while the tie cut into her wrists.

"Why—why—why are you doing this?"

Fallbrook pulled Brynna's head back by the hair; she could feel the individual strands breaking in his grip. She pinched her eyes shut, waiting for the feel of the cold, steel blade as it ripped into her flesh.

But it didn't happen.

Instead, he wound a long length of duct tape over her mouth and another over her eyes. Before her eyes could adjust to the relative dark behind the duct tape, Fallbrook picked her up and shoved her, headfirst, into what Brynna assumed was his SUV. She tried to struggle and kick, but he looped her feet with the zip ties just as easily. He shoved her to the ground, and she landed on the itchy interior carpet with a heave when her ribs crashed against the center hump.

When she tried to scream—a pathetic, muted cry—he threw something soft but heavy over her and said, "We're going to play a game, okay? It's called you scream and I kill you. There's only one rule: you scream, kick, or make any sound, and I kill you. Maybe I'll take the tape off your eyes so you can watch it. Maybe I won't so you have no idea when it's coming. Wanna play? Of course you do."

Helpless, terrified, and unable to move, Brynna stayed pressed against the floor, her forehead resting on the carpet as the tears started to fall. She heard Fallbrook slam a car door then open another; once he slammed that too, she heard him start the car and gun the engine.

A song she used to like—something she and Teddy had even danced to last night—filled the car and Fallbrook hummed along. Brynna tried to remember anything she'd learned from the litany of public safety assemblies the schools had made her attend, but the only thing that stuck with her, the only thing she could remember was a female officer telling the students, "If he gets you in his car, you're as good as dead."

After a few short minutes, Fallbrook slowed the car and Brynna lifted her head, trying to listen to everything. She heard his window roll down and the muted voices of the funeral procession floating through the car window. She could make out Mrs. Shaw thanking someone for coming.

Brynna's heart went crashing against her chest.

"We'll be right over," Brynna heard in the distance. "We're just waiting for Brynna."

Her whole body seized. It was her father's voice.

"Shhhh," Christopher said from the front seat. "Remember our game."

Sweat and rage poured through Brynna and she struggled, trying to scream. If he was going to kill her, he could do it right now. But Christopher simply rolled up the window, stepped on the gas, and went right along humming to the radio.

They could have driven for minutes or possibly hours—time

ceased to exist in the blackness where Brynna lay pinned—when Christopher turned down the radio.

"You know," he said, "I am being so rude. You asked me a question and I didn't even answer it. What was the question again now? Oh, right, don't trouble yourself; I remember. You asked me why I was doing this."

Brynna winced, tasting salt tears and metallic blood on her lips.

"Well, obviously you've figured some of it out by now, haven't you, Brynna? I mean, I know you're relatively smart. You were doing pretty well in my English class. Too bad you won't have a chance to bring that grade up. It did take you a long time to catch on, and I left you so many signs. Well, Erica did. If she can't speak, I figured I should speak for her."

Brynna gritted her teeth, trying to pull her palms apart, trying to will the plastic tie to loosen.

Christopher clucked his tongue. "Nice room, by the way. You might want to remind your pops to lock the doors the next time he goes on a bender."

Heat exploded in Brynna's cheeks, and she found herself feeling strangely ashamed, as if impressing a psychopath was something she should do. Then she thought of Mr. Fallbrook—Christopher, whoever he was—walking around her house when she wasn't around. Sweat broke out on her brow. Or had he been there when they were asleep? Had he been in the house while her mother worked upstairs, painting, oblivious to the world outside?

Fallbrook went on, and Brynna wished she couldn't hear him. "My name is Christopher. Shaw, not Fallbrook. Fallbrook was my stepfather." Christopher's voice tightened into a low growl. "Talk about an evil son of a bitch. Bastard paid me no mind unless he was beating the snot out of me." His voiced lightened again, the quick change eerie. "Don't worry; he paid for it. I made sure of that. See, that's kind of what I do. I make sure that the people who are responsible for things—bad things—don't get away with it. The world would be a very fucked up place if we let people get away with murder, wouldn't it be, Brynna? Don't answer that; I know you're listening. So why did I do this…"

Brynna pressed against the floor as the car shifted. She felt the motor slow down, and her fear became a striking terror.

If he slows down, he's going to stop. If he stops, he's going to kill me.

Brynna worked against the restraints on her hands and ankles, not caring as the thin plastic tore into her skin.

"Remember when I put up that one daily topic? It was, *Write about a time you were really scared.* Do you remember that, Brynna? I remember. I remember what you wrote. You wrote, 'I don't remember ever really being afraid.' And I got your paper and I thought, hmm, that's funny. Because I would have been scared in the ocean at night. I would have been scared if someone I loved went into the water and was left there to die. Don't you think that'd be scary? I know it was scary for Erica. I know, because I saw it."

Brynna's stomach dropped.

"I was following her to keep her safe. I always tried to keep her safe. And I did until you and your stupid dare."

Everything inside of Brynna broke down. She stopped struggling and cocked her head to listen, feeling the tears loosen the back of the duct tape.

"Did you like the phone call, Brynna? The little replay of memory? I thought it was neat. I replay it a lot. There's more of it, you know. It keeps going on. It keeps going on to the point that Erica was begging for her life. You should have seen her out there, trying to hang on. She was a good swimmer that one, and feisty too. She begged me to help her. She kept saying, 'Pull me in. I need to come in so I can help Brynna.' She knew you weren't a good enough swimmer."

Brynna opened her eyes behind the strip of tape. Erica was looking for her? Erica didn't drown? Her heart started to thud as a dark realization came over her.

"I told her I would help her. She was my stepsister, you know? What kind of brother would I be? I got down on the pier ladder—I don't swim—and held an arm out to her. And you know what that little bitch did? She told me no. She told me she could climb up the ladder by herself."

Brynna remembered Erica's words, so haunting that night as she pulled the blinds over her bedroom window: "It's probably my creepy stepbrother… He's got some crazy obsession, Brynnie."

"It didn't take long for her to get desperate. The tide was pretty heavy. She got close enough and I grabbed her. Just grabbed her arm. She still flinched. I mean, I was risking my life to save this little bitch—I was in water up to my waist! And she flinches. But I caught her. Caught her by that beautiful long hair of hers." Brynna could hear him breathe deeply. "I was going to save her. I pulled her toward me and she struggled. She said some awful, hateful things. But it was nice having her body against me, struggling like that." He giggled, a sound so evil it made goose bumps shoot up all over Brynna. "And then I pushed her down. It made her struggle more, you know? Being held under the water. I wrapped my arms around her and held her there. I could feel her kick and scratch."

Brynna's body wracked with sobs. She wanted to make Christopher stop, would have begged him if she could talk.

"She fought real hard for a minute and then…then I could feel it when the life left her body. It was magical. I never felt anything like that. I couldn't wait to do it again. There was another girl, at a pool where I used to work. But she wasn't like Erica. Erica was special. That spot, Harding Beach? Special. I knew there was only one way to get the feeling back."

Brynna bit back bile, the tears coming so full and so hard that her whole body shook, the zip ties continuing to dig into her limbs. Finally, her body thunked against the seats when Christopher lurched the car to a sudden stop. She strained, listening for anything she could use, anything that could help her. She prayed for noise, for people, but everything was silent in the car until she heard the click of Christopher's seat belt.

She held her breath, squeezing her eyes shut and doing her best to make herself smaller under the blanket as she heard Christopher round the car and pull open the back door. He pulled off the blanket, and shards of light flit in through the gaps in the duct tape over Brynna's eyes.

But she didn't need her vision to know exactly where she was.

EIGHTEEN

In one fell swoop, faint light burned Brynna's eyes, and her skin screamed from the quick rip of the tape. Christopher was smiling down at her, the smile that looked so calm behind his desk in her English class looking nothing short of maniacal as he studied her. He took a heavy, deep breath, and Brynna craned her neck, looking around her. Twilight was setting in.

"Don't you love that smell, Brynna? The sweet sea air. I don't think I can ever get enough of it."

He reached in and grabbed her by her clothes, dumping her with a thud in the parking lot on the edge of Harding Beach. He shut and locked his doors, and Brynna found herself laughing uncontrollably, the idea of a murderer locking his car doors against burglars suddenly seeming incredibly ridiculous to her. Christopher whirled.

"What the hell are you laughing at?"

Tears were running down Brynna's cheeks. She was hysterical, knowing that Christopher wanted to kill her—was going to kill her. He crouched forward, his face screwed up in fury, and ripped the tape from her mouth.

"You're going to die today, Brynna. You find that funny?" He gave her a swift kick in the ribs, pain shooting out like a starburst from her chest. She whimpered.

He gathered her up, and even through her clothes, Brynna's skin crawled when his body made contact with hers.

"If you really loved Erica, if you were a really good friend, you would have stayed out there to help her. You could have saved her."

"But you…it was you."

Christopher shook his head sadly. "If you had been there for her, if you had been looking out for her, then I wouldn't have had to. I wouldn't have gone into the water. I was just trying to save her, but she started to scream." A biting anger crept into his voice. "I was just trying to put my arms around her to keep her afloat, but she kicked and she bit me. She called me a freak." He paused, eyes flashing silver. "You should have been there. You should have been there when she stopped kicking."

He looked at her with a bizarre kind of sorrow in his eyes, and Brynna's mind raced, trying to figure out what to do. She could scream, but Harding Beach was far back off the road and off the beaten path. Even if she could run, there was nowhere she could go.

"You don't have to do this now. You don't have to."

He kicked her feet while he held her up, his lips at her ear. "I have to do this. You *made* me do this. You and Erica. You could have stopped me." He paused, his knife-sharp eyes burning into hers. "But you just let her die."

"No," Brynna mumbled. "I didn't know. I didn't know where Erica went. It was dark and I couldn't see her."

"She was so, so scared all alone out there. Especially before she knew I was watching her."

Brynna's stomach churned.

"And now I've been watching you."

She tried to turn away, but he pressed his lips harder against her cheek, wrapping her hair around his hand. "I've learned a lot since Erica though."

He gave her another kick and lifted her as they slowly made their way to the beach. The tears rolled over Brynna's cheeks, and she did her best to look around, eyes darting for anyone who may be nearby. She saw the remnants of a bonfire—a couple of smashed red party cups and a forgotten, sand-covered blanket—but no people. Christopher's eyes followed hers and then he grinned. "No one to hear you scream."

His voice sent a tremble of fear shifting down her spine, and she lost her breath when he swept her up and carried her to the tide line.

"Don't do this. Oh god, please don't do this." Brynna struggled against her restraints, feeling her feet and hands move just a slight bit more than they had in the car. Not by much—not enough to free her.

Christopher gazed down at her then rolled her from his arms. She landed with a sickening thud, her body falling like the dead weight that it was, smacking against the wet, hard-packed sand. Brynna struggled to catch her breath, tried to steel herself against the sudden pain ripping through her whole left side.

Christopher pulled her onto her back, bracing himself over her. Brynna's hands and feet dug into the wet sand, doing anything to put distance between the two of them.

"Wondering why I didn't just toss you off the pier? So I could hold you under like I did Erica?"

The glee on his face—the brightness in his eyes—was nauseating. Tears rolled from Brynna's eyes into her ears but were immediately washed away by the tide coming in. It was shallow, just about an inch, enough to wet her hair and flick a few drops into her ears.

"It'll take longer this way. When the tide comes in, I can watch you die." He grinned, a hideously dark grin. "It will take a long, long time."

Christopher pushed off her, sitting up on his knees, watching as the tide went out. Brynna stared at him, paralyzed. He shot her another grin then pushed her up on her side so that she was facing the water, facing the crashing waves. He patted her head. "Don't worry. We've still got time."

Brynna watched in terror as the tide came in, wave after wave crashing over her. She turned her face away as best she could, avoiding the first few crashes of water, but as the tide got higher, the water splashed over her chin and her lips then washed over her nose. She tried to remain calm, to hold her breath, because just as soon as the tide would come in, it would go out again.

She watched Christopher stand up, still with that weird, serene smile on his face, and walk behind her. She could feel the sand fall as he burrowed one foot under her then kicked her again. She flopped on her stomach, and the water crashed over her, an icy wave breaking over the back of her head, flittering sand into her eyes, nose, and mouth. She coughed and he laughed, then the water was back, crashing over her. She watched it recede, the terror ratcheting up each time she noticed that the tide would go out less and less, the depth of the water increasing, closing the gap between the water and Brynna.

"Please, Mr. Fallbrook, don't do this!"

"Or what?"

Brynna had no answer. Her neck ached from arching it back each time the water closed over her. Her ribs felt splintered, broken and useless. Sand and salt water burned at her eyes.

She wanted to beg for her life—or beg for a quick death—but she didn't want to give Christopher the satisfaction. Besides, she had let her best friend die. If she had just waited for Erica...

A wave came, this time deeper, and Brynna's full body was plunged under. She held her breath, her lungs screaming with the effort as the water seemed to recede more slowly. When it finally drew back, it licked at her right shoulder, splashed over the arch in her back.

"Won't be much longer now."

She felt Christopher's foot dig underneath her again and she winced, holding her breath even as every inch of her exploded in pain. The wave crashed as he lifted her, and suddenly, she was weightless, free, being sucked into the surf.

The water crashed over her head and plunged her down. She tried to claw, to paddle, but her hands were bound uselessly behind her. The water swirled, and she kicked her legs together, trying to find ground, trying to find a way to push her head out of the surf. Tension burned all through her, the adrenaline breaking into a hot, coursing rush through her system.

She wasn't going to die this way.

With a burst of strength that almost seemed otherworldly, Brynna cracked the zip tie that bound her ankles. The water sucked her in, disappearing behind her, spitting her out onto the rocky curve of shore.

She edged herself onto her feet, waves behind her, just in time to see Christopher rushing toward her, his face twisted in anger, his mouth open as he released a primitive scream that Brynna knew would stay with her whether she lived or died.

The waves crashed into her back and shoulders just as Christopher rushed her, knocking her hard against the water. She felt her whole body fly and then plunge back into the water, the rush of the ocean cruelly spitting her down. Her forehead hit the sandy bottom and she gasped, drinking in a mouthful of salt water. It burned her nostrils and felt as if it were searing its way through her body. Her lungs screamed. She kicked, trying to right herself—and then Christopher was on her. He yanked her up, and she began sputtering and coughing as the cool night air hit her cheeks. She gulped desperately, feeling her bruised ribs protest.

Christopher bear-hugged her and pulled back toward the shore, but he wasn't fast enough. The water swelled and crashed over them, lifting them both, sucking them further out. She felt Christopher's fingers digging into her flesh, then his fingernails as he tried to hold on to her. He was crashing into her, struggling against her, and Brynna remembered he couldn't swim.

She took a chance, plunging into the surf, kicking toward the pier. Christopher's grip on her tightened before the waves crashed again, breaking his hold on her. She was buoyed by the swell and shoved hard away from him. She thought of Erica, of the nights they had raced lane to lane, and dove hard, kicking until her legs burned and her heart hammered against her chest.

She didn't know how far she swam, but when she turned, she saw Christopher go under, disappearing into the dark water. Behind him, an ambulance and a police cruiser roared down the beach, casting red and blue lights across the water. Suddenly there were people charging down the beach, and she could hear voices and sirens against the sound of the surf.

Brynna blinked, the feeling of déjà vu overwhelming her. Her whole body ached, heavy with effort, and her legs started to cramp. She felt her chin slip into the water.

"Brynna!"

She couldn't recognize the voice. She thought maybe if she just closed her eyes… The water swirled around her ears, blocking out any sound. The water felt good, finally, caressing her, easing her into the tide.

It's over now, she thought. *It's all over now.*

The water lapped over her face and she slid down low, looking at the milky moon above her through the swirling, clear water. All the pain left her body. All the anxiousness, the stress—it was all gone, and she was going to keep her eyes closed and just rest, just rest for a minute or two.

NINETEEN

It was loud where Brynna was.

She could hear things humming and whirling, the rhythmic crash of the surf. And then a hand found hers and squeezed it gently.

"Can you open your eyes, Brynna?"

Brynna did as she was told, her eyelids fluttering open without much effort.

"Mom?"

Her mother smiled down on her then called over her shoulder, "She's awake, Adam."

Her father came through the door and went straight for Brynna's other hand, holding it gently around the needle.

"Am I in the hospital?"

"You are, hon, but everything's going to be okay. We can even take you home today."

Brynna tried to sit up then blinked at the sea of flowers around her bed, balanced on the sideboard and meal tray. "What happened?"

"You nearly drowned." Her father's eyes were rimmed in red and his voice was soft.

"How did you know where to find me?"

"Evan did. When we couldn't find you—when someone said you had gone off with friends—we called everyone in Point Lobos. Then we started with your friends in Crescent City."

"Evan didn't know where I was. He wasn't even speaking to me."

"You didn't make it easy..." Evan was standing in the doorway, Lauren, Darcy, and Teddy behind him. "We went back to the café where you and I had coffee. I remembered what you told me about that night, about Erica. Can we come in, Mrs. Chase?"

She nodded, tears streaming down her face.

"I thought he was crazy," Lauren said sheepishly. "I mean, I know how much you hate water, so..."

"But I never told you it was Harding Beach. How did you know?"

"Darcy told us."

Brynna looked at Darcy as she shyly avoided Brynna's gaze, instead studying the edge of the hospital blanket.

"She showed us the pictures," Teddy said. "We made her."

Darcy's cheeks blazed a fierce pink.

"I knew why you hated the beach but I thought that..." Evan paused. "I thought that maybe you would be able to make peace with Erica and you'd want to do it there."

"We all went," Lauren volunteered. "We saw two people struggling in the surf when we got down there. You went under and Mr. Fallbrook—or whoever he really was—was yelling your name."

"Lauren and Teddy took off at a sprint," Evan said. "Just dove right in."

"Lauren found you," Teddy said. "She swam you back most of the way."

Brynna felt tears misting her eyes. "Thank you, all of you." She glanced at her parents. "Christopher?"

Her father shook his head. "They never found him. Assumed he'd been swept out with the riptide." He turned toward Evan, Teddy, Darcy, and Lauren. "You know, we're going to go downstairs and grab a couple of coffees. You mind keeping an eye on the patient?"

"Sure."

Brynna's father rounded the bed and held a hand out to her mother. She took it, blew Brynna a kiss, and they disappeared out of the room.

"I—I can't believe, after everything, that you guys would come find me."

Darcy sat at the edge of the bed while Evan and Lauren fought over the single chair. Teddy pulled Brynna's hand into his.

"We're your friends, Bryn. Real friends never really let go."

Brynna thought of all the times she "saw" Erica. In her mind's eye, she could see her smiling now. "No," she said, "they never really do."

ACKNOWLEDGMENTS

No book is ever written alone. I'd like to thank the amazing team at Sourcebooks Fire for everything they do to make our books the best and cheer them along every step of the way. Thank you! Thanks to my wonderful agent Amberly Finarelli for seeing this puppy through its infancy and all the way out into the world. I owe a debt of gratitude to my Club One gang for keeping me going—Shirley, Penne, Marilyn, Nadine, Gary, and Dave. Thanks to my parents for not sending me directly to the nuthouse when I told them I was going to write books for a living (I was seven). Thank you to my Rogue girls with an extra special nod to Marina Adair who has actually seen me cry (probably over this book), and to all the wonderful "resources" who've turned into invaluable friends: Lee Lofland, Dr. Jonathan Hayes, Kasey Halcon, Chief L. Scott Silverii, PhD, and Dr. Cyrus Yocum.

And most importantly, to all you amazing fans out there who keep reading and writing—I love you guys! Thanks for letting the nerdy book girl into your world.

She thought it was an accident.
She was wrong.

Don't Miss
Hannah Jayne's

Truly, Madly, Deadly

ONE

"Thank you for coming."

The words rose and fell on the soft pile carpet, and Sawyer wondered whether she should brush the small ball of fuzz from Kevin's earlobe. It stuck there, stark and white against the dark navy blue of his suit.

"I couldn't have gotten through today without you," Mrs. Anderson said, squeezing Sawyer's ice-cold hand.

Sawyer knew she should say something comforting, something warm and thoughtful, but all she could focus on was that little bit of fuzz on Kevin's left ear.

"They said it was immediate," someone whispered. "They said he was drunk."

Sawyer had heard those words tumble over and over in her mind every minute for the past forty-eight hours. *It was immediate, Kevin was drunk, he didn't stand a chance*. She wasn't crying—couldn't anymore—as she stared down at Kevin. His eyes were closed, his lips slightly parted, and his hands were gently crossed against his chest. Sawyer couldn't help but think from somewhere dark, somewhere deep inside of her, that at least he couldn't hurt her anymore.

"You must be devastated."

Sawyer felt Mr. Hanson, her Spanish teacher, lay a gentle hand on her shoulder. She shrunk away, the smell of lilies suddenly overwhelmingly cloying. "I'll be right back."

She took the stairs two at a time, her black ballet flats falling soundlessly on the carpet. She paused on the top floor landing when she saw the girl at the end of the hall.

The girl blinked at Sawyer.

She was tall and thin—unfortunately so—with a boyish body that was all edges and angles. Her long brown hair was looped in a herringbone braid that fell over one shoulder, and baby hairs stood up in a static-y halo around her head, shot out from the loose weave of the braid. The girl's eyes looked like they may have been velvety brown and deeply alive once, but they were sunken and flat now. Her full lips were barely pink and pulled down at the edges. This girl wore her mourning black like a second skin.

Sawyer swallowed; the girl swallowed.

Sawyer paused for a full beat before tugging self-consciously at her braid, then averted her eyes from the mirror that reflected a girl she scarcely recognized. She continued down the hall, moving quickly.

She knew from nights lying to her parents and sneaking, shoeless, past his parents' room that Kevin's door was the last one on the left. She slipped in there on a sigh, clicking the door shut softly behind her. A curl-edged painting was scotch taped to the back of

Kevin's door and Sawyer, stunned, fingered it softly. It was a beach scene she had painted the first day Kevin spoke to her. They were in art class and she was lost in her own brush strokes, squinting, leaning close to make the crush of the waves as realistic as possible.

"You're really good," he had said, his chin jutting toward the scene. Sawyer could still feel the overwhelming heat in her cheeks as her index finger followed the curl of foam on the forever-still water.

She heard a soft breath in the yellowing light that filtered through the blinds and cracked across the painting. "The recruiter came to see him, you know."

Mr. Anderson said it without turning around. Kevin's father was perched on the end of his son's bed; his head was bowed and his back was toward her, but Sawyer could see that his fingers were working the silky fabric of Kevin's number twenty-one Hawthorne Hornets football jersey while an army of gold plated football trophies looked on.

"He talked about marrying you." Mr. Anderson looked over his shoulder then, his watery blue eyes finding Sawyer, a reminiscing half smile on his chapped lips. "He said that he'd get into Cal and you'd get into the Art Institute and that would be it."

Sawyer tried to smile, tried to remember the moments when she and Kevin would sprawl in the grass, her hand finding his as they talked about a future that was far off and pristine, that sloughed off divorce and jealousy and high school pressures and rivalries. She remembered telling Kevin that she wanted to go to the Art Institute, remembered the far-off look in his eyes when a smile snaked across his lips.

"What?" she said, barely able to keep the grin from her lips.

Kevin shook his head and squeezed Sawyer's hand gently. "How perfect is that? I'll go to Cal, be the dashing football star, and you'll be across the bay at the Art Institute painting portraits of your beloved."

"Portraits of John Lennon? I think I'd get tired of that."

Kevin tugged at her arm—gently, softly—and Sawyer slipped into his lap, loving the feeling of his arms wrapped around her. She felt so safe, so warm, and when his lips nuzzled her ear, she felt the spark move low in her belly.

Now the memory caught in her throat. *That was when things were good,* she told herself.

Mr. Anderson sucked in a sharp breath that brought Sawyer back to the present; she looked up just in time to see Kevin's father double over himself, heavy hands hugging his sides. There was no sound except the ragged tear of his breath as he cried.

Sawyer felt her bottom lip quiver, and when she pinched her eyes shut, she saw Kevin, cheeks pink and alive, lips pressed up into that half smile he shared with his father. In her mind's eye, that grin turned into a snarl. She heard the sickening smack of skin against skin in her head. She reeled, feeling the sting again.

"He loved you so much."

Sawyer felt Kevin's warm breath, heard the deep rumble of his voice as he told her he loved her for the first time. She remembered the shiver that zinged from the top of her head to the base of her spine, amazed, delighted, enraptured. Kevin—Kevin Anderson, the most popular boy in school—loved *her.* She was everything in that moment when Kevin's fingertips brushed against the small of her back, when his lips pressed up against hers. Her life—her family—had splintered. Her mother had moved across the country, her father loved another woman, but Kevin Anderson wanted Sawyer. He wanted Sawyer Dodd, and that made her feel *real.* She wanted to hold on to that moment, was desperate to hold on to that moment and nothing else—not when he got angry, not when she made him mad, not the tear-racked apologies that followed.

Sawyer nodded, the tears slipping over her cheeks. "I loved him too."

• • •

The mood at school on Monday was somber, and Sawyer was tired of people averting their stares when she walked by. Third-period choir was her favorite escape, and when she slipped into the band room, she couldn't help but grin when Chloe Coulter, seated on the piano with long legs kicking, caught her eye.

"Sawyer!" Chloe vaulted off the piano, her blond ponytail flailing behind her. She tackled Sawyer in an enthusiastic hug, not caring as students shoved past them.

"How are you?" Chloe's eyes were a bright, clear blue, and today they were wide and sympathetic, framed by too-dark black lashes and heavy brows. "Are you okay?"

Sawyer nodded slowly, and her best friend squeezed her hand, then blew out a sigh. "Did you just get back in town?"

Chloe waved a pink late pass. "Yeah." Her eyes searched Sawyer. "I'm so sorry, Sawyer. I wish I could have been there. Was it awful? It was awful, wasn't it? I should have been there with you. God, I suck."

Sawyer swallowed hard. "It was your grandmother's ninetieth birthday. No one expected you to come back."

"But I would have," Chloe said, blond ponytail bobbing.

"I can't believe he's gone," Maggie Gaines said, her ski-jump nose a heady red. She was flanked on either side by stricken onlookers who offered condolences and Kleenex as Maggie murmured to them in a voice just loud enough to be overheard. When she caught Sawyer staring, Maggie's glossy eyes went immediately hard and sharp.

"Look at her," Chloe spat. "Kevin was your boyfriend, but Maggie needs to be the inconsolable center of attention. That should be you."

Sawyer shrunk back into her baggy sweatshirt. "Let her have her moment," she mumbled. "They dated for a while too."

Chloe snorted. "Like a hundred years ago."

Mr. Rose kicked open the side door and shoved a costume rack into the choir room. The student chatter died down and kids leaned forward, eyes glued to the new choir uniforms.

"Ladies and gentlemen," Mr. Rose started, "I know you've all been waiting with bated breath to see what you're wearing for this year's regionals."

The group groaned as a well-tuned whole.

The Hawthorne High Honeybee choir was known for only two things: being four-time back-to-back national champions and having the ugliest uniforms known to man. Sawyer's freshman year featured an army green taffeta number with balloon sleeves and lace inlays for the girls, and equally unattractive green velvet blazers for the guys. Sophomore year the budget was cut, and the Honeybee choir showed up looking like an exceptionally well-tuned army of white-vested waiters. At the end of last year, the school had taken "pity" on the choir and offered up some leftover graduation gowns onto which the costume department had stitched fighting hornets and musical notes. That was what the group was expecting when Mr. Rose began his excited introduction.

"So, without further ado…" Mr. Rose pulled the black sheet off the costume bar and a collective "ah" sailed through the classroom. Maggie stopped sniffing into her Kleenex, Chloe gasped, and Sawyer sat up straighter.

"OMG!"

"They're gorgeous!"

With one hand, Mr. Rose held up a simple black satin sheath dress, its waist cinched with a thick red satin sash. In the other hand, he offered a black blazer with a red tie. The Honeybees cheered.

Mr. Rose, apple cheeks pushed up into a full-face smile, beamed. "The school board heard your fashion protests and decided—finally—that the Singing Honeybees should look like *five*-time regional champions!"

Once the students had dropped back into some semblance of order, Mr. Rose handed out the plastic-wrapped garments. When he got to Sawyer he paused, giving her the sympathetic smile she was so quickly growing tired of seeing. He rested a soft hand on her shoulder, cocked his head. "Are you doing okay, Sawyer?"

Sawyer took her dress and offered him a small smile. "Yeah, I am. Thanks Mr. Rose."

"You know, I'd like for the Honeybees to add a small tribute number to Kevin in our set list. He was such a big part of the Hornet community."

Sawyer felt a lump growing in her throat and she nodded. "That sounds nice. Kevin would have liked that."

"I'd like to feature you in a solo for that number." Mr. Rose's eyes were kind, his puffy gray eyebrows high, expectant. "Would that be okay with you?"

Sawyer nodded mutely, dread, excitement, sadness, and anxiety welling up inside her all at once. "Thank you, Mr. Rose," she finally managed.

Mr. Rose passed Sawyer and Chloe, continuing his costume distribution to the other Honeybees. Chloe leaned in, excitement evident on her face.

"A solo?" she asked breathlessly. "Oh my God, that's awesome! It just sucks that—" Chloe avoided Sawyer's eyes, looked at her own hands folded in her lap. "It just sucks that Kevin couldn't be here to hear you."

Sawyer tried to form a response or a cohesive sentence, but nothing came out.

Mr. Rose took his spot behind the piano, and the Honeybees did their warm-ups. At the last note, he beckoned to Sawyer. She made her way to the front of the class, feeling the heat of all eyes on her. When she turned, it was just Maggie, her eyes narrowed, challenging. Sawyer offered a small noncombative smile that Maggie ignored.

We used to be friends, Sawyer heard herself plead silently.

Maggie's hate rolled off her in waves.

When the bell rang, Sawyer and Chloe gathered up their backpacks and new uniforms, and headed toward the door. Maggie, arms crossed in front of her chest, stopped Sawyer dead in her tracks.

"A solo?" she said. Her eyes raked over Sawyer, the distaste evident.

"Can you move, please? I need to get to my locker before fourth." She was too tired to deal with one of Maggie's jealous rages.

But Maggie remained in Sawyer's way.

"Do you think I'm going to fall for you and your stupid little 'woe is me' act? Doubtful. You don't deserve this solo, and you didn't deserve Kevin. A real girlfriend wouldn't be able to pull herself together, let alone do a solo."

Sawyer wanted to fight back, but she was exhausted and emotionless. Maybe Maggie was right—she didn't deserve to be Kevin's girlfriend—didn't deserve to be at the blunt end of his anger, a small voice inside her head nagged. Sawyer shook it off and shoved Maggie aside with more force than she meant.

"Lay off, Maggie."

"Get over yourself," Sawyer heard Chloe growl. "Sawyer doesn't need to play the chick who can't get herself together—you do it too well. It's just too bad you've been doing it ever since Kevin dumped you. When was that exactly? Nine, ten months ago now? Little long to be carrying a flame, don't you think?" Chloe flicked a lock of Maggie's long hair, then wrinkled her nose. "It's probably time to drag your obsessively depressed ass into the shower. It'll make us all feel better."

Chloe shoved past Maggie and linked arms with Sawyer, steering her down the hall.

"You didn't have to do that," Sawyer said, hiking her backpack over one shoulder. "I can handle Maggie."

Chloe's blue eyes went wide and baby-doll innocent. "Oh, honey. I didn't do it for you." She blinked, a wry smile spreading across her passion-pink lips. "I did it for me."

"*Hola, señoras.*" Mr. Hanson was the school's sole Spanish teacher, but at barely thirty years old, he looked more like a student than a faculty member. He edged his way between Sawyer and Chloe and grinned, while a hallway full of girls drooled. "*Perdón, perdón*. Ah, Sawyer! *Has estudiado para la prueba?*" he said, looking expectantly at her.

Sawyer felt the redness bloom in her cheeks and shifted her weight. "Um, *si, señor.*"

"*Bueno!*" A wide smile spread across Mr. Hanson's face, his eyes crinkling with the effort.

"Ohmigod, what did he just say to you?"

Sawyer shrugged. "Honestly, I have no idea. My stock answers are *si, no*, or the often used 'how do you say menstrual cramps in Spanish'?"

Chloe wrinkled her nose. "Ew."

"They never ask you to translate that sombrero thing if they think you've got cramps."

Chloe watched the back of Mr. Hanson's head as he disappeared into Principal Chappie's office. "Screw French. I'm transferring into Spanish."

"You were bound to waste it on some French Canadian anyway."

"Don't you love him?"

Sawyer glanced over her shoulder, caught the last of Mr. Hanson's dark hair as he disappeared into the office. "Don't you think he's a little overeager?"

"Please. Half my teachers don't even know my first name. Hanson's like, fresh out of teacher school, or whatever, and still hopeful. He still believes in us." Chloe batted her eyelashes sweetly.

"Whatever."

"Besides, I heard he gave Libby a ride home the other day."

Sawyer unzipped her backpack. "And I'm sure she thanked him appropriately."

Chloe crossed her arms in front of her chest, bored now. "Are we still on for tomorrow night?"

"You mean our convocation?"

"Ooh, convocation. SAT word?"

Sawyer laughed. "My ticket out of suburban hell. Let me call you about tomorrow, though. Dad and wife number two are finding out the sex-slash-species of The Spawn. I'm sure they'll want to do something educational and emotionally satisfying out of their *Blended Families/Blended Lives* book."

"Ah, another evening rubbing placenta on each other and worshipping the moon?"

Sawyer sighed. "Are you sure you don't want me to come over and watch your parents' passive aggression as they avoid each other while showing their extreme disappointment in your choices?"

Chloe folded a stick of gum into her mouth and chewed thoughtfully. "Hell no. Wednesday is fried chicken and mac-and-cheese-as-vegetable night at the double wide. That dysfunction is all mine. And they're not my parents—Lois and Dean are my guardians."

Sawyer cocked her head, her arms crossed in front of her chest. "Not mom and stepdud anymore?"

"Hopefully not. Haven't seen Dean in over a week. And I'm using the guardian thing so hopefully Lois will finally cave in and admit that I'm adopted."

Sawyer grinned. "Except that you are the spitting image of your mother."

"Sawyer Dodd, that is a horrible thing to say."

"Of course. A thousand apologies. I take it back."

"Better." Chloe blew Sawyer an air kiss. "I'll be waiting by the phone with greasy fingers for your call."

"I'll have the ambulance on standby," Sawyer called over her shoulder.

She grinned, watching her best friend skip down the hall. For the first time in what seemed like forever, things felt normal and light again.

"Excuse me." Logan Haas smiled shyly at Sawyer and she stepped aside, letting him get into the locker under hers. Logan bore the unlucky high school triumvirate of being slight, short, and nearsighted, but Sawyer liked him.

"Hey, sorry," she said.

Logan stacked his books, slammed his locker shut, gave Sawyer an awkward salute, and headed down the hall, eyes glued to his shoes. Sawyer spun her combination lock and yanked the door open, her lips forming a little *o* of surprise when she did so. Amongst her neatly stacked binders and books was a short, fat envelope in a pale mint green. Her name was printed on it in a handwriting font. She took the envelope and looked over both shoulders; no one milled about, red-faced or smiling, indicating that they had slipped the note in her locker.

She tore the envelope open and pulled out a matching mint green folded card, a tiny plain oak leaf embossed on the bottom. When she opened it, a clipped newspaper article slipped out. Sawyer didn't have to read the headline to know what it said: "Local High School Student Killed In Car Wreck." She swallowed down a cry and read the note on the card.

It said, simply,

You're welcome.

ABOUT THE AUTHOR

Hannah Jayne is the author of nine books, including the national bestseller *Truly, Madly, Deadly*. She lives in the San Francisco Bay Area where she slays demons from her couch, chases serial killers in her pajamas, and bows to the whim of two very spoiled felines.

You can track Hannah down at www.Hannah-Jayne.com, Hannah Jayne Author on Wattpad, or @Hannah_Jayne1.